Sphyxia

Paul Cody

Fomite
Burlington, Vermont

ISBN-13: 978-1-947917-91-0
Library of Congress Control Number: 2020945549

Fomite
58 Peru Street
Burlington, VT 05401
www.fomitepress.com

For Liam and Austin

I have been half in love with easeful death.

—John Keats

One

DR. MANCHIN SAYS TO put it all down in notebooks. Every bit of it, particularly about last summer, which was months ago. Write especially about that one stretch in summer, in August or September, when you were sixteen, he says. When the really strange stuff happened. When it came to a crisis, a head. When you might have died.

Now I'm seventeen.

Dr. Manchin gives me three big, blank notebooks, with college-lined pages, and he gives me two pens. One with black ink, one with blue ink. The notebooks have red and green and black covers.

He'll lower the dose of my meds, at least some of them, so I won't be so sleepy during the day. Right now, I take five pills in the morning and four at night. I take two of one pill in the morning, and a third dose of that pill at night. Another pill, a pink tablet, I take one in the morning and two at night.

The meds are for mood disorder, depression, anxiety, and one or two other things, I think. Dissociative something. I'm not sure.

I'm also not sure how long I've been here. A week or two, a month or two. Maybe less, maybe more.

Possibly half a year. I don't know.

Nothing stays the same. Or almost nothing.

Kids come and go. Kids get discharged, get admitted. Staff come on-duty, then go off-duty eight hours later. Nurses, aides, doctors, people from housekeeping and the kitchen.

We kids, we sit in our chairs, stand against the wall or in doorways, and we watch. We listen and we watch and we feel them too, I think. The way staff move, light and quick sometimes, and other times heavy and slow.

They come in from the main entrance at the back of the ward. The entrance is off a big hall, in the regular part of the hospital. They stop at a locked metal door, at a sign that says Behavioral Sciences Unit. There's a keypad next to the door, and they punch in a passcode, hear a click, and then they pull the metal door open.

Then they're standing in an empty foyer, double doors straight ahead, a single door to the left, and a solitary black button on the wall next to each door. The doors are locked. Straight ahead, through the double doors, is the adult unit. To the left is the adolescent unit.

They press the button next to the single door, wait, press it again, wait more. Then a staff person appears in the frame of the small window on the door, looks out. The door opens.

They step through and they're inside. They're looking around, down the long hallway, at the big, glassed-in nurses' station, at the people standing and sitting. They don't hear the door click and lock behind them.

I remember all that from when I came in. A week or a month or a half year ago. I don't remember much else. Everything was fog and mist and veils, and happened far away. Even my hand, at the end of my arm, was a long way away.

I knew the door had clicked and locked. That I was inside, and couldn't get out.

There's always mist and fog, and a good deal of sleep. There's still that faraway feeling, like everything's happening way over there. The other side of the hall is the other side of the world. The grey-blue carpet on the floor is an ocean.

I sit in a chair, in the dayroom, as they call it. Bobby Collins is sitting in another chair, tapping his hands, his feet, tapping everything that can be tapped. The floor, the arms of the chair, tapping his thighs with his fingers.

Bobby Collins is fifteen, and has only been here a week. He's short and very thin. I never see him eat much. He pushes food around on his plate with his fork at meals, and rarely puts anything in his mouth. He has a high, thin voice, as though he hasn't hit puberty yet. But he has acne, and his hair is so short that his nose and ears stick out.

Bobby talks almost all the time, to go along with his tapping. He talks about hunting, and he talks about his rifle. He talks about cool fall mornings, out in the woods before sunrise, with a little dusting of snow on the ground. How quiet it is before the sun comes up.

Bobby tells me things, and I almost never say a word. I look at his face, his eyes, and I nod sometimes. Sometimes I smile.

Real low, I say, Hmmmm. I say, Really. I say, Right.

He has a small, pushed-up nose, dark and lively eyes, a thin mouth. His two front teeth, on top, are crooked. One of them overlaps the other.

There's nothing like the hour before the sun comes up, he says. He looks out the window, and his fingers are tapping his knees.

If he could be out there with his gun, right now, he wouldn't have to be in here.

Bobby smiles.

If I was there, he says, I wouldn't be here.

I think, He's right. If I was somewhere else, then I wouldn't be here either.

But I don't say it. I say pretty much nothing. Pretty much all the time.

Once in a while, with Cara, my social worker, or with Dr. Manchin, I'll say things. A sentence or two, in a soft, soft voice.

Speak up, Trey, they'll say. We can barely hear you.

I almost want to say more, and to say it louder, but I also don't want to say anything either. Everything is like that now. Wanting to say things, and not wanting to say things at the same time. Wanting to go to sleep, and not wanting to sleep. Wanting to stand up and walk around the ward, and wanting to stay in my chair, or at my position on the edge of the dayroom, leaning against the wall.

Bobby Collins stands up and starts pacing, around one side of the nurses' station, then back and around the other side. He stops to talk to Lisa, one of the aides, then he moves along, stopping to talk to Amanda, a patient, who is very tall, and looks powerful.

Everyone likes Amanda. She talks to everybody, even to me, although I never say anything back. Sometimes Amanda gets quiet and withdrawn, and for days at a time, she won't come out of her room.

She says they have her on lithium, but it takes a while to get the correct, or clinical, level of lithium in her body.

I'm still sitting in the chair, watching, then my eyelids get real heavy, the way they usually do this time in the morning. I close my eyes, rest my chin on my chest, then voices and sounds are coming from far away. I can feel people walking by now and then. The air moves, and the swish of their clothes make whispery sounds, and you can feel their weight, the feet lifting and falling on the floor, even through the carpet.

When I'm still, when I'm half asleep, I can hear and feel everything. Drafts of air from the heat or air-conditioning vents, cool or warm. I can feel the light on my eyelids, on my face, on the skin of my arms.

Were there really bodies in the basement? The sweet, strangling smell of formalin? The embalming fluid? Was there the smell of flowers?

I'm drifting like this, and then I hear the outside door, on the far side of the nurses' station, and I know it's Dr. Manchin. I open my eyes and look up, and he has a black wool overcoat on, open at the collar. He's wearing a blue shirt, a red striped tie, tied into a small tight knot at his throat.

When he smiles his eyes shine behind the glass.

I try to keep my head up because I don't want Dr. Manchin to see me sleeping, not at this hour of the morning. He thinks I'm far too withdrawn as it is.

My head has to weigh fifty pounds, and I could easily hold it up if I was not so tired. But it feels as though I've walked twenty miles, and have not eaten or slept for days, and I would give almost anything for a bed in a darkened room and one or two pillows. I could stretch and yawn, could push a cool pillow around under my head until I got just the right fit, and then as I was drifting away—the sweetest moment in the day—I'd feel the pillow change from cool to warm, from the heat inside my head.

Then in the chair, I close my eyes. I hear Amanda laugh, Dr. Manchin talking to Wendy, the nurse, and to Lisa, the aide, and then to the social worker, Cara.

Did someone try to kill me? Someone I know? Is that even possible? At some weird, witchy part of night?

This is winter now, I think. This is January or February. Out there in the world. Snow in the trees, snow on houses and on the sidewalks and roads.

In here, it's always seventy degrees.

The hills, Lisa says. My goodness, the hills.

Bobby Collins says, Waffles, and I wonder if that means there will be waffles for breakfast this morning.

No, Amanda says. Pancakes.

My eyes are closed and it's all very far away. It's like there's a television talking in a distant room, and the volume gets loud then soft then loud again. It's hard to know when it's a commercial or a regular program.

Mrs. Harcourt, my second grade teacher, is saying that it's such a lovely day outside that if we get our vocabulary sheets done, maybe we can go out for an extra recess. Mrs. Harcourt has skin like coffee with milk in it, and a slight accent from an island somewhere, that's almost musical.

After Miss Levy in first grade, Mrs. Harcourt is the second teacher I've fallen in love with.

Sometimes she laughs and calls me, Three.

Trey means three, she says, and she calls us beautiful children. Beautiful, beautiful children.

Mom and Dad, known as Ellen and Henry, they're not here. They haven't been here for a while. They used to be around all the time, more or less. Morning, noon, night. At three in the morning, at seven o'clock Saturday night. At noon and all other times.

Then I came here. I was brought here by my sister Nora, who's very nice, and it's like Ellen and Henry disappeared.

Nora has come several times. Three or four or five times, I think.

Nora is tall and has light brown hair. She looks like me, with the long nose, the huge brown eyes, but with Nora everything is pretty. With me, with the same features, I'm not pretty at all. I'm strange looking. The big Adam's apple, the long neck, like a creature that should be in the water or air, but is stuck awkwardly on the ground.

Nora is three years older than me, but has always seemed older than that. She seemed old when she was young. She's a student at the big university on the hill, here in our town. She wears a red down jacket, and a black scarf, and a wool hat with the strings hanging down from each earflap that looks like something from the mountains of South America.

Whenever Nora visits, her cheeks are red from the air outside, and she smells like summer or fall or winter, like cut grass or leaves falling or snow and ice.

What do snow and ice smell like?

I don't know, but they smell like snow and ice. They smell cold and bright. They are not anything else.

How can you explain some things?

I feel someone very close by, and I open my eyes.

Cara, the social worker, my social worker, is standing in front of me. She's smiling. She's looking down at me in my chair, and she's smiling that big sad wonderful smile.

You sleeping? she asks, and I shake my head and say, Thinking.

Cara is short and heavyset. She has very pale skin and gray eyes, and thin lips.

It's good to think, Cara says, and she smiles, and I'm looking at her white, white teeth.

I wanted to let you know that Dr. Manchin wants to meet with you and me later this morning, around eleven.

I nod.

That okay? she asks.

I nod again.

Okay. I'll come find you, she says.

Then she says, You can't stay here forever, Trey. And we don't want to send you to a state hospital. That's the last thing we want. It's the last thing you want.

She pats my arm, once, twice, a third and fourth time. Then she turns and goes.

The big room has become suddenly quiet. I don't know when it got that way. People seem to be anywhere but here. Amanda is gone, Bobby Collins, the aides and social workers, Dr. Manchin. They're all somewhere else. They're everywhere except here.

My eyelids blink and settle down, over my eyes, my chin goes to my chest, and a door might open and close, footsteps may pass, but it's as quiet as it ever gets in here.

My head is heavy beyond belief. It's always heavy, but right now, in the chair, it must weigh a thousand pounds.

The main door of the ward opens and closes, and there are low female voices.

Lisa, a voice says. This is Maggie.

Hey, Maggie, Lisa says.

My eyes blink open, without raising my head, then there are footsteps way off, and then my mother is looking at me and smiling, and Mrs. Harcourt, from second grade, is smiling too.

Three, she says. Beautiful boy. Mrs. Harcourt says that.

Then there are footsteps that stop very close to me, very close to the chair.

Sometimes it is hard to go from way back then to now. It can be confusing, disorienting.

Don't we want to know where we are?

I look up, and a girl, maybe sixteen, is standing two or three feet away.

Is this Maggie? A new patient?

She's wearing a deep blue hoodie, the hood up, and there is dark hair poking out around the side of the hood, surrounding her face. She has very pale skin that almost glows. She has big dark eyes, a small nose, a wide mouth with lots of teeth, and she's wearing blue lipstick.

She's sixteen, or she's fourteen or seventeen.

She's very thin, fairly tall, and she's looking at me frankly.

What do you say to her? I ask myself.

She keeps looking, and I look back at her.

What's in those eyes?

Maggie? I finally ask.

She smiles, she nods slightly.

Trey is three, she says softly. Then walks away.

Two

THE HOUSE WAS HUGE and stood one house in from the corner, on North Tioga Street, two or three blocks from downtown. It had gables and two turrets, but I didn't know what those things were called back then. Just that they were high up, and looked like something from a castle made of wood.

There was even a small porch on the third floor, where you could step out from Mom and Dad's bedroom and look around at people and cars on the street down below, or in one direction, you could see the tops of the buildings downtown, and in the other direction there was the Fall Creek neighborhood and the roofs of houses.

This was our house, and this was our town. There was Ellen and Henry, there was Nora, and then there was me.

We were the Burnes family. The four of us.

The rooms were enormous, and hard to heat in the long winters. Mom and Dad said that the heating bills would land us in the poorhouse.

I asked Nora where the poorhouse was and if it was like our house.

Nora laughed and said she doubted it was like our house. Then she said to ignore them, that they were just talking. There was no such thing as a poorhouse anymore.

At least she thought there wasn't.

Maybe in olden days. But not now.

Out front, on the lawn, there was a small sign that said, Burnes Funeral Home.

That was us. We were a funeral home.

Down on the first floor, and in the basement. That's where the funeral home was. And Nora and I, we were never to go down there. Not ever. Especially to the basement.

That's where the dead people were. That's where Mom and Dad got the dead people ready to be looked at by family and friends.

The bereaved, Mom called them.

The bereaved came in the late afternoon or evening, dressed up for church, and they came inside.

Nora said they signed a book, and then they stood or kneeled in front of the long shiny box with the dead person, and they said a prayer or looked at the dead person and felt sad.

At school sometimes, Nora said, kids said that she lived in the dead house, and that her father was really Dr. Death.

I was too young to go to school yet, but I would probably hear the same kind of thing when I went to school, Nora said.

Nora said that Mom said they didn't know any better. That kids could be pretty ignorant.

Ignorant meant not knowing. It was the same as ignore. Sort of.

There were six or seven rooms on the second floor, including two bathrooms, and the third floor had four bedrooms and a bathroom, and windows all over where you could look out over rooftops, and you could see the steeples of churches all around downtown.

Steeples were tall because they were reaching their skinny arms toward God in the sky.

The sky was where the dead people went after they were buried in the ground. The sky was full of dead people in their suits and ties and dresses and shiny shoes, walking stiffly around. Plus there were angels all in white and they had giant wings on their backs like birds. Only angels were much bigger than birds.

Michael the Archangel was the head angel, and he was close to God, and he was the boss of all the other angels. God was Michael the Archangel's boss. God was the boss of everything.

God knew everything and saw everything and heard everything.

He was everything and everywhere. Unless God was a she.

Nobody was ever alone because, even if they didn't know it, God was there all the time, in all places. So you didn't need to think or argue about God. And you didn't ever have to be lonely.

When I woke up late at night, at midnight or three or four in the morning, I'd lie in bed and think of the dead people lying in the basement. I didn't want them to stand up from the stainless-steel table Nora told me about, or from their coffins downstairs, and begin to walk slowly, with unseeing eyes, up the stairs, their arms straight out in front of them.

I was on the third floor, in a corner room away from the stairs. But no matter how slowly they walked, they had the whole night to reach me.

Lying on my back, feet together, my hands folded on my stomach, looking up, I shuddered because I realized that this was the way the dead lay in their caskets.

I hurried.

I moved quickly to my side because I didn't want someone—God or an angel or Mom or Dad—to mistake me for a dead person and put me in a coffin. They could easily make that mistake, especially in this house.

They were always flying around and looking everywhere for dead people.

Please, God, I whispered, but so soft and low that I didn't even know if I had whispered out loud or just in my head. I wasn't sure if it mattered because even if you just whispered something in your head, it probably still counted, I was pretty sure.

I prayed Hail Marys and the Lord's Prayer, one after the other, over and over in my head. Five or ten times.

Then the window on the far side of the room, near the bureau, began to get light. Morning was coming, and the dead people wouldn't try to move in the daylight.

But there was the chemical smell then, which was always there when there was no cooking going on, and no food smells. The smell made it a little hard to breathe, and made you want to open windows, though I never did.

The smell was from the basement, and I had once heard Nora ask Mom what it was. formalin, Mom said. To preserve things.

What things? Nora asked.

Why, bodies, of course, Mom said, as though it was as common as milk or coffee.

That way, I thought, the dead people would arrive in heaven as fresh as the flowers on the first floor.

But the smell also meant that a new dead person had arrived in the basement.

Sphyxia, someone said. Mom said, or Dad said, or maybe Nora said.

I heard, Sphyxia, again, and didn't know what it meant.

I could hear the van with the tinted windows pull into the parking lot behind the house. I heard the engine turn off, the doors of the van slam, and I went to Nora's room on the third floor, at the back of the house, because it overlooked the parking lot. Down below was the hearse, the black limousine, and the van backed up to the big doors to the cellar.

Mom and Dad, who wore black, stood by the doors to the cellar, and behind the open doors of the van. They slid a long, thick white package, a white package that had a zipper on top and nylon handles, out of the van and into the doors to the basement.

After a few minutes, I heard Mom on the stairs. I knew it was Mom because her step was so much lighter than Dad's. She reached the second floor, and I got there from the third floor at the same time as her.

She was wearing her dark green, rubber apron, and she had clear thin gloves on her hands. Already, she smelled like formalin. The green apron smelled like formalin all the time.

It was like a mask was on your face and you couldn't breathe.

Like sphyxia.

Sometimes, I thought, Mom was going to point for me to go downstairs, to the first floor, then to the basement, and she and Dad would both be wearing rubber aprons, and masks, and they would point for me to lie down on the big, shiny steel table.

They wouldn't say anything out loud, but I knew they were thinking, It's his turn.

On the second floor, Mom squinted at me, as though she wasn't used to the light.

What have you been doing? she asked, and I said I'd been in my room.

I didn't want her to know I'd been watching from the third-floor window.

The new bodies almost always arrived in the middle to late morning, it seemed, because many people died during the night. So first thing in the morning, people called Mom or Dad, who always said they'd pick up the body by nine or ten.

Around one or two in the afternoon, the dead person's family would come to pick out a coffin, to make arrangements, as they said, to sign a contract, and Mom or Dad were very busy.

Me and Nora stayed on the third floor, if we could. The smell of formalin was overtaken by the smell of flowers, and flowers had a smell as rich and thick as formalin.

We sat on Nora's double bed, on the third floor, and Nora would say that the dead person's name was Norma or Patrick or Nancy.

She was eighty-seven years old, Nora said, and died of a heart.

Nora knew because she asked questions all the time. Mom and Dad didn't mind when Nora asked questions, but when I asked questions, maybe because I was so young, they'd stare at me.

None of your business, they usually said.

Though Mom was nice once in a while.

Dad had a lot on his mind, Mom said.

Dad was usually not real nice, except to dead people and the bereaved.

Dad wore a black suit, or Dad wore a rubber apron and a mask over his face. Dad wore the gloves.

Three

MOM WAS NOT TALL, but she was not short either. She was in-between, and she said sometimes that in-between was a good place to be. She said that most regular people were in-between. As they should be.

Should was one of Mom's favorite words.

Mom was straight as boards, in front and in back. She had wide shoulders, narrow hips and skinny legs, and she was very strong. Almost as strong as Dad, and that was real strong.

Her nose was narrow like her hips, the nostrils so small that Nora and I wondered how she could breathe. Her eyes were small and dark, and she wore glasses with silver frames and very thick lenses. Her mouth was thin and wide, her teeth a little crooked, but the thing you noticed about Mom was her forehead.

Her forehead sat over her face like a great white cloud. It was very wide and very deep, so deep that it almost looked like she was going bald.

She wasn't going bald because her light brown hair was thick and frizzy. It was just, Nora and I thought, that her white forehead was big because it had to protect Mom's powerful brain.

If Mom didn't pull her hair back into a tight bun at the back of her head, her forehead wouldn't seem so huge. But hair around a woman's face was vanity, Nora said Mom said. Vanity was when you were vain. And vain was a love for your own appearance.

That wouldn't be practical either. Hair getting in the way of your work, hair flying around your face. Getting in your eyes, your nose, your mouth.

How would you get your work done if you were trying to be pretty and if you worried about how you looked?

Mom believed in no-nonsense, in getting the job done, in the shortest path between two points being a straight line.

No fussing, no dawdling, no beating around the bush.

Life was short and time was precious.

Precious was extremely valuable, like gold or diamonds or rubies or emeralds. Gold was yellow, diamonds white, rubies red and emeralds were green, like the Mother Country, like Ireland.

That was where Mom and Dad came from. Dad came to America from Connemara when he was sixteen, Mom came from Galway when she was twelve.

You could hear just a little of Ireland in Mom, and a lot in Dad.

Mom said Ireland was bewitched. She said it was a place of poverty and poetry. She didn't ever want to go back there, even though she loved the place the way she loved her mother and father. With all her heart, she said, but from a distance. The deep green fields, the rocky stone walls covered in lichen.

Oh, she said to Nora, don't get me started. Please, for the love of God, don't get me started.

When Mom was in the kitchen, making scones, the room warm from the oven, there was flour on her hands and a white smudge on her cheek, and she seemed in-between. Her hair would get loose from the bun, and her face was hot and red from the stove.

She looked like a mom.

Usually her face was pale, and she wore a little pink lipstick, not from vanity but because it reminded her, she said, that she was a woman after all.

That was another thing Mom noticed and had settled on. Who you were, and where you came from, and who you thought you were. Because people didn't know their place, Mom said. Almost never.

There was a big difference, she said, in who people were, and who they thought they were. That was a big problem with the world.

Sometimes, when I said something, Mom would pause. She'd turn to me and look down through her thick glasses, and say, Who do you think you are?

I wouldn't say anything, and Mom wouldn't say anything else, but I was pinned by her eyes, dark behind those thick lenses. I was something small, impaled by her stare.

Or she would say to me or Nora, I'm your mother, as if we didn't already know.

I'm your mother, she'd say again, loud, and we didn't know what to say. Because what did it mean that she was our mother? Did it mean that we had forgotten she was our mother, or that we were acting as if she wasn't our mother?

What did it mean to be a mother?

Mom would tell us that Dad worked very hard, almost all the time. He worried and stayed up nights, not sleeping as he should.

And God knows he needed the sleep.

Dad had ulcers from worrying, and that meant he had holes in his stomach. You couldn't see them from outside, but they were there, underneath the black clothes, and underneath the skin, like dead people under the grass at a cemetery.

But Dad had to drink lots of milk for his stomach problems, and he chewed yellow and pink tablets that made his stomach feel better, and he took other ulcer drugs.

You could see him, Mom said, tight and nervous as a squirrel in a tree. His hands shaking, a nerve in his cheek or lips jumping and twitching.

Mom said we kids thought it was easy. It was just a big walk in the park, a stroll on a sunny day.

I looked at Nora because I didn't know what she was talking about.

A walk in the park? A stroll on a sunny day?

Nora was looking at Mom, and Nora's face was serious, which worried me. Nora would almost always be calm and alert at the same time. She didn't often get worried, I thought. That's how it seemed to me.

Nora was pretty and Nora was smart and she was strong. Nora looked after me. She always said that things would be fine, that things would be all right.

Her bedroom was on the third floor, right next to mine, but in a back corner of the house. I could hear her very late at night, turning over in bed, getting up for the bathroom, getting back in bed, and then later, murmuring things in sleep that only I could hear.

The moonlight that fell in my room from the window fell in her room too. It was milky, like the glasses of milk that Dad drank for his stomach.

Mom and Dad seemed to get in bed and go to sleep, and stay that way until morning. Almost all the time.

I nearly always woke up in the middle of the night, and stayed awake for hours, even when I was four or five. Worrying about everything.

I didn't know what Dad worried about, but somebody had to keep things in order by worrying about them, and somehow, that was my job.

The dead people in the basement on the first floor. Mom and Dad. Nora, me. Bad things could happen to any of us.

Well, maybe not to the dead people. Mom said dead people didn't care.

Maybe I would go sleepwalking down the stairs, and then to the first floor, and finally to the basement.

That could happen. People sleepwalked. They didn't even know they were doing it.

Or lying in bed, very late, I could hear creaks and groans, and I'd listen, careful and still as a hunting cat.

What was that? Who was that?

It always came from downstairs, but was it from the second floor or the first floor? Or even from the basement?

I listened for more creaks, more groans, and once I thought something whispered my name.

Trey, something said. Trrreeeyyy, it said again.

Was that real? Did that happen?

I had to pee, but I was afraid to go to the bathroom. I didn't know what was out in the hall.

Going to bed in the evening was hard. It was hard to go to sleep, and hard to lie awake in bed for hour after dark hour. Staring at the ceiling and walls. Listening, feeling the pale cool sheets all around me.

The white sheets surrounded every part of me except for my head. Except for my white moon face. The moon way overhead, and the moon of my face. Here, and way up there.

The moon, Nora had told me, made the oceans move, the tides rise and fall. High tide, low tide, over and over.

Just as the moon was full, and days later, it was a sliver of white silver in the sky.

Maybe the moon didn't look like it was doing much, just sitting near heaven. Getting round and fat as a ball, then skinny like a sickle they used in Ireland to cut grass. But just hanging there, looking like it was doing nothing, was a trick. Just because it was calm and still, like Mom or Dad, didn't mean it didn't have terrible power.

The power to move whole oceans, to destroy cities like in Japan, to drown sailors in boats all over the world.

Up there on the third floor, the moon fell through my window, and made a lacy pattern on the floor, the wall, on the side of my bed. So pretty, and so like a ghost too.

Could ghosts be pretty? Could ghosts be like angels, only without big wings?

Were ghosts sweet or nasty?

Ghosts were white like the moon and like angels. Ghosts wore white sheets and you could see right through them.

In bed, I wore white sheets too.

Maybe I was a ghost, and people could see right through me. Maybe I floated the way they did. Down hallways, into rooms, in and out of windows.

You became a ghost when you died. So a ghost was a dead person, only later. All the blood had been drained out of them.

I must have fallen asleep again, and it must have been two or three or four in the morning. I didn't know for sure, because I don't think I could tell time yet. All I knew was how the moon was, how the light was or wasn't.

The dark was still deep and pure.

Maybe I had been dreaming, and there was a veil between me and the regular world. Maybe there were creaks and groans that I could sort of hear.

They could be the old boards of the house, they could be dead people.

Half asleep, half awake. Part of a dream, part of the deep-night world.

Then I knew that someone or something was standing in the doorway, and the huge house was all around me. Over and under and on every side.

I couldn't open my eyes quick because then the thing in the doorway would see me, would know I was awake.

I stayed very still, and the thing was still there. If I stayed like this maybe it would go away.

Then very very slightly, moving just a tiny piece of my eyelids into a slit, I looked.

Mom was standing in the doorway, looking at me with strange eyes. With eyes that didn't seem to know me.

There were lacy shadows on her face from the moon.

She was wearing her green rubber apron, she had a mask covering the lower part of her face, she wore the gloves.

Mom and the apron smelled of formalin.

The sphyxia again.

Four

S O TERRIBLY SLEEPY TODAY. Head as heavy as bricks, as gallons of water, as a big round bag of dimes. They slosh and clink and knock around inside the walls of my skull, which tries to hold my brain.

I'm in the dayroom, in the chair where I usually sit, and there's very little activity. Things get slow or real busy here very quickly. The halls and rooms will be swarming with staff and patients, and then five minutes later there will be nobody and nothing except the walls, the floor and ceiling, the furniture. And me, and I am like a piece of furniture.

A fly can land on me, and I will not move.

Dr. Manchin has lowered the dose on two of my meds, so instead of two tabs in the morning and one at night, or one in the morning and two at night, I now take one of each in the morning and one of each at night. That's better because it's not as confusing.

This was supposed to make me less sleepy during the day, but it's done the opposite, I'm pretty sure. I wake up in a deep and lightless hole, and the things I think in those first few minutes awake are dark beyond measure. That there is no such thing as hope, and that I will die soon, and that will be a good thing, because then I won't feel like this. I think. I hope.

In those dark moments, I see my body, wrapped in a shroud, sliding into the oven to be cremated.

But after I am moving for a while, after I have taken my morning meds, things get less dark. For an hour or two it evens out, and I can reason with the day.

Then the sleepiness comes, around mid-morning, and that's where I am right now. In my chair, my head a thousand pounds. So heavy that I can't keep my head up.

My chin is on my chest, and I see at the edge of my vision that Maggie, the girl with blue lipstick, who I now know is seventeen, has come into the dayroom, and is sitting way over in a corner, under a window. She curls up in a chair, pulls her hood tight around her head, and closes her eyes.

I shut my eyes, and think, We both have closed eyes. We're both the same, just like this. Closed eyes, sitting in chairs quietly, in the same dayroom, not bothering anyone. Like normal people. Exactly like regular humans in the real world.

If you saw this from a little ways away, you wouldn't know that we were on a ward for the mentally ill. That the doors were locked, and that all the glass, in the windows and in the nurses' station, was shatterproof.

Two days ago, I'm pretty sure, I met with Cara, the social worker, and Dr. Manchin. We met in a windowless room, with a table like a dining room table, and plastic chairs, and nothing on the walls except a whiteboard.

I don't think the door of the room was locked.

They were nice. They spoke softly. They are always nice and they always speak softly.

Cara began. She said that I had been here on the ward for many months.

I wanted to ask, How many months? But I didn't.

She said that insurance was asking how long I would be here, and insurance wanted to know if my treatment could not be adequately addressed in a state facility.

The state facility that insurance was talking about was Malvern.

Had I ever heard of Malvern? Dr. Manchin asked.

I shook my head.

We don't want you to go there, Cara said. It's not a bad place. I'm not saying that. But it's primarily custodial.

Dr. Manchin said, There's heavy mesh on all the windows, the television, which is usually broken, is bolted to a table, the furniture belongs in a dump, and there's a very high staff-to-patient ratio. You might see the doctor for ten minutes every two or three weeks.

The patients at Malvern, Cara said, are often pretty far gone, and some have been at the hospital for years. You'll see psychotics, people with schizophrenia, with bipolar I, which is serious manic-depression, people with severe alcohol or drug addiction issues. There are the mentally ill coming out of state prisons.

Cara and Dr. Manchin both looked at me. Their eyes were dark in the shadows of the room.

Trey, Dr. Manchin said. It's pretty rough at Malvern, and we don't want you to go there. Last year a young man was raped at Malvern.

Really, Stanley, Cara said, as though Dr. Manchin should not have said that.

He needs to know, Dr. Manchin said.

Cara turned to me and said, Some people don't ever come out

of there, once they're in. Or if they're lucky, they might get released to a group home. But very few ever get back to normal life.

She looked at me some more with her dark eyes.

How could they rape a young man? I wondered. Then I thought about it, and said out loud, Oh, no.

Oh, no, what? Dr. Manchin asked, and I shook my head.

We're fending off your insurance company, Cara said, and so far we've got another month out of them. And they may go for a second additional month. But they're mainly interested in saving money, and they could cut you off at any moment.

You've been stable for a while, Dr. Manchin began, and Cara said, You've done really well in some respects. But you're still kind of stuck at this point.

My eyes, I think, had question marks.

You're withdrawn, you don't speak very much, and you don't interact with either the staff or patients, Dr. Manchin said.

We'd like to see you press harder, to work at some things, Cara said. We'd like to see you making more visible progress.

You need to elevate your game, Trey, Dr. Manchin said.

I thought, Elevate my game?

I'll write in the notebooks, I said.

Good, Cara said. That's a start.

Yes, Dr. Manchin said. Very good. A good start.

And please try to talk more, to interact with the people on the ward, Cara said, and her eyes stayed deep and dark and full of some kind of feeling.

Dr. Manchin's glasses had slipped halfway down his nose. He didn't push them up, and I worried they'd fall off his face. Then he wouldn't be able to see.

Please don't make us send you to Malvern, Trey, Cara said. You're only seventeen. You have an entire life in front of you.

Malvern, I thought, was the state hospital. It was where the chronic mentally ill were sent. The broken TV was bolted to a heavy table. There were no carpets on the floor. The couch had springs coming through the cushions.

They raped boys. At least someone raped a boy.

They could rape me, and I wouldn't have a voice to yell.

Could that be me? I thought. A boy who got raped?

Could I be the one they were thinking of, whose insurance was running out, and who might go to Malvern?

Back in the dayroom, I am tired everywhere—in my head, hands, legs, belly.

I am like a little kid who stands silent and still in a corner of a room. If you stand very silent and very still and tired, and if you close your eyes tight, then maybe you become invisible. Nobody could possibly see you. Nobody could possibly harm you.

If you stand and say nothing, and barely breathe.

I did that so often. I did that almost every day. And when I was very young, it worked. I was invisible.

Just as when I was very young, when I was three or four or five, I could flap my arms very hard and even though I couldn't really fly, it seemed as though I did lift myself off the ground, a foot or two, at least.

If I could have flapped my arms longer and harder then I might have flown, even though Nora thought it was funny, me flapping my arms as though they were wings.

Nora said I didn't move off the floor.

And I wasn't invisible. Not really. And I'm not invisible in the chair in the dayroom. I'm just quiet and still.

Once in a while my stone-like head will roll from one side of my chest to the other. My hands will twitch, my fingers will tremble, from the drugs, I think.

Drugs are why I shake, and drugs are why I am as tired as someone who has not slept in a long time. Tired as someone who has worked almost forever without rest.

We're not supposed to sleep in our rooms during the day. Some people would sleep all day. Some people would almost never come out of their rooms.

But they mostly leave me alone. They must know all these drugs make me tired.

Maggie is sleeping in her chair, I'm pretty sure.

Then I am nodding deeply, and the air in the vents, the heat, is getting farther and farther away. There are a few footsteps now and then, but they seem to be from the big hospital corridor, outside the locked doors. A place I have not been in months.

It's another world out there.

There are no voices, or almost none. A single word floats, murmuring, then there's silence, then another single word.

It's spring because the grass everywhere has turned from brown to green. Trees have buds that thicken and blossom, and the earth itself, where there was just dirt, is pushing up small yellow and purple flowers. The air smells like earth thawing, it smells like wood, dead leaves, clean air, new life.

In the evening, after dinner, the light is thrilling as the sun moves closer and closer to the horizon in the west. There are deep rose colors, and pale blue, and the sunshine on red brick is so sharp and clear and beautiful that I often stand and stare.

A month ago there was snow. A month ago I was seventeen

years old, but I am suddenly six years old and the world, in April, is big and mysterious and surprising.

How can the world be so beautiful? I wonder, at six, standing on the sidewalk in the Fall Creek neighborhood. How can it contain all these things?

A dog barks, a car goes whooshing past, another small dog makes yipping sounds.

A red cat sits in the middle of the sidewalk, and as I approach, she does not move. I stop and look at her.

Her eyes are gold, with tiny black centers, and she has a square handsome face. She licks her paw, cleans behind each ear, and then looks at me some more. The inside of her mouth, her tongue, are bright pink.

She continues to not move, to look at me as though to say, Who are you? What are you doing here?

What does a cat think? I want to know.

Then I wonder, standing on the sidewalk, what I think. Who am I? What am I doing here?

Then my head is so low on my chest, and continues to weigh a thousand, a million, pounds. The vent overhead has stopped, now it kicks on again, and it is so warm that it makes me even more sleepy. Deeper than dreams or death. Deeper than oceans. Down where there is no light or air.

I lift my head, and Maggie and her blue lipstick are sitting in the chair next to me. Her arm on the armrest is almost touching mine. Her hood is still up, and she is looking at me the way the red cat looked at me.

Why're you here, Trey? she whispers.

Five

DAD WAS HENRY BURNES, Funeral Director, and he was Funeral Director more than anything else. He wore dark suits and white shirts and deep blue or maroon ties. His black shoes were always so polished that you could see reflections of light in them.

He was only a little taller than Mom, and his black hair was curly. He was thin and very strong. He had wide shoulders and thick arms. His nose was long, his mouth a lean line, and his eyes were black and shiny like his shoes. His nostrils were long and black like his shoes also, but they were not shiny. They pulled in air, then let it out from between his thin lips.

He spoke in a low, full, comforting way, the way he spoke to the bereaved.

He said, Ellen, I'd like a word, and he and Mom went downstairs to the office on the first floor, or up to their big bedroom on the third floor, and they were almost sad, the way they moved so slowly.

Me and Nora never went to the first floor, and we never—not ever—went to the basement. Down there was the underworld, down there was the place for the dead. They were there all the time, Mom and Dad, the corpses, in body or in spirit.

You couldn't see the spirit, not really, not if you looked. The spirit was like air or light. You couldn't see the thing itself, only what it did to other things. You could see the curtains blow out, or leaves shuffle in trees, or when the leaves were dead on the ground you could see them move on the grass or on the sidewalk or street.

They didn't have invisible strings attached to them. They moved from the wind.

Light was the same. You couldn't see it. Not really, even with a flashlight. But when you turned the light on, the room would no longer be dark. You could suddenly see chairs and lamps and the ceiling and rugs. But light was trickier.

You couldn't hold air or light in your hands. You couldn't put them in a box and send them to someone.

Spirits were the same as air and light, only they were even more slippery, they were even harder to see. A spirit was like a ghost or angel, but different too, Nora said.

At the funeral of a very old man named Rupert, who lived by himself in an apartment and died alone, you could feel his thin spirit even down on the first floor, where Nora and I never went. I could feel it even on the third floor.

There were calling hours only on a Tuesday afternoon, and very few people came. An old lady, then an old man and an old lady together, then two women in nurses' uniforms, white shoes and stockings, the flowery tops.

They were coming from work, Nora said, as we watched from her bedroom window. They must have taken care of him when he was sick, she added.

Then just before the end of calling hours, a priest in a black uniform, with a white square at the Adam's apple, arrived, holding a book with a black cover in his hand.

He'll say prayers, Nora told me. Rupert must have been a Catholic.

Mom and Dad were Catholics, and so were Nora and me, in a way.

The Holy Roman Church. The Mother Church.

Saint Peter, Nora said, said something about building a church on a rock, but that didn't make sense.

Upon this rock, she said. Upon this rock.

She said it twice, but she said there's more, only she couldn't think of the rest of it.

Rupert's spirit was old and sad and not very strong. His spirit had shrunk down like his old body. His spirit couldn't glow very much, couldn't float around and touch people, even though people wouldn't know that a spirit was touching them.

But then a boy named Kyle, who was only eighteen, died in a car accident, and there were lines all down the back and front walks, and around the corners, all down the sidewalk. Hundreds of people lined up to come in and look at him in his casket. To shake his mother and father and brother's hand, to hug them, to say how sorry they were. To say that they almost didn't know what to say.

Kyle's spirit was very strong. I could feel it as I looked at all the young people. Did anyone else feel it?

The young people lined up to pay their respects?

That's what Mom called it, Nora said. Paying your respects.

They were high school students, and not a single one of them, from the third floor, looked old. They were sixteen and seventeen and eighteen.

They don't belong here, Nora said.

She said they should be doing homework, or playing sports, or hanging out at each other's houses or on street corners or in parks. They should have been flirting with each other.

Flirting was a way of fooling around in a romantic way. Making moon eyes and winking, touching someone else on the shoulder or arm or hand. You were sort of saying you liked a person.

You were saying you liked them. You may even like-like them. Maybe some time down the road you might have even begun to love them. Like a girlfriend or boyfriend.

Instead, many of them were crying. They had shiny eyes, and big silver drops slid down their faces.

This was very sad. It made me and Nora want to cry too. It made us want to go somewhere else, somewhere alone, and cry into a pillow or into the sleeves of our shirts. But we didn't. We stayed at the window and we watched.

After the funeral of Kyle, Mom and Dad were nice to us for a day of two. Dad tried to teach me to play chess, and in his slow, comforting, half-Irish voice, he told me how each of the pieces moved. The pawns could move forward in the same row, and they captured an enemy piece at an angle.

The horse could move two down, and one sideways, or two sideways, and one up or down. The horse could jump over other pieces. The bishop went at an angle, the castle could go up or down or sideways, the queen could do almost anything, and the king could just move one space in any direction.

You tried to capture the enemy king. That was the whole point of the game.

I asked Dad if Ireland had a king.

He said, What? in his low comforting voice, but there was no comfort in his voice.

Dad was scary, and I couldn't even say why.

Just to be near him, to sit across a table, over a chess board, was scary. Near Dad, my hands shook as though I was very cold. I had to press my legs together hard because I was afraid I'd pee in my pants.

Dad might be happy or sad, but his voice was always the same, as though he was speaking to the bereaved. He always talked that way.

Nora wondered if Dad spoke to the dead people the same way, as he was fixing them up on the steel table to get ready for the presentation, as he called it. For when the bereaved came in to see the dead person for the last time.

Dad slapped me once, on a winter afternoon, and I didn't even know why. His hand flicked out so hard and fast that I almost couldn't see it. It was a lizard tongue. I was four or five years old. I nearly fell, and my face was stinging, and I began to cry. I began to cry louder and louder.

Mom and Nora came in, and asked what was the matter, and I didn't know what to say, just that one side of my face felt as though bees had stung it over and over.

He, I began. He, I began again, but he was looking at me with those eyes, with that thin line of a mouth. So I just cried even louder.

Nora put her arms around me, and Mom went to Dad and took his arm. Mom said, There, there, to Dad, like he had been slapped. Dad put his arm around her shoulder, a thing you almost never saw.

Later, behind the closed door of their bedroom on the third floor, I could hear Dad crying. I could hear that weird, unnatural sound, even though I couldn't see him.

I felt sad. I wanted to knock on the door, and put my arms around him and say that I was very sorry. I wanted to tell him it was my fault. That whatever I had done to make him angry, I was sorry. That I wouldn't do it again, no matter what.

But we didn't do that. I never put my arms around him, and he never touched me either, not in the usual way.

Not long after that, a few days or a week or a month later, I was lying in bed once again, and it was late and dark and silent everywhere. I had been asleep, and then I heard the soft murmuring sound of an Irish voice.

I opened my eyes in that hiding way. Barely a slit, so nobody would know that I was awake. And there was Dad, kneeling down on the floor, on the little rug next to my bed. His elbows were on the edge of the bed, his eyes were closed.

He was wearing a dark suit and tie, a white shirt, and in this soft, low voice, he was praying.

I knew three prayers. I'd known them as long as I could remember knowing anything. The *Hail, Mary*. The *Our Father*. And the one he was saying. *The Act of Contrition*.

Contrition meant sorry. It meant you didn't want to do a bad thing again.

Oh my God, Dad said. I am heartily sorry, for having offended thee. And I detest all my sins, because of the loss of heaven and the pains of hell. But most of all, because they offend thee, my God.

Then his voice dropped, and he seemed to mumble.

He began again, Oh, my God, and he finished with, Who art all good and deserving of all my love. I firmly resolve, with the help of Thy grace, to confess my sins, to do penance, and to amend my life. Amen.

His elbows shifted on the edge of the bed. In a low, quiet way, he cleared his throat.

I know you're awake, he whispered. You think I don't know, but I know. And I need to tell you that this is a struggle, that it's very hard. That none of this is easy. Not for me, not for your mother.

I kept my eyes closed tight. I didn't move.

He didn't say anything else and he did not move. I wasn't sure if I was breathing.

Please, please, please, please, I said in my brain.

Then it was later, and I must have been sleeping.

Dad was no longer there.

Six

NORA WAS TALL FOR her age, even in first grade. In second grade she was still tall. She was taller than every girl in her class, and she was taller than all but two boys.

She seemed much older than her age. Even Dad said so.

She had blond hair, which was funny, because neither Mom or Dad had blond hair. Dad's hair was black, and Mom's hair was lighter, but it wasn't blond. And Mom and Dad were not especially tall either. So maybe Nora was delivered by the gypsies, Mom said. By the tinkers.

Tinkers were also called Travellers in Ireland.

Mom winked, to say she was just kidding.

Nora's hair was straight, with a little bit of wave, and Mom's hair was frizzy, and Dad's hair was very curly.

Mom said that Dad had an older brother named Padraic in Galway, and Padraic was tall. He was taller than six feet. He was a turnip farmer in Connemara.

Dad was from Connemara and Mom was from Galway. Mom said that that was a long time ago and it was very far away.

Dad didn't talk or write letters to any of his family in Ireland.

He had two brothers and four sisters, and for all Dad knew, Mom said, they might, the lot of them, be in jail or dead. And good luck to them, Mom said Dad said.

Not that your father's bitter, Mom told us. It was just that he wanted to put the past far, far behind him.

They had known poverty in Ireland, Mom told Nora. They had known hunger and want and squalor, and Nora would never know or imagine what that was like, thank God.

Dad's father was a fright, Mom said.

Now go look after your brother, Mom said. We have work to do downstairs.

Mom was wearing a black skirt and black sweater over a red blouse, and Dad came in wearing his black suit.

Black was everywhere.

Nora and I sometimes joked that Dad wore his black suit to bed. He wore it all the time. Mornings, nights, weekends.

I think he must wear it when he takes a shower, Nora said. Or else, how would it ever get clean?

The best time was with Nora. She wasn't like the rest of us. She was funny and warm and she was really smart. She read books all the time, and she had taught me to read already, before I even went to school. She seemed so old.

We would sit in chairs next to each other, or we would sit on my bed or her bed, shoulder to shoulder, the open book on our laps.

Now sound it out, Nora said, and I looked at the picture for clues.

Th, th, the, I said, because that was a tricky sound, and wasn't like the letters. The letters were, T like tea, and HE, like he. So it would be tea-he, only it wasn't.

Instead, you put T and H together like TH. One sound for both letters. Then E.

Then you read about the red hen and the yellow ducks.

All of them in the barnyard, maybe like in Galway or Connemara.

There was brown cow, there was white seagull, there was blue in the sky up above. Everything had a color. Green grass and trees. Red flowers.

You could write down all of it, and anybody could pick up that piece of writing on a page at any time, and they would see what you had seen and written. It was kind of like magic, Nora said.

Nora had brown eyes, and red lips. She smelled like talcum powder and lemon and vanilla. And when you leaned against her arm and shoulder, you could feel how warm she was. When her hair brushed against your face, it was very soft and smelled beautiful, like a peeled orange.

Nora was a gift to life from God, Mom said when she was sipping from a glass at night. She'll break some hearts, our Nora will.

Dad nodded and sipped from his glass.

Learning to read with Nora was a little scary, because I didn't want to disappoint her. But it was fun too because I was learning the secrets behind the black marks on the page.

After we read for a while, Nora closed the book and kept it on her lap.

For a long time, neither of us said anything.

Mom and Dad were working on a body down in the basement.

I practiced not saying anything almost all the time. I was invisible. Then when I was with Nora it was hard to start talking all of a sudden.

Nora looked at me and saw me. She smiled as though she liked what she saw. Nora was not like anybody or anything else.

She was in second grade, and she said that usually, in the middle of every morning, all the kids in the class would take a break. Ms. Laster, their beautiful teacher, would hand around a little carton of milk and a small packet of crackers to each kid.

Is every teacher beautiful? I asked.

Nora laughed softly and said, Almost.

Then she said, And if they're not beautiful, they're really nice.

Her first grade teacher, Miss Levy, was beautiful, and her second-grade teacher, Mr. Crowe, wasn't beautiful, but he was handsome and very funny. He called all the kids, Pal, or Buddy, or Champ or Ace.

Sometimes he called a girl, Flossie or Daisy.

Mr. Crowe was almost always joking around, and the kids liked him a lot.

Mr. Crowe and his wife Renee had a baby during the middle of the second-grade year. He brought in a picture to show them the baby, and it had a scrunched-up face and wore a little knit cap that was blue. If it was a girl, the cap would have been pink, and the blue cap meant that it was a boy. It was a he.

The cap was how you could tell.

But at mid-morning, in Ms. Laster's class, they would eat their crackers and drink their milk. The crackers were in a small plastic package, and there were two crackers in each pack.

The milk was cold and fresh and good, but sometimes, when the milk carton was almost empty, Nora said, you could smell the empty carton inside, which was made of heavy paper that was waxed. It was a funny smell, a distinct smell, that you didn't find anywhere else.

Like formalin? I asked, and Nora laughed.

Oh no, she said. Not that. Not unpleasant at all.

Nora said that at school there were no dead people. She said there were just kids and beautiful teachers. Or almost all beautiful teachers.

Is everyone nice? I asked.

Almost. A few kids were nice most of the time, but sometimes they would not be nice. They could be mean once in a while. Once in a blue moon.

What's that?

What's what? she asked.

A blue moon?

Oh, Nora said. I think it's something that doesn't happen very often. It's pretty rare.

Have you ever seen a blue moon?

Nora laughed again.

You're a funny boy, Trey, she said. You ask such curious questions.

Is that bad?

No, she said. She pushed my hair off my forehead with her fingers. It's a good thing. It's a very good thing. It shows that you want to know things.

I didn't say it, but Nora was the only person I could ask. Mom usually said to stop asking questions, then she'd make a funny face, like she smelled something bad. And Dad—well, you didn't ask Dad questions. You didn't know what he might do.

Nora said that after everyone had finished their milk and crackers, Ms. Laster told them to get their blankets from their cubbies. It would be naptime for a half hour.

They all had small blankets, and they spread them out on the floor. The floor had a rug so it wasn't too hard. Then Ms. Laster shut the lights off and pulled down some shades, and the room wasn't dark, but it wasn't too light either.

Nora said she always put her blanket down next to Asia and Emma, and not too far from Talia. They were her best friends in school, and Emma lived right near us, one street down and two streets over. Emma was half Japanese and half English, and smiled all the time, and just looking at her, Nora said, made other people want to smile too.

Asia was not from Asia, but from California. Then her family moved to New York. Her real name was Anastasia, and Asia was just the last part of her name, standing alone.

Nora said it was the same as Liam, which was a shortcut for William, and she bet that that was true of a whole bunch of names.

Do you go to sleep on your blanket? I asked.

Sometimes, she said. Not all the time, but once in a while.

She said she always tried to stay awake because she loved the feeling of being awake and lying there among all these kids, and almost all of them would be sleeping. She said that usually they never stopped moving.

Most of the kids rested their heads on their arms, and even after they were asleep, when their breathing deepened and slowed, their legs or feet, their arms or hands, would twitch or flutter.

What's flutter? I asked, and Nora said it was what a butterfly did. Kind of float and flap its wings.

Flutter, float, flap, I thought. Like butterflies and sleeping kids in school.

She said that she sometimes drifted between awake and asleep, opening her eyes every once in a while, not moving her head, but looking. Ms. Laster was sitting in the chair at her desk, leaning back, her eyes closed, smiling. Even with her eyes closed, even resting, Nora said, Ms. Laster smiled.

Emma, who was probably her best friend in the world, was sleeping just to her right, her mouth slightly open, now and then whispering things in her sleep. Okay, and, Sure, and, I think so.

Asia breathed so slow and deep that Nora worried sometimes that Asia had stopped breathing. She almost wanted to reach over and shake Asia, to make her breathe again, but every time, when it seemed as though she couldn't possibly be alive, Asia did breathe. And sometimes she gurgled in her throat.

Nora said that she had never known these kids before school, and now she knew almost all of them. Because of coming to school, she said, she had so many friends. Kids she didn't know were even alive.

School was good that way. School was so much fun.

Different than here? I asked.

Nora looked at me with her eyes like a summer sky. Her face softened. Her face was warm.

We were in her room on the third floor. We were sitting on the bed. There was a picture on the wall of a painting of a smiling boy. There were little bottles and containers on top of her bureau. Small, colored cloth elastics for her hair.

Outside the window were the bare branches of trees, and a bird high up in the sky, going somewhere.

Nora said, You won't always be here, Trey. I promise.

Almost nowhere is like here, she said.

School's different? I asked, even though she had already said it was.

She nodded.

Nothing could be more different, she said. Nothing anywhere is like home.

Seven

WE SIT NEXT TO each other nearly every day. Maggie and me. When the ward is busy and crowded, and when the ward is quiet.

We say pretty much nothing. A word or two. We say, Hey, or, Hi. We say, Maggie, or, Trey. Doing okay? Behaving?

We nod or wave or shrug our shoulders in response.

We sit in a small alcove, under big windows, in a corner of the dayroom.

In the eight days that Maggie has been on the ward, we have sat next to each other six of those days. For hours. Sometimes for an hour in the morning, two hours in the afternoon, for an hour in the evening.

We hardly touch, though our chairs are so close, are against each other, that we feel every shift that each of us makes. When one of us crosses or re-crosses our legs, or moves an arm, or when Maggie pulls her legs onto the seat of the chair and folds them under her lotus-like. Or when she pulls her knees to her chest. Once or twice a day our arms brush against each other, and on two different days, a Wednesday and Saturday, our hands brushed the other's.

I could feel in that half-second how smooth and warm her skin was, like satin or velvet, like warm water or a late June breeze. That silkiness seemed like the whole world.

Her fingers are impossibly long, the nails chewed down and ragged, and her palms are square and look too small to anchor those fingers.

On a Sunday evening, the saddest evening of the week, we are sitting in the alcove, not saying anything, and Amanda sits down near us. Amanda is quite tall, she has big shoulders, and she is a person everyone likes. She has been here almost as long as me.

Nobody, not even Cara or Dr. Manchin, seem to know exactly what's wrong with Amanda. She seems normal most of the time, but then she withdraws from everyone and everything for days. She stays in bed in her room, or if they force her to come out, she'll bring a small afghan her grandmother made for her. She'll curl up on one of the couches in the dayroom, the afghan covering everything but her nose and eyes. She'll wear a wool watch cap pulled low on her forehead.

The afghan is red and black and green. Red, black, green, over and over, in small squares.

Amanda will stay like that for two or three or four days, and nobody can touch her when she's in her blue period. Then she'll come out of her room, always in the morning, after a long sleep, and she'll be Amanda again. Laughing and talking, the Amanda everyone likes so much.

She sits down in a chair opposite Maggie and me, and she looks at us and smiles.

So, she says, can I ask?

Maggie and I just look at her. Then Maggie smiles.

Are you two a thing? Amanda asks.

We continue to look at her, Maggie keeps smiling, but I only look.

I suppose I can't expect an answer, Amanda says, and I know it's incredibly rude to even ask. But you two do sit here with each other. I know you don't say anything. Of course you don't say anything.

Maggie keeps smiling. Bobby Collins paces the dayroom, circling the big nurses' station. Dennis, a new overweight kid, walks with Bobby for one lap, but then he has to stop. Dennis looks winded. Bobby is wearing a new, blaze-orange sweater his dad brought him, and he keeps pacing, nodding at people he passes.

The heat kicks on, and we can feel warm dry air coming from a vent overhead.

I have never been a thing with anyone. Not ever. I have wanted to be, in my mind, but the space between my mind and the regular world is vast.

The reason I ask, Amanda says, is because everybody's wondering. I mean, the whole ward. Staff and patients, she goes on. Even Dr. Manchin said, It's nice to see Maggie and Trey becoming friends.

I wonder if that's what we are. Friends.

Amanda says, So I kind of got appointed to ask, not that I expect an answer.

Maggie stops smiling for a few moments, Bobby circles the station once more, and I sit and watch. The air in the vent stops blowing.

Okay, I'm sorry if this was rude, Amanda says.

I almost feel bad for her.

Maybe you two don't even know. Maybe all of us, including the two of you, will have to see, she says.

Amanda stands up from her chair, begins to turn, and Maggie reaches up and pats her on the forearm. One, two, three pats. Then very briefly, Maggie strokes the spot she has patted.

Now and then, I feel the eyes of other people on us. Lisa the aide, Cara, my social worker, Kaylee and Sue, who are nurses. Bobby looks, Dennis, Juliet, Amanda, Clea, who are patients, also look. Just briefly, then they look away.

There's room for twelve patients on the ward. Eight single rooms, and two doubles. But most of the time there are anywhere from seven to ten patients here. If you're thirteen, they will admit you. And when you turn eighteen, they kick you out. This place is for adolescents.

I'm pretty sure I won't turn eighteen until the fall, the early fall. Near September or October.

Then at eighteen, if you have to, you go to the adult unit next door, or they send you to a state hospital, or they send you home. I don't know where or what home is anymore.

I feel Maggie's eyes on me, and unlike the eyes of the people on the ward, who look briefly and then look away, Maggie's gaze is steady, her gaze is true. I don't even know why I think or feel that, but it's something I'm sure of.

Her eyes are very big, and they are so dark that they may be black. Or a deep deep brown.

I look up and she is staring at me. She is looking closely and carefully, and somehow that doesn't make me uncomfortable.

Most of the time, when people look at you, you can tell what they feel. You can see or feel anger or mockery, humor, hate, curiosity, warmth. You can feel almost everything that's inside of a person. You can feel it in your own eyes, you can feel it on your skin.

With Maggie, I'm not exactly sure. There's no anger or mockery or hate. There's humor and curiosity. I think there's warmth.

She's wearing a hoodie with the hood up, and as usual, there's black hair peeking out from the front edges of the hood. She's wearing bright red lipstick. She always wears lipstick, and she seems to have all the colors. She has blue, green, black, red, and I think a few others.

This hoodie is maroon, and she has hoodies in at least two other colors, dark blue and gray. She also has several colors in sweatpants, and lots of socks that are part yellow, purple, lime green, gray, white and black, all in one pair of socks.

I hold her gaze for what seems a long time. I almost think she's going to say something, announce something, and that both scares and excites me. But we just relax into the gaze, eyes locked, seeing whatever's there to see.

Then Maggie looks away, and Clea sits down across the day-room. She's thirteen and the youngest person on the ward. Clea's chunky, has dirty blond hair and wears a shawl. She's only been here for a few weeks, but I've never seen anyone of any age so depressed.

Clea seems to be moving underwater, against the current. She spent her first week more or less in bed, and when they got her up for meals, she fell asleep at the table, her chin falling to her chest.

They must have her on meds, and they're talking about E.C.T., about shock therapy, which they'd rather not do because she's so young. This is what Bobby Collins tells us.

For most of the last week, they've been locking her room during the day, so she can't hide out in there, and she falls asleep in a chair in the dayroom, or she sits and silently sobs, big silver tears rolling down her face. All of us walk by. All of us see the tears, and all of us, I'm pretty sure, want her meds to begin to work.

The patients, we patients, we know each other. We know nothing about each other, really, but we know everyone's name and where someone is from, and we sort of know, or we find out, who visits each of us. We guess what's wrong with everyone.

There's Bobby, Amanda, Maggie, Dennis, Juliet, Clea, then me. There's a small, muscled fifteen-year-old named Elliot, who spent his first few days pacing and talking. Talking, talking, talking. Elliot apologized for talking so much. He said he couldn't stop. He said he'd like to stop.

Then Eliot plunged. He stopped talking and pacing, and now he barely comes out of his room.

And there was a boy named Gerald, who was almost eighteen, and he believed that he could control other people's thoughts. He said he could Jedi people. Now he's on the adult unit, we think, and we never see him.

Amanda heard that Gerald might be schizophrenic. That was not good because she didn't think they could cure that.

Juliet is very tall, the tallest person on the ward, and her legs are so long that she moves like a colt. She's sixteen. She wears very short shorts, even when the rest of us are freezing, and wool sweaters on top that have snowflake patterns. When two people are standing and talking, Juliet will go stand with them, she will nod and smile and say nothing.

Nobody knows why Juliet is here, other than that she is a little bit odd. But we are all odd, Amanda says. Even the staff. They're a little bit odd, too.

I'm in the chair, and I can feel Maggie in her chair, right next to me, and everything has grown quiet. People have gone into their rooms, or gone to meetings with a nurse or social worker or with Dr.

Manchin, or with the other, part-time psychiatrist, Dr. Altemio.

My eyes are closed, and this is when I can really feel the drugs, all over my body. I can feel them in my feet and hands, my stomach and chest, but most of all, I feel them in my head. Not my ears and nose and lips, so much, but taking over my brain.

My brain grows so heavy and sleepy that it tilts my head to the side, and then back, so my throat is exposed.

It doesn't matter, then, how I look or who sees me. Just that I can rest my head somewhere. Just that I can meet that heaviness with sleep.

My eyes are closed, and I'm sliding deeper and deeper into darkness, into distance, and I'm in the house, I'm on the third floor, and this is a long time ago, and it's very late and very dark.

The whole house is heavily asleep. I can feel that. Maybe they were drinking earlier in the night.

I get up, and without putting my slippers on, I move into the moonlit hall, and go silently down the stairs, and then I see the back door to the first floor, and I start down. I have only been on these back stairs to go outside. At the bottom, there's a big hallway, with a door to outside, another to the basement, and a third door to the first floor, which is open.

I can smell flowers, many many flowers, and the rooms of the first floor are very big. I go from room to room. There is glass in the French doors, and then there is a long room with rows of folding chairs. At the front of the room, on a stand, surrounded by flowers, is a big long shiny box. Its cover is pushed up, and in the moonlight washing the room, I can see puffy white fabric lining the cover.

Then I see folded hands, I see a still white face pointed at the ceiling.

There's a hand on my arm.

A voice says, Trey, then says, Trey, again.

Then a hand is shaking my arm, and I'm gasping. I'm gasping for air.

I say, Please. I say it again, and I'm trying to breathe.

It's okay, Trey, Maggie says.

Trey, she says again.

It's Maggie, I start to realize. But I'm still breathing as though there's not enough air.

Eight

EMMA WAS PROBABLY NORA'S best friend. Or she was one of Nora's two best friends. BFF. Best friends forever. Asia was the other one. Nora loved both of them as much as anyone could love another person. All three of them were in Ms. Laster's second grade class at Fall Creek School. They had met in kindergarten there.

They ate lunch together in the cafeteria, they played together during recess in the gym or on the playground, they talked on the phone or by the computer, and they knew everything about each other.

Emma and Asia both had very dark hair, but Emma's hair was darker. It was black. That was because Emma was half Japanese on her father's side. Asia's hair was dark brown. It had little hints of red in it when she was outside in the sunshine. Inside, in the shade, it was only dark. It was so deep brown that it was almost black like Emma's hair.

Nora's hair was blond, and Nora said that hair was something girls thought about. They thought about hair way more than boys thought about hair.

Unless it was later, and boys grew up and went bald, and then they thought about the hair they didn't have.

Will I be bald? I asked, and Nora said, Like an egg, like a cue ball. Then she laughed.

I felt the thick hair on my head with my hand.

No, she said, and put her hand on my hand, on top of my head.

Just kidding, Nora said. Everyone doesn't go bald. Not all men. I doubt you'll lose your hair.

How come? I asked.

Because Dad has lots of thick hair, Nora said. So you will too.

Will I be like Dad? I asked.

Only with your hair, Trey, Nora said.

Nora went to Emma's house for the first time on a Saturday, in first grade. It was only a few blocks away. Nora was six, but she walked there by herself, and she said afterwards that it wasn't too scary. Just that everything—houses, trees, telephone poles, cars— seemed huge. Seemed like giants.

Nora walked one street down, in the direction of school, and then she went left and walked one and a half blocks over, in the direction of Cayuga Street, and at number 214, at the big red house with the green door, she was there.

Emma had two older brothers who loved video games. They were sitting in a small room they called the den, their eyes fixed on a television screen, clicking and clicking small controllers in their hands.

When Emma said, This is my friend Nora, neither boy looked up, but they said, Hey, and, Hi, Nora, and kept clicking and watching the screen.

Emma's mom wore jeans and a gray sweater, she was a little chunky, and her smile was big and her eyes smiled too, Nora said.

She asked if Nora walked all this way by herself, and Nora

said, Yes, but it wasn't too far. Just one block down and almost two blocks over.

Emma's mom's name was Mia, and she said to call her Mia, and then her dad was there. He was small, wore thick glasses, and he smiled almost all the time. He was Akira.

Akira taught mathematics at the university, and Mia was something called a psychologist. That meant she listened to people who had problems and tried to help them. They were studying at a university in North Carolina. They got married and moved to the university here a long time ago.

They were so nice, Nora said. They smiled, and Mia even gave Nora a hug, and said they hoped that Nora would visit more often. They had heard so much about her from Emma.

They didn't ask her about her parents, but Mia did ask if she had a brother or sister, and Nora said, Yes, she had a brother named Trey, and he was three and a half years younger than her.

He's very quiet and shy, Nora said, and I wondered if I was quiet and shy.

Nora was glad that Mia and Akira didn't ask her about what her mom and dad did for work. Kids at school did that. Kids at school knew that Nora's mom and dad were in charge of dead people. Walter Rusher, in her class in first grade, asked Nora if dead people ate dinner with her family every night, and if they all slept in coffins.

Peter Crawford said it was weird, working with corpses, and Wendy Vaughn said that the dead must smell really bad. They must smell like poop, Wendy said. She couldn't imagine how anyone lived in the same house with all those bodies.

They were standing outside on the playground, and the buds on trees and bushes were growing bigger. That had been April, Nora said, the end of April, and spring was finally coming to upstate New York.

Nora ignored them. She barely even blinked, but she wished that her mom and dad did something else for a job. She wished her dad was a mathematics teacher at the university, and that her mom was a psychologist. She wished that her mom and dad were doctors and took care of people the way Asia's mom and dad took care of people.

One girl, Rose Hanlon, who was so fat that her legs rubbed against each other when she walked, said that the ghosts of the dead stayed around, a long time after the body was gone. They went, Woo Woo, and Sss Sss, and they hovered in hallways and rooms.

Rose lived in a big old house on Utica Street, in the middle of the Fall Creek neighborhood, and trees and bushes were all grown up and pretty much covered the windows and porches of her house. There was a cracked window on the second floor, in front, and most of the paint was peeling.

Some kids said the house was haunted, Nora said, because Rose's father had died of alcohol in a bedroom on the second floor, three years ago. Rose and her mom were visiting New York City for three days at the time, and Rose's father was lying on the floor all weekend, his dead eyes staring at the ceiling.

From across the street on Utica, you could see that the third-floor window of Rose's house was always open. Summer and winter, spring and fall, the window was always open, Nora said.

Rain and snow could blow in, cold or hot air, but it was never closed.

Nora said that some kids were pretty sure the window was left open to let the ghost of the dead father leave. He hadn't left because the window was still always open. When he was gone, Nora thought, they could close the window, and stop the rain and snow from getting in.

Is that true? I asked, and Nora said she wasn't sure. She didn't think so. But from the way she was avoiding looking at me, I could tell she wasn't sure.

She said the strange thing was that Rose and her mother came home from New York City, from their fun weekend, and there was their father and husband, not moving on the bedroom floor, his eyes just staring, looking at something nobody else could see.

Is Rose nice? I asked.

Yes, Nora said. Really nice. She's funny, and she does math really quickly. She already knew all her multiplication tables at the start of second grade. And even though she's really fat, she's kind of beautiful. She's very pretty. She has big green eyes.

Are those other kids nice? I asked.

Walter, Peter and Wendy?

I nodded.

They're not the nicest kids, Nora said. But they're not that bad.

Why'd they say mean things?

Nora shook her head.

Everyone says mean things sometimes, Nora said. Most of the time they're pretty good. Except Walter, I guess. A lot of kids don't seem to like him much. I don't think he has friends.

Nora often sounded like a grownup. She was strange that way.

Not one?

I don't think so. He always eats alone at lunch.

I pictured him with red or blond hair, wearing glasses, and having a long thin nose. With wet, red lips and crooked teeth. Making funny faces by moving his lips and squinting.

Will I have friends? I asked Nora.

Of course, she said. But you have to talk and you have to be friendly.

In a little over a month I was starting school. I would be in kindergarten at Fall Creek School. I would walk to school with Nora.

In a little over a month, Nora would be in third grade. And from then on, I would be just a little bit behind her. When I was in second grade, she would be in fifth. It would be like that all the way. That would never change.

That was in July, in the second half of the month. July was very hot and very humid. Except once in a while, every week or two, when a big thunderstorm would rumble in from the northwest, and Mom and Nora ran around the second and third floors, and slammed all the windows shut.

Then it grew very dark, and almost cold, and the branches on the trees outside were whipping back and forth in the wind. Rain and wind lashed the windows, until it seemed they would break, and there was thunder, there were jagged shots of lightning that were so fast that you wondered if you had really seen them.

The thunder was bigger and louder than anything in the world, thunder made you vibrate. Mom said that when she was a kid, the nuns used to say that thunder was the sound of angels bowling in heaven.

The nuns said a lot of things, Mom said, and sometimes you didn't know what to believe.

Believe what? Dad said, because he was suddenly in the room.

He moved so quietly because he had rubber or something on the bottom of his shoes.

When the nuns said angels were bowling, Nora said, and Dad smiled at her, remembering.

Dad liked Nora. She was the opposite of me.

What do you think, Quigley, Dad said to me.

Dad often called me by an Irish name. Quigley, O'Connell, Madden, Riley, O'Brien, Burke, O'Toole.

When he said the name in his almost Irish voice, the sound was nearly like music. It was a brook moving over colored rocks, it was a breeze touching the leaves in the trees.

Dad was wearing his rubber apron, and I thought that there must be a body in the basement. Maybe they brought it in late last night, after Nora and I were asleep. We always knew if there were one or two bodies in the house.

But sometimes, we both slept though the night, and Mom and Dad brought dead people home in the van at midnight or at one or two or three in the morning. One of them would go out in the van, or both of them, because we would never know, sleeping way up on the third floor.

People died at all hours of the day and night.

When Dad called me Quigley, I shrugged and smiled.

Dad stepped over to me. He reached out his hand, and I was going to duck. But I didn't, and he rubbed the hair on top of my head.

I could smell formalin.

Almost as fast as it began, the thunderstorm stopped, and when Mom and Nora opened the windows, the air was cool and dry and smelled like rain.

Another few weeks, Quigley, and you'll be in school, Dad said.

I nodded.

Dad's hands were on his hips, as though he was about to do some work.

You excited? he asked.

Yes, I said, because I had not yet said anything. He might know how scared I was.

Good, he said in his low voice. I hope it will be grand, Quigley.

Me too, I said.

We could hear Mom and Nora on the third floor, opening windows and talking. Their voices were bright.

That night, after dinner, when Mom and Dad were both working in the basement, Nora said that she had gone down the back steps, earlier in the day, to go to the backyard. The doors to the first floor and basement were not only unlocked, they were both wide open. She could see carpet on the floor in a big room on the first floor, and through the door to the basement, she could see a second door that looked like steel, with a sign that said New York State Law: KEEP OUT in big red letters, on the door.

I felt the tiny hairs on my neck and back rise.

No, I said. Don't go there.

Sooner or later, Trey, Nora said.

Not ever, I said.

Nine

IN LATE AUGUST, THE week before school, the body of a four-year-old girl who died of cancer in the brain came to our house. Cancer was a terrible thing, Mom said. It grew inside you, and kept growing and growing until it took over everything.

It ate you alive, Mom said.

Do I have cancer? I asked.

Mom said, Not that we know of.

Even a four-year-old girl could get it, and she wasn't much younger than me. Because I was five, and the little girl was four, and I wondered if they knew she had cancer at first, but ignored it, or if they just didn't know.

I thought, How would you know? What did it look or feel like, eating away inside? Did something smell or taste different? Could you feel it, eating at your heart or at your brain?

Did it make you very sick from the beginning? Or did it take a while to know?

Nora asked Mom questions. Nora wanted to know too.

The little girl's name was Alice. Her Mom and Dad owned two restaurants, and they worked very hard. They knew a lot of people in town because their restaurants were busy and popular.

Mom met with Alice's mom and dad when they came to the funeral home. Mom said they did not look good. She said they were thin and gray and looked like they had been crying for a long time. Their eyes were red and swollen.

They had three other children, who were older than Alice, and Mom said that had to be a comfort. Like if she and dad lost me, they would still have Nora.

For a long time, the mom and dad did not know Alice was very sick. She had terrible headaches every day. Headaches so bad that she would cry and moan from the pain. After a while, after headaches every day for a month, after tears and moans, they took Alice to the doctor.

The doctor ordered a CAT scan, which was not a regular cat. It looked inside, and found a mass, a lump, near the bottom of her brain. That was bad. That was very bad.

Alice had had surgery, she had drug treatment, she had radiation on her brain like X-rays, to kill the cancer. Her hair fell out so she was bald like an old man. Then she went blind, Mom said.

The cancer was stronger than Alice. The cancer killed her.

She fought hard, Mom said. She fought long and she fought hard.

It was an awful, awful thing to lose a child, Mom said. A mother and father were not supposed to outlive their children.

She knew people were always saying that, about outliving a child, but it was still true. She couldn't think of a worse thing.

Then Nora said that Mom excused herself because she had work to do on Alice, down in the basement.

Nora said she didn't want to even think of that, the work Mom had to do in the basement. She said she didn't want to think of Mom or Dad in the rubber aprons, standing over Alice, who lay on the stainless steel table.

Most people who died and came to our house were old, sometimes very old. They lived a long time and it was time for them to die. Not all of them, but most of them.

When old people got sick, pretty often they would die. Like an old tree losing its branches, and then falling over in the big wind of a storm.

The disease that made them sick was like the storm and the big wind. It was like gravity, Nora said, that pulled everything down to the ground.

An old tree wasn't strong like a young tree. The big wind wouldn't take down the young tree, although sometimes it would. You could never tell really.

I tried to think about school, which was only one week away. It was right after Labor Day, which Nora said marked the end of summer. It was also to be nice to working people.

There was Memorial Day at the start of summer, she said, and Labor Day at the end. Memorial Day was for dead people, and Labor Day for workers. People had cookouts with hot dogs and hamburgers and burning red charcoals to cook them. They drank beer and wine to feel good.

I don't remember ever going to a cookout with Mom and Dad and Nora. I don't think Mom and Dad drank wine or beer either. They drank something that looked like pee, only browner, and it was whiskey. It made them happy and relaxed and talkative at first. Then it made them tired and sad, and then you didn't know what they would do.

They might cry or yell or sing or laugh or hit you. They might fall asleep on the couch or on a chair. Anything could happen.

But now, they were busy with Alice, and I could tell that they were thinking of Alice. She was down in the basement, or on the first floor in her tiny casket, and she wasn't an old person, she wasn't even an adult of any sort. Old people and adults had had a chance to grow up and to live, at least a little. The list of things Alice had not been able to do went on and on. She never drove a car or fell in love or cut her hair the way she wanted it. Never got married or rode a bicycle or shoveled snow in the winter or walked in the woods by herself or learned to swim.

Alice hadn't done any of those things. She hadn't even gone to school yet, and that was something that I would be doing in only a week. If I didn't die for some reason.

I didn't think I would die soon, but Mom and Dad always told Nora and me that you could never know. They said every person alive carried around his or her death.

There was a silver clock in the big living room, on a mantle above the fireplace, and it ticked and ticked and ticked, all the time. It never stopped, not even for a second.

Whether you thought about it or not, whether you heard the ticks or not, if you were asleep or if Nora was looking at her computer, or if I was in the bathroom, taking a bath, the clock continued to tick, one tick every second.

Dad said time never stopped, that it moved constantly, for very small children who didn't even know time existed, for kings and queens and presidents and prime ministers, for everyone who lived and breathed. The only time it did stop was when you died. Because then you were out of time.

I didn't think I knew what he was talking about. It felt slippery and foggy, and almost made me dizzy, the more I thought about it. Out of time was so strange. It meant ran out of time, but it also meant removed from time. Like you were moving on a busy street, but then you stepped off the street, and time was over there, on the busy street, happening to other people.

Mom told Nora a little bit about Alice, something she and Dad never did. They never told us anything about what they called their clients. That would be unprofessional. To be professional meant to do your job, without a lot of song and dance involved.

You had to respect the dead, Mom said.

Nora told me that Mom had told her that Alice was being buried in her favorite corduroy overalls, which were blue. She'd wear a white turtleneck under that that had clocks on it, and white sneakers that flashed red lights from the heels. She would hold her favorite stuffed animal, a purple elephant.

Mom told Nora that they'd found a small blond wig with short hair that looked like Alice's hair before her own hair fell out from cancer drugs. They'd put the wig on Alice, and she would look the way she used to look. Only thinner, and sleeping.

Nora said that they had ordered a special small casket for babies and small children for Alice. It was years since they had done a wake and burial for a baby or small child. Mom said it was very hard for everybody when a child died. It was even hard for funeral directors.

Nobody knew where to put all that sadness.

And Nora said that people always said the dead person looked like they were sleeping, looked natural, but she didn't think that was true. Not at all.

One time, back in the spring, when Nora was looking for Mom

or Dad to see if she could go over to Asia's house, she couldn't find them. She looked on the third floor, she looked on the second floor, and finally she went downstairs to the first floor, something she was never supposed to do.

The rooms were big, they had high ceilings, and every room had carpets, and everything smelled like flowers. She went from one room to another, and she came to an office with a desk, two computers, and comfortable chairs in front of the desk. But no one was there.

She went to a lobby by the front door, and there was a stand with a book on it where people were supposed to sign in, she thought.

Then she went through another doorway, and there was Dad standing in front of a casket, adjusting the tie of a dead man. Dad was wearing his black suit with a white shirt, but no tie. For a moment Nora thought that Dad had taken off his tie to put on the dead man, but the dead man's tie had a flowery design, something Dad would never wear. Not in a thousand years.

He turned, and looked surprised, and then Dad said, Nora.

Daddy, I'm sorry, she said. I looked all over but I couldn't find you or Mom.

Sweetheart, he said in his sweet low voice.

He motioned for her to come to him.

She went over and leaned against his side. He put his arm around her. The smell of flowers was very powerful. It was almost like the smell of formalin, only nicer, sweeter.

She tried not to look at the dead man in the coffin. She closed her eyes at first, but even leaning into Dad's side, with his arm around her, Nora couldn't help but open her eyes and look at the man.

He was old, Nora said, and mostly bald. He had a pointed nose and heavy eyebrows that were white, and his thin lips were closed and not smiling. There were rosary beads wrapped in his folded hands, and his suit was dark gray.

The white lining of the casket was like pillows, and there was a small, real pillow under his head.

That's a deceased person, Dad said. That's the work your mom and I do. We try to make them look good for the family.

Nora nodded, under Dad's arm. She thought the casket was like a jewelry box, like the ones for Mom's rings and her pearls. You opened the top, and the ring was set in soft white satin. That's what she thought it was called. Satin.

The dead person was precious like rings or pearls.

But the dead person did not look like he was sleeping, and he did not look natural. He was more still than a stone. His lips were slightly red, but his nose, his ears, his fingers were all faintly blue.

He almost looked like he was made of wax, like he was a statue, only not made of metal or stone, but colored wax.

Nora kept thinking, even standing there with Dad, This is the first time I've seen a dead guy. This is what's on the other side of the door.

Late in the afternoon before Alice's calling hours, when people would come to look at her, and to say how sorry they were that she was dead, Mom asked Nora and me if we wanted to go downstairs to view her.

I shook my head, but Nora said that she did want to, as long as Mom would go with her.

Mom looked at me, and I kept shaking my head.

That could be you in the casket, Mom said to me. Some day it will be you.

I continued to shake my head.

Nora went down the stairs with Mom, and I pictured Nora and Mom standing at the casket, looking down at Alice in her corduroy overalls, holding the purple elephant, her eyes closed forever.

Ten

ALL THE TIME, FROM the moment I wake up, everything I hear and feel, everything I think and see, is swimming and drifting and crackling, inside my brain, I'm pretty sure.

This was not supposed to happen. They were supposed to lower the dose of my drugs, to give me a little less of each med, three times a day. I was pretty sure they had done that. For a few days, maybe for a week, I thought that things were more steady, more clear. There was less fog, it seemed, and things didn't waver and drift, didn't move around so much.

But like everything else, that has sifted away. It was vapor that hung in the air, near the ceiling, for a while, and when you looked again it was gone. Into cracks or into tiny holes in the acoustic tiles of the ceiling.

That's one of the problems in here. You don't notice, you don't see why or where or who, and then it's all different. You're sitting in your chair in the dayroom, you close your eyes, and when you open them the vapor is gone. And you can't count on your brain anymore. It's doing funny things.

We line up at the back window of the nurse's station. Kaylee or Sue, or one of the other nurses, comes over, from inside the glass, unlocks the window, and begins giving out meds. Me, Bobby, Amanda, Elliot, Juliet and Clea. A few others. But no Maggie.

Kaylee has a big cart in front of her, and on top of it are two pitchers of water, a stack of tiny cups that have pleats, and another stack with slightly larger cups. Kaylee hits buttons on a panel on top of the cart, and a drawer opens. She takes three or four or even five bottles of pills from the drawer, opens them one at a time, taps a pill or two into the pleated cup, then does the same with each container.

She pours water into a larger cup, and hands both cups out the window to Clea.

How you doing, Clea? Kaylee asks, and Clea mumbles, Fine.

Kaylee watches Clea tilt the pills into her mouth, sip water, then crumple the cups, which she hands to Kaylee.

I'm third in line, behind Bobby and Elliot. Amanda's behind me.

No Maggie again? Bobby says to me and Amanda.

I don't say anything, but I've noticed. I'm pretty certain I haven't seen her in two or three days. Maybe four or five days. I'm not sure.

She's in her room, Amanda says. Not feeling too good.

Bobby and I look at each other.

How long? Bobby asks.

Three or four days, Amanda says.

I watch Elliot get his pills.

For some reason he doesn't talk all the time the way he used to. Kaylee asks if he's doing okay, and Elliot says, Great, in a very quiet voice.

He hands the empty cups to Kaylee, and she drops them in a plastic trash can near her feet.

Then it's Bobby, and he says, Kaylee, so nice to see. How you be?

Great, Kaylee says, and she smiles at Bobby. You're rhyming today, she says.

I am, he says.

That's a good sign, right? she says.

He smiles. Oh yeah, he says.

Bobby still taps things with his fingers, but he doesn't talk as much. He used to talk all the time, I think. Weeks ago. I believe. I'm pretty sure.

Is it meds? Like with me?

Is it meds, or our brains?

Kaylee takes out four pill containers for me. She taps out two pills from one container, another two from the second container, then one each from the last two. One is a pink triangle, two are oblong, the rest are regular white tablets.

I can't remember if this is different from before. I think maybe there used to be a pale blue pill, a green and yellow capsule, and another white capsule. Is that possible?

How is it, Trey? Kaylee asks.

I nod, then say, Thanks.

I take my pills, and swallow all the water.

Be good, she says, and I hand her the empty paper cups. I don't say anything else.

I had thought to ask her if these pills were different from before. Were there more of some, and less of others? Are the different colors and shapes just a change of dose?

I feel weird, I wanted to say. My brain is on fire, I almost said. Or my brain is in a deep freeze. I can't tell.

But there were too many people around to say anything.

Now in the dayroom, in a chair, sounds are so loud that I almost have to put my fingers in my ears. Just footsteps and voices, a door opening and closing. But they sound like crashing pots and pans, like gunshots and bombs.

How long can something like this last?

I want Maggie to get up from her bed, put her hoodie on, and come out here to sit next to me. She wouldn't need to say anything at all. In the week or two or three that we sat next to each other, we never said more than a few words.

She could be silent, as she always was, and I would be silent too. When her arm or shoulder or hand brushed against my arm or shoulder or hand, that would be enough. That would be so much better than words. That would be nearly everything.

Three, four days ago, Maggie seemed the way she always seemed. She sat in the chair next to me, and she didn't say anything, but I didn't either. A few times, our shoulders and hands brushed against each other.

We sat for hours, in the morning, the afternoon, the evening. That seemed ridiculous, just sitting and not saying anything. How boring.

But I could feel her openness and warmth, at least to me. And she could feel mine to her, I think. Just sitting on our chairs. Next to each other.

This is the bin, the farm, the monkey house. We may be on the ward, we may be in need of Behavioral Science, of the Unit, but we know where we are.

I've thought of going to her room, knocking on the door, going in. Sitting on the side of the bed. Talking to her. I don't what I might say. Probably, I'd just sit on the edge of the bed, my side touching her side.

She would know it was me, and I'd know it was her.

But in here, to go into another patient's room is like murdering someone. It's a major rule, and a major infraction of the rules. I'd be kicked off the ward, and for me, that would mean going directly to Malvern, the state hospital.

I may be going there anyway in a few months. In two months or six months. Lisa and Cara keep mentioning it. They say, You can't stay here forever, Trey.

As though that was my deepest wish.

They say it every few days.

Malvern, I hear them whisper. And I'm not sure, sometimes, where the sound is coming from.

Malvern, they whisper. Malvern, Malvern.

I don't think I can go home. Nora is no longer there. She lives at the university on the hill.

Mom and Dad? I don't know.

Do they even live in this town anymore?

Did Dr. Manchin say that he asked them not to visit me? Did he tell them that I needed respite from the home and the parents in the home?

What does Dr. Manchin know about what happened? Did he talk to Mom and Dad on the phone? To Ellen and Henry?

Did he know how it was?

Henry would use his low, comforting voice. His funeral director's voice that said how sorry he was, and how in this time of grief, this was not when you wanted to be worrying about every little detail. Please let him worry about the details. He would take care of everything.

Mom would sit in a chair next to the bereaved, in front of the chair in their office on the first floor. Mom would nod sadly. Mom would understand.

Is that how they were with Dr. Manchin?

But Mom and Dad are now absent, just as Maggie is mostly absent. Just as Elliot and Bobby are talking much less.

When did all this happen? And how did it happen?

More than anything else, why do these things happen?

Did I really almost die? In July or August?

Some people go to bed as one person, go to sleep and wake up the next morning, and they're a different person.

Amanda does that sometimes. She's so nice and normal. She's the best person among us patients. She's nice, she has good manners, she's cheerful.

Amanda's appropriate, I heard Cara, the social worker, say.

That means she does the right thing at the right time in the right amount.

Then she goes to her room and stays there, for a night, a day, for another night and day.

Half of us hardly talk. Me, Maggie, Clea, Juliet.

We sit and we stare. We fall asleep in our chairs.

Mom used to call that being a bump on a log.

We suck energy from a room. Someone, I think, said that we're a waste of space.

Amanda's been out of her room now for at least a week, maybe two weeks. She's on two new drugs, Cymbalta and Zoloft. They're both antidepressants, but they're a little different, I guess. Dr. Altemio is her doctor, and Amanda says that Dr. Altemio likes to try cocktails of drugs.

He tells her that one drug will potentiate another drug. She says potentiate means make something else stronger. She says that's why they often give opioids, the pain medicines, along with Tylenol. Tylenol makes the opioids stronger, and the opioids make the Tylenol more effective. Amanda doesn't know how that works, just that it does work.

Dr. Altemio knows.

He's a small man with thick black hair and a big Roman nose. He doesn't look like he's long out of medical school, and he's very handsome, Amanda thinks.

He has dark eyes that are kind, and he never wears a tie. Just striped dress shirts and V-neck sweaters. Dr. Altemio has hiking boots, and he has a two-year-old daughter. Amanda knows because Dr. Altemio has shown her a picture of the daughter.

Her name, Amanda says, is Grace.

Amanda doesn't know the name of Dr. Altemio's wife. She thinks it should be Sofia or Isabella. Something like that. She says that the wife must be very smart and very pretty. Dark hair, dark eyes. Big smile, thin lips. A professor of something at the university.

You know what I'm saying? Amanda asks, and I nod.

We're sitting in the corner where Maggie and I usually sit, and Amanda fills the chair, she's so tall and has such wide shoulders. Her hair is long and brown with specks of red in it, and it's pretty wavy.

Our shoulders are touching because, even though I'm skinny, I have wide shoulders like Amanda.

She has big green eyes that are hard to look at. You can see almost everything in her eyes. Sadness, longing, laughter, the birds cross the sky of her eyes, I think. Just dark flickers that move quietly and quickly.

When you go to your room and stay there—I say. Why?

She looks at me with those eyes. I look away.

Cause I have to, she says. I can't be around people. Everything's loud and violent. I gotta get away.

Maggie? I ask.

Is that why Maggie's in bed? Amanda asks. Is what you're asking?

I nod.

Probably something like that. I don't know. You'd have to ask her.

We sit some more, and it's very quiet on the ward. It always gets real quiet for an hour or two after meds. I start to nod a little, and I feel Amanda move. She stands up, pats the side of my head, and I can sense her walking away.

People move a little on the far side of the dayroom. The big door to the hallway out front opens and closes. There are footsteps, there's a snatch of television. Music, laughter, loud voices. Then the TV is turned off.

Outside is gray, and outside is raining, and the rain is drumming on the roof of the big house, above the third floor. The rain moves down and almost sideways outside the window, and it seems to want to flood the world.

I can't imagine where it all comes from. I can't imagine where birds and squirrels, cats and dogs, where people go to stay dry.

It must be the middle of the afternoon, but it seems much later. It seems almost like dusk, like sunset, because it's so dark. People can get into their beds, and listen as the rain gets farther and farther away. And when they wake up the rain will be gone. Then it will be full dark.

But there are footsteps. Footsteps climbing stairs. Footsteps on carpet. Movement somewhere. Movement in several places.

Somebody, close, wisps of hair touching my cheek.

A light kiss on my cheek.

I blink and blink, half wake up, but nobody's there.

Eleven

KINDERGARTEN. THE FIRST DAY. Three days into September, and past Labor Day. Nora and I were walking on North Tioga Street, past so many houses. Houses and houses and more houses. Cars were going both ways on Tioga, and cars were going on the cross streets.

There were so many kids. All of them wearing backpacks. There were tall kids and short kids and medium kids. Kids with every color hair in the world, and every color clothes too. Stripes and polka dots, lightening bolts, swirls and squares.

There were shorts and skirts, tee-shirts and button shirts, some sweaters and sweatshirts, and all kinds of sneakers. Cranberry sneakers, and bright green, and electric blue, Nora said.

Electric meant the color blue or yellow or orange looked like it was plugged into a light socket. It meant you might be able to see it in the dark.

Some girls had electric pink sneakers, and bright yellow socks. Many of the girls had ribbon in their hair, or hair clips, or elastics covered in cloth. Some of the boys had hair as long as the girls' hair, and a few girls had hair as short as the boys.

We passed Marshall Street, Yates Street, and then Tompkins Street, and on the far side of Tompkins, Asia and her little sister Pippa were standing and waiting, looking at us and smiling. They looked mostly the same, only Asia was taller and a little chunky, but they were both pretty. They had brown eyes, and pale skin, dark hair, and big teeth.

I had never met them, but Nora had told me Pippa was in kindergarten too. She was nice like Asia, and she had been playing the violin since she was three years old.

Nora didn't know what kind of name Pippa was, just that it was a name and she thought it suited Pippa. It was bouncy like a ball, and kind of happy, Nora said, and she thought Pippa was bouncy and happy like her name.

Nora and Asia walked in front of Pippa and me. We didn't say anything because we were so shy and scared of the first day, but Nora and Asia talked constantly, and when they didn't talk they laughed.

They both had Ms. Masik for third grade, and Pippa and I had Ms. Macbride. Each grade at Fall Creek had two classes, and each class had twenty or twenty-five students. Nora had never had Ms. Macbride. She had only come to Fall Creek a year ago, but Nora's friend, Talia, had a brother who was in her class and liked her.

He said she was funny, Nora told me.

A big woman in an electric orange vest, carrying a red Stop sign, was crossing kids at Tioga and King Streets. She held up her sign and all the cars stopped and the kids crossed.

The school was only a block away. There were moms and dads with some kids, with really small kids, and there was another crossing guard at the corner of King and Aurora. Fall Creek School was on the far corner.

Thousands of kids played on the playground in front of the school. Maybe not a thousand, but it seemed that way. There were a hundred kids. There were more than a hundred.

Everything was huge. Everything was tall and wide and bigger than at home. Trees, fences, telephone poles, the school building, made of red brick.

We stood, Asia, Nora, Pippa and me, and then Emma came over. I had seen Emma once when she came to play at our house. Emma waved to Pippa and me, and then she and Asia and Nora starting talking. Emma had very dark hair like Asia.

They laughed.

Pippa and I stood like bumps on a log. We didn't say a word. Every minute or so, I looked over at her, but mostly I looked down at my white sneakers. Then I could feel her eyes on me, and when I looked at Pippa, she looked scared. Her dark eyes were big.

I wanted to say something. I wanted to ask her why she was so scared. I wanted to tell her that I was scared too. But if I did say I was scared and she asked what I was scared of, I wouldn't know what to say.

All these kids were scary. Maybe Ms. Macbride was scary. Maybe I would walk in the building and I would disappear. I wouldn't be able to say anything, wouldn't be able to do anything, and they would make me go home.

A loud bell rang, and Pippa said in a small voice that that was the first bell. Asia had told her there was a first bell, and that meant that in five minutes a second bell would ring and you had to go to your classroom.

The first bell was to warn you about the second bell.

I thought, What if you don't hear the bell?

Asia had told her all about school. About bells and playgrounds, about going to the bathroom, about classrooms, about lunch and gym and recess. Pippa knew all about almost everything.

When Pippa talked she moved her hands around as though she was conducting the words. Nora had shown me a video on her computer of a woman conducting singers with her hands. The singers all wore black and they stood in rows, each row higher than the one in front of it.

The singers were loud, and then they were soft, then they were loud again. Nora said it was a chorus, like birds in the trees, all singing on a sunny morning. She didn't know why they all wore black like a funeral, like Dad's suit. They just did, was all.

All the kids were drifting in small sideways steps to the big door of the school. It was as though they were flowing like water, like someone had tipped the ground up on the far outer edge of the playground, and all the kids flowed toward the doors.

Then the bell rang again, and I could see a speaker on the brick wall near the door. That's where the bell lived.

A man and a woman were standing outside the doors, and a second woman held one of the doors open. The two women and the man called out the names of kids.

Tara, Tamar, Wendy, Peter, Spencer.

Let's go, the man said.

C'mon, the woman holding the door said.

They did not look mean. They were smiling.

A tall girl poked a medium sized boy in the back. He turned quickly and said, Charlotte, stop. He grinned. She's poking me, he said.

He had long brown hair and his sneakers were untied. He was smiling too.

The girl said, Stop, Harry. She had frizzy blond hair piled on top of her head.

Harry had red lips and cheeks, and his blue eyes were bright.

And all the time, all the kids were moving to the door. Some parents were standing together near a play structure.

Inside, in the hall, it was darker and cooler than outside. There were stairs to the right, and a hallway that went off to the left.

The bigger kids were all going to the stairs and the second floor. They were almost all loud, were calling out to each other, were joking and laughing. The little kids all went left on the long hallway, and I went left with them.

There were signs next to big doors. One said, Mrs. Harcourt, with a big 2 next to it. Farther down the hall a sign said, Ms. Levy, 1. A tall woman stood next to each sign. One had gray hair, the other had brown hair.

Pippa was four or five steps in front of me, and she seemed to know where she was going.

Near the end of the hall were two doorways on the left. There was a small woman next to a sign that said Ms. Crowe or Ms. Crow. And a giant letter K. Then a door with a very young woman, very thin, strong, and her sign said, Ms. Macbride and another letter K.

Both K teachers were smiling. They had beautiful big smiles, and they both wore glasses. Ms. Crow wore a tan dress with small blue flowers, and Ms. Macbride wore dark pants, a white shirt, and a vest that was made of electric blue and red and orange and purple colors.

I stopped in front of Ms. Macbride, and she put her hand on the top of my head and kept it there. Her hand felt light and cool.

She said, Hello, there, and I didn't know what to say, even though she had a sweet voice.

I'm Ms. Macbride, she said.

I nodded, and her hand stayed on my head.

You are?

I still didn't know what to say.

She squatted down, and then she put her hand on my arm.

What's your name? she asked, and I said, Trey, so softly that I didn't think she could hear me.

Trey, she said. Of course. I've been looking forward to meeting you.

She smiled more, and I looked at her grey eyes floating behind her glasses, a few inches from my eyes.

She smelled like orange or lemon.

Everything will be terrific, Ms. Macbride said. Trust me.

Inside the classroom there were big windows that looked out onto the front playground. There were pictures on the wall, there were charts, and there was so much color. Greens and purples, yellow and raspberry colors. There were pictures of rainbows, lions, dogs, trees, bugs, clouds, and the sun in five or six shades of yellow. There was a whale and a dolphin. There was a bear. There was a large orange cat with stripes of darker orange.

There were small tables and chairs on one side of the room, and a big thick carpet on another side of the room. There was a sink in one corner, and low down on one wall were cubbyholes, with each of our names on one cubby. There were hooks on the wall with our names on tape under a single hook.

Kids were standing around the room, almost every one was standing by himself or herself, except for two boys who stood next to each other, almost leaning together. They were small and had dark eyes and hair.

More kids came in, and then Ms. Macbride came in. She seemed to nearly walk on her toes, and to bounce when she walked.

She did something then, in that first minute in the classroom, that made us love her. She stood in front of a desk, her regular big teacher's desk. She squatted down, then swung her arms back then forward, and jumped in one movement from the floor to the top of the desk.

She stood on the desk, smiling.

Kids laughed, kids said, Wow. They said, Whoa. They said, Oh my goodness.

Her jump was one of the best things we had ever seen. Ms. Macbride might have been in a circus once. Ms. Macbride could jump over a parked car if she wanted.

She jumped down, and it was like we were now expecting her to fly. Instead she got us to sit in a circle on the big rug, and most of us sat with our legs crossed. I was next to a tall, sleepy fat boy on one side, and a tall regular girl on the other side. The fat boy had red hair, and the regular girl had light brown hair.

Ms. Macbride asked us to go around the room and say our names out loud. There was a Tom, an Emily, two Sarahs, a Hannah, a Matt and a Samson. There was Pippa and Trey, a Daniel and Julia and Owen, a Toby, a Cora, a Madeleine and Maddy, a Sophie, girls named Dylan and Sydney. The two boys who stood together were Max and Major.

There was a husky boy who looked like a bulldog, and he was named Ronnie. A very thin shy girl with curly hair name Renee, and a boy with light brown hair named Bjorn. There were other names too, but sometimes it was hard to keep track.

When it came around to Ms. Macbride, she said her name was

Aubrey, but that we should always call her Ms. Macbride, because that was the rule of the school.

Aubrey was a nice name. Aubrey was a good name for Ms. Macbride.

Then it was later and we had learned so many things. Where the bathrooms were, and how we had to raise our hands and ask permission before going to the bathroom. Where the gym was, and how the cafeteria was just past the gym. How we were not supposed to run or yell in the halls. How we were required to treat each other with respect at all times.

Then it was time for snack, which was milk and crackers. And then it was time for nap, which Nora had told me about. None of us had blankets at school yet, so we all lay down on the big carpet. Ms. Macbride shut the lights off, and the room was so quiet that we could hear a teacher's voice all the way down the hall.

I was lying next to Renee, who was very thin, and Matt, who was short and had a sweet round face. Pippa was lying sideways, just above our heads, and the sleepy red-headed boy was near our feet, and he was already snuffling and almost snoring, asleep.

This was all of us, that first day of school. All us kids lying there like we'd known each other forever.

My eyes were closed and I could feel all the breathing, all around me. Then I opened my eyes and Renee was looking at me.

I looked at her, and then she smiled.

Twelve

DAD WAS AWAY FOR three days to meet with many other funeral director people, in New York City, the biggest city in America. He would eat fancy dinners and drink whisky in glasses, and talk and talk and talk to people who cared for dead people the way he did.

Mom didn't know if they would all wear black suits, but she said there was a good chance that many of them would.

Why not? Mom said. That's part of the business. That's what they have.

She said New York City had streets like canyons, with buildings so high that they almost touched the sky. She said there were millions and millions of people there. All kinds of people. More people and more kinds of people than Nora and I could ever imagine.

Did they have dead people too? Nora asked, and Mom laughed.

She took some sips from her clear glass and said, You bet. Wherever there are people there are dead people. Everyone dies.

Even little kids died. Little kids like Alice. She was only four years old, she was younger even than me, and that was very young. Alice was so young that she had hardly been born, but that didn't matter because death wanted her.

And Nora had gone downstairs to the first floor with Mom to look at Alice, in her blue overalls and white shirt with clocks on it. She held her purple elephant, and Nora said her casket was almost as small as a bread box, like the one in our kitchen.

She was pretty, Nora said. Even dead.

Her hair was light and curled, and her face was white, with red smudges on her lips and cheeks. Her eyes were closed, and she really did look like she was sleeping, and not like she was dead.

Except that she was very thin. Nora wondered if Mom or Dad had put something in her cheeks to make them puff out. Tissue paper or cotton balls.

She didn't ask, although she almost asked. She wanted to know if that was part of taking care of the dead.

Mom was glad that I was in school now, because that meant that I was no longer underfoot all day long. She could get on with all the things she wanted to do.

I couldn't think of a single time I had been caught under her feet, but Nora said that wasn't what she had meant. She meant that I wasn't around during the day, and she didn't have to worry about where I was and what I was doing. Mom could come and go the way she wanted to.

She does anyway, I wanted to say, but I didn't say that.

Nora said, Do you miss Ireland?

Mom had taken enough sips from her glass, and had refilled the glass, so it was safe to ask.

Ireland was way back in the murky past. That's what Nora said. The past was always murky, or it was misty sometimes. Nora thought the past, murky or misty, was the biggest secret. That Mom and Dad were back there, and it was hard to see and know much of anything. Because of the time that had gone by, and because of the murk and mist.

Nora was always saying almost grownup things. Mom said she was an old soul.

I love Ireland, Mom said. Ireland was my home. It was where I was born, and where I began to grow up.

Then Mom looked out the window, and kept looking, as though Ireland was out there on the street.

Ireland was so green, she said. It was more green, and brighter green, and deeper green than anywhere in the world. There weren't as many trees there as there were in America, but there were rocks everywhere, all over and under the grass. And rock walls that were everywhere too, and went every which way. So many rock walls.

Mother and Father did their best, Mom said. God knows, they did. Bless them. But it was hard with so many mouths to feed. With all these kids with dirty faces, and needing their diapers changed. Hungry all the time.

And children dying from one thing or another, Mom said.

Did your brother or sister die? Nora asked, and I was waiting for Mom to look hard at Nora or shout.

But Mom was back in Ireland, and it was a long time ago. Her eyes were big and soft.

No, thank God, Mom said. But a family down the road lost one, and in the village, a family lost two to the influenza. Two little babies, five and eighteen months old.

I thought of Alice with her purple elephant, and I thought of Mom and Dad saying everyone had a death in them. One death for every person.

Does Dad miss Ireland? Nora asked.

Oh, you're a nosy one, Mom said, and she put her hand on the side of Nora's face.

Inquisitive, Mom said. Curious.

Mom smiled.

Curiosity's a good thing, Love, Mom said to Nora. That's how you learn. It can do a lot more than kill a cat.

Mom took another sip from her glass, and then she took a pack of cigarettes and a lighter from the drawer of a table. She lit a cigarette, which was long and thin and white, and blew smoke at the ceiling.

We were in the living room on the second floor. The room was big, with a tall ceiling, and three large windows in a curved bow that looked onto Tioga Street down below. There was a patch of grass, a tree with white flowers in the spring, and the funeral home sign, that had a white light inside it so you could read the sign at night.

There were two nice couches that had blue and gold stripes, and chairs and tables. There was molding along the edge of the ceiling that Nora said was from a long time ago. The molding was shaped like small seashells, and came from when the house was first built over a hundred years ago.

In olden days, Nora said, the workers took more time and made beautiful things. Not like now, she said, when nobody cared. Except about money.

Was that true? I had asked her. That now nobody really cared?

She had looked quickly at me and away. Well, maybe not everybody. Maybe just some.

Mom said for us not to breathe the smoke, that it was bad for us. Nora said, Isn't it bad for you, Mom?

Mom laughed again.

She had a low, rumbly laugh, like a train whistle in a tunnel.

What was Ireland like for Dad? Nora asked. Was it the same for him as for you?

Mom said that Dad grew up in Connemara, and that was way out in the country, most of it. Dad's father was a farmer, when he worked, but he drank more than he farmed as the years went by.

His mother was Mary, and she had had eight or nine babies, but some of them were born dead. You didn't have babies in a hospital over there, not the way you do here, and sometimes the babies didn't make it when they were born.

Did they have funerals? Nora asked, and Mom said, Not like here.

Just something simple, with the priest blessing the child, and the body wrapped in a holy cloth.

She said that Dad's family only had thirteen acres of land, and that they farmed turnips. And everyone worked the land, not with machines or plows, like here, but with sticks and rakes and hoes.

There were four rooms in the house. The big room with the fireplace, and a bedroom for his mom and dad, and two other small rooms, separated by a blanket. One side for girls, one side for boys.

There was only one bed in each bedroom, so all the girls slept in one bed, and all the boys slept in the other bed.

One winter, Dad's little brother John, who was only four, got sick, and died in his sleep, right next to Dad, in the middle of the night. Dad could hear him struggling to breathe, and then Dad heard him when he stopped breathing.

It was a very dark and very cold night in Connemara.

Dad didn't get up, he didn't tell anyone, because he didn't think there was anything to be done. He snuggled close to his dead brother, because he wanted to keep John's body warm. He stayed like that for hour after hour, but he could feel John's body losing its heat.

John had freckles, and he was a lovely boy, Dad said. He used to sit near Dad when they ate, all of them around the one table. Sometimes John climbed into Dad's lap, and smiled at Dad. Dad was almost like John's father, because his real father didn't pay much attention.

How old was Dad? Nora asked.

When John died? Mom asked.

Nora nodded.

Six. Maybe seven, Mom said.

I thought, What would happen if Nora died? What would I do?

Even though she wouldn't die in the same bed?

Was Dad angry with me because I was like John and I wasn't dead?

I couldn't think of a single kid in my class who had such a family. I had never heard of a dad who had a brother who died in bed, right next to him, very late on a dark night.

That must have been terrifying for Dad to lose John, not just because John was a lovely boy, but because it happened very late at night, in the middle of winter, when Dad was lying next to John. Dad listened to John breathe, then he listened to John not breathe. Then he tried to keep John's body warm, all during the rest of the night.

That was sad. It must have been terribly sad.

John had freckles and I had freckles.

Dad was only six or seven years old when John died. That was at least a year older than me, but six or seven was still very young. Nora was eight years old already. Nora would have known what to do.

Did Dad worry that his mother and father might think he had done something to hurt John? Did Dad worry that they would accuse him of killing John? For a reason that nobody could explain?

Lying there in the dark, on a freezing winter night in Connemara, snuggled next to John's cooling body, Dad must have thought so many things, Nora said. About John, about his brothers and sisters, about his mother and father. He must have remembered how his mother, when one of her babies was born dead, would stay in bed for weeks, for months even, in her dark bedroom, and would barely bother to blink or breathe. Like she was dying, and would soon join her dead baby.

Would she do that now, trying to join John?

Mom puffed on her cigarette, and blew smoke at the window overlooking Tioga Street.

Poor Dad, Nora said. That's the saddest thing I ever heard.

That is as sad as anything, Mom said. So don't be so quick to judge your father. You haven't walked in his shoes, Trey.

I looked up and blinked, hearing my name.

No, I said. Never.

Mom sipped from her glass.

That was October, and Dad was coming home later in the evening from New York City. Already, by late in the afternoon, early in the evening, it was getting dark sooner and sooner. Winter was coming.

I was in kindergarten, Nora was in third grade.

Mom lit another cigarette, and blew smoke toward the edge of the ceiling, at the mold that was like small shells.

Later, when it was full dark, Dad came home. Nora had gone upstairs to read, and I sat at the kitchen table with Mom and Dad.

They were drinking from their clear glasses, and they were both smoking cigarettes.

I ate Cheerios, and they talked quietly. Then they were silent.

There were freckles on my nose and cheeks.

I looked up and both Mom and Dad were gazing at me and smiling. This had never happened before. Something warm and strange flooded me.

As though, at that moment, they loved me and were glad that I was there.

Thirteen

AMANDA AND CLEA ARE sitting near me in the dayroom. Outside the window, it's April, and I think, still pretty cold. When staff come in for their shifts, they're wearing winter coats and hats and gloves.

Amanda is sitting opposite me, and a half hour ago she saw Clea standing by herself, against a wall, and she waved Clea over. Amanda patted the seat of the chair next to her, and Clea sat down carefully, as though there might be tacks on the seat.

You doing okay? Amanda asked, and Clea smiled weakly. It looked like it was painful for her to smile.

Clea nodded. She said, Okay. She paused, then added, I'm okay.

Clea is the youngest patient on the ward. She's only thirteen, we heard. She's medium sized, as tall as most of the girls, and a few pounds overweight. Her brown hair frames her face closely, and she wears a bright orange watch cap most of the time. She even wears her hat at meals.

The only person Clea is friendly with is Bobby Collins, and that's a surprise. Clea, we've heard, comes from a fancy neighborhood in the city, and Bobby, we're pretty sure, lives in a trailer with his dad, out in the country.

Bobby hunts. Clea seems like she has never been within a half mile of a gun in her life. But you see them talking sometimes. When Bobby paces the ward, and Clea stands near the wall and stares at her feet, Bobby stops and talks to her.

Bobby's fifteen, only two years older than Clea, and we're pretty sure he's one of the youngest people on the ward.

Bobby talks to Clea, and though we don't know what he says, we can see her talk back to him and even smile. Almost nobody else has heard her say more than two or three words at a time.

Even Amanda, who talks to everybody, who looks after everybody, has not gotten more than a few words out of Clea.

Some of the staff joke that Amanda should be paid staff. Maybe they'll fix whatever's wrong with her. She'll grow up and she'll work on a ward like this. Everybody will like her a lot, just as everybody likes her now.

Except when she comes tumbling down. Then she stays in her room, and there's a thick gray cloud in the room and spilling out into the hallway. It's like you'd need special equipment to go into the room. You couldn't breathe in there, unless you were Amanda.

Amanda tells me that Maggie got her first E.C.T. treatment today.

I noticed, a little while ago, that Maggie's door was closed, and doors arc only supposed to be closed when someone is getting dressed or undressed.

E.C.T. is electro-convulsive therapy. It's shock treatment to the brain, and it's used for bad depression, when other things don't work. Amanda said they don't like to use it too much with someone so young.

Amanda says she saw Maggie come back in the morning. Not

long after breakfast. She was in a wheelchair, and she had one of those light blue surgical hairnets on her hair. Her head was lolling over to the side. She didn't look like she was about to play chess anytime soon, Amanda says.

Maggie's door is still closed, Amanda says, and it's like there's a huge electrical storm in her brain, with lightning bolts, and winds so strong they're knocking over power lines.

I keep picturing the brain as deep sky on a winter night. With pinpricks of stars and a slightly clouded moon, and vast black space where the air is so thin and cold you can't breathe.

Now there are lightning bolts and crackling electrical charges from star to star in Maggie's brain.

The world down here hardly exists for Maggie anymore.

Are they hurting her? Clea asks.

No, Amanda says. They sedate you first.

Clea looks at Amanda as though Amanda is her mother or teacher.

Will they do that to me? Clea asks.

Probably not, Amanda says. At least you're getting out of bed.

In Maggie's room, the shades are probably drawn, and there's a bottle of ginger ale on the nightstand. They always give you ginger ale.

Not too long ago, a week or two or three, I'd guess, Maggie and I were silent buddies. We'd sit for hours, right next to each other, and even though we hardly said anything, we'd still sit. And not saying anything was okay.

I don't know how that was exactly. How it happened or what was going on. For hours and days, our two chairs were less than an inch apart, and sometimes they touched.

Sometimes we touched, though it was usually—maybe always—by accident. An arm or hand, now and then a shoulder. One or two times, when she was pulling her legs up into a lotus position, her shoulder and head leaned over, under her hood, and her face brushed my face. There was hair sticking out all around the hood, and the hair touched my face.

The hair was very soft and smelled like vanilla. Vanilla and something like citrus. Orange? Lime? Lemon?

Did Maggie think what I thought? That we seemed to accept and understand each other? That there was comfort or solace, if that's the word? That we understood what it meant to say almost nothing, and to just sit there next to each other?

I had been sitting in a chair in the dayroom for weeks, and probably months. Just sitting. Once in a while, Bobby Collins would sit down and he would talk. Now and then Amanda sat down.

But neither of them stayed for long. Bobby would talk on and on, and it almost didn't matter that I was sitting there with him. He would talk about hunting, about his dad, about things he'd seen on television.

Amanda would bring news of the ward. About Dr. Altemio getting in a small accident in his car, sliding on ice and getting the passenger side door dented. About Lisa being out sick with a migraine.

Amanda knew patient's full names, their ages, their diagnosis.

But when she sat and talked, she always said something and then paused, as though she was waiting for a response. Even when I never had a response, she still paused.

Amanda told me that Maggie was sixteen. That her mom was a heart doctor, and her dad a professor. She was a student at the alternative high school in town. She lived two streets over from where Clea lived.

Maggie had never been a patient on the psych ward before. This was Amanda's second visit. Maggie had been depressed since she was twelve. She had what Amanda said were called mixed episodes.

She'd be depressed, and she'd pop up into a little mania, just to confuse the doctors. She'd talk all the time, where before she wouldn't talk at all. She didn't sleep very much, where she had been sleeping all the time. She'd eat a bunch when she hadn't been eating hardly at all.

Then she was stuck on the low end. The very low end.

Maggie had been on all kinds of drugs to get her mood stabilized. Lithium, Depakote, Effexor, Lexapro.

Amanda knew a ton about drugs. She said Maggie's drugs were mood stabilizers and antidepressants. Amanda had been on most of these drugs at one time or another.

Amanda knew about diagnoses too. She knew the difference between bipolar I and bipolar II. She said they didn't even call it bipolar anymore. It was a mood disorder, which she said, sounded nicer.

Amanda is as tall as me, and has broad shoulders. She has beautiful pale skin, and red spots in her cheeks and lips. She has small pretty features, that don't seem to go with the rest of her, and dark brown hair that doesn't fit either. As though her face belongs with a small body, and blond hair belongs with her face.

It makes her striking, a contradiction, and you keep looking to see how all this fits together.

Maggie's had a very tough time, Amanda says. But, Trey, she says, and she looks at me.

I want to say, But what, Amanda?

But I don't.

I just look, and keep looking, at Amanda's dark eyes.

Her hair is brushed back, and held at the back of her head with a tortoiseshell clip. The clipped hair bounces when she talks. In the overhead light, there are deep red highlights in her hair.

How can such dark hair have red highlights? How can a girl with these shoulders have such delicate features?

Trey, Amanda says, I'm pretty sure Maggie likes you.

I keep looking at Amanda.

I wonder if Maggie has said something, even a few words, to Amanda.

I want to ask how she knows. How she can tell. If, being a girl, she has some special sense of this.

All I can do is look at Amanda. Clea's looking at Amanda too.

How do you know? Clea asks, and I almost shout, Thank you.

Clea is staring steadily at Amanda, and she looks very intent. It's as though she needs to know as much as I do.

Then Amanda pushes hair off her forehead, stray strands that escaped her hair clip.

Clea and I are both watching her.

I asked, Amanda says. You wanna know something, you ask. Then she smiles. She has full lips.

So last week, Amanda says, she asked Maggie. She said, Do you like Trey?

And? I think.

And? I think Clea thinks.

Neither of us says anything, though. We just look, and Amanda just smiles.

Do you like Trey? I say to myself.

Well, I need to know, I think quietly. Do you like Trey?

But Amanda is still smiling, and Clea and I are staring.

Amanda, Clea finally says.

What? Amanda says.

You were about to say, Clea says. And Clea sounds like she talks all the time. As though talking was normal.

We can't ask Maggie, who has lightning bolts in her brain, in deep cold space.

Finally, I say out loud, Amanda, please.

Amanda looks at me, and then Clea looks at me. As though I'm the family cat and I just started speaking.

Amanda smiles wider. She says, Thank you, Trey. I needed some response from you. I needed to know if you cared.

I do, I say, and Clea says, We really want to know. There's not much other excitement in here.

Well, Maggie didn't say anything, not in the usual way, but you kind of expect that from her, Amanda says.

But she was looking at me, she was paying attention, Amanda goes on. Maggie's eyes—they were totally on me the whole time.

This was in the doorway of her room, and this was after dinner, I think, on Thursday, Amanda says. I could see into her room, and the bed was very neatly made, the way you just don't see in here. Unless your mother came in and made it for you.

Amanda, I say. You busting my chops?

A little, Trey, she says. But making sure you appreciate what I do for you.

Can we cut to the chase? I ask, and Clea and Amanda stare at me. The cat has continued to speak.

Okay, sorry, Amanda says. In the doorway, I said to Maggie, Do you like Trey? And she didn't say anything. But remember, she was really really low at that point.

But she was looking at me the whole time, and she stopped moving when I asked. She was really still. Her eyes were huge. She was very sad.

She moved her head up and then down. It was an emphatic nod. And she started smiling like the sun rising over the ocean. Which was even more striking in that sad face.

Really? Clea asks. No joke?

I wouldn't joke about a thing like this, Amanda says. Then she fixes me with her stare, and then she smiles, and Clea is staring too.

I'm in my chair, and they're staring, they're smiling, and I feel as though I've done something good. Although I haven't really done anything.

I close my eyes for a while, and feel Amanda and Clea move, and later, five minutes or an hour later, I'm still sitting and my eyes are closed. I'm in some space where the walls and floor and ceiling close in on me, and press and press, and where I may not be able to breathe very well. I lie there, I sit there, and each breath is shorter and smaller and more shallow.

Then I blink, and move my hands, and keep my eyes closed tight. I'm wrapped in a heavy wool blanket, I'm wearing a thick wool hat and socks, and I'm floating in vast cold darkness, and there are stars and stars and more stars very far away. There is a planet with very large rings around it, a planet that's red, a beautiful blue planet that floats and spins so slowly.

How does this happen, that you are inside a closing space, then you are in deep space? And it changes in an instant? You don't even need to blink your eyes sometimes, though sometimes you do.

When I open my eyes slightly, the day has grown deeply overcast outside, and nobody has turned the lights on in here. There are several people bent over screens in the nurses station, and Dennis, a big, overweight kid, is asleep in a chair on the far side of the dayroom, near a dark gray window.

I look at the wide hallway, and then I look again.

Standing in her doorway, wrapped in a large blanket that covers everything but her face, hands and feet, is Maggie.

She's watching me, and now I'm watching her, and as far as I can tell, there's no expression on either of our faces.

Her face is pale, and in the gloaming, it seems to almost glow.

I blink and blink and blink, and she does not disappear.

Fourteen

KINDERGARTEN MADE EVERYTHING DIFFERENT. Kindergarten made the whole world double in size. There was still the Burnes Funeral Home, and the second and third floors. We went to bed there, and slept there, and woke up in our rooms on the third floor. But I didn't stay there all day long the way I used to. Near Mom and Dad, and the dead people. Near the heavy sweet smell of formalin and flowers.

Kindergarten meant going out every day of the regular week, and walking with Nora to the Fall Creek School. From Monday to Friday. To see Ms. Macbride and the hundreds of kids. Kids with red cheeks, and high voices like a flute. Kids who ran and skipped, kids who jumped, kids who sometimes stood still as deer, and then skipped away, sudden as a heartbeat.

There was Pippa, who we often saw on the walk to school, and there was Max and Major. There was Dylan, who was a girl. Dylan was tall, and Major had brown skin like the coffee with cream that Mom drank in the morning. Major was sweet, and he had a small shy smile, and his best friend was Max who lived two houses away from Major.

Max and Major had been best friends since preschool, when they were two years old.

Max had red hair and more freckles than I had ever seen in my life. Max was skinny and short, and Major was regular.

Dylan had a piping voice, and she smiled all the time, and sometimes she smiled because someone said something funny, but other times because it seemed that she'd thought of something funny. When she thought of something funny she smiled a smaller smile that didn't last as long.

One Sarah, skinny Sarah, was best friends with Hannah, since preschool, though not the same preschool as Max and Major. The other Sarah was big Sarah, though she wasn't fat exactly. Just very tall and solid as a tree trunk.

Big Sarah wore glasses with red frames, and they were always slipping down her nose.

Skinny Sarah was not friendly, but big Sarah was.

Ms. Macbride called skinny Sarah *Sarah B.*, and she called big Sarah *Sarah W.* All the kids called them skinny Sarah and big Sarah, but not to their faces.

Hannah had thin blond hair, and she was maybe the smartest kid in the class. She didn't say much, but she could already read and write and add and subtract like a big kid. Like a kid in second or third grade.

I could read and write too, but so could a few other kids. Maybe they had a big sister like Nora to teach them.

Renee and Pippa started to become friends. Renee was tiny, and always had ribbons in her hair. Red, blue, orange, green and yellow ribbons. Her hair was pretty much black.

How do you make the color green? Ms. Macbride asked one day.

You mix blue with yellow, Hannah said, and we all looked at Hannah.

How could she know that? we wondered.

Max said, No way.

Way, Ms. Macbride said.

She took a little blue paint, added some yellow, swirled them around with her brush, and she got: green.

You took one thing, added another thing, and you got a third thing. It was magic.

When I told Mom at home about taking blue and adding yellow, she laughed and said, Well, there you go. And laughed some more.

I couldn't tell if she was being mean or not.

Did you know that? I asked, and she looked at me and didn't say anything.

So I left the kitchen, went to the hallway, and up the stairs.

Dad was standing in the third floor hallway. Just standing, still as stone.

I thought, Uh oh.

I didn't know he was up there by himself, and thought that if I had known, I wouldn't have come upstairs.

He said, Trey.

Dad was wearing black pants and a white shirt, and he wore his watch with the black face and yellow numbers.

Hey, I said.

Hey Trey, he said.

I went around him to my room, took my shoes off and lay on the bed.

Whenever I saw Dad now I thought of him and his dead brother John, on a freezing winter night. I thought of John being dead, and Dad lying next to him all night, and I wondered if that was why Dad became a funeral director. I thought of Dad at just seven or eight years old, and how that wasn't much older than me.

He must have been a boy with freckles on his nose and cheeks.

Then Dad was standing in the doorway, and he was smiling at me, but not in a mean way. Sometimes you could see Dad and know there were heavy clouds in his brain. Sometimes you could see that there were no clouds.

It's like the sun appeared in his eyes, and then it disappeared. A storm gathered in his brain. High chilly winds grew strong. Branches whipped the air.

Dad put his hand on my knee and squeezed it. He had big hands, and long thick fingers that were square at the end. There were blue veins on the backs of his hands.

I put my hands behind my head, and tried not to look at Dad. It was scary to have him so close. I looked at the white ceiling and the wall and the frame of the door. He wore black pants and a white shirt, but for some reason he was barefoot. His feet were very white, but there were blue veins on top of his feet, same as his hands. His toes were long and squared like his fingers.

You okay? he asked.

Good, I said, but so softly I didn't know if Dad heard me.

What's that? he said, and he smiled.

Outside, a car went by on North Tioga Street, and then another car, and then something bigger and heavier passed. Maybe a truck. Maybe a fire engine, though there was no siren.

So how's school, Trey? Dad asked. Are you enjoying school?

I looked quickly at Dad, then away. His eyes were dark, and

there was no storm in them that I could see. But sometimes, in the darkness, it was hard to tell.

Good, I said again.

What's that, pal? he said.

Sometimes Dad called me or Nora pal or buddy or sport. Once or twice he called me handsome. Like, Hello, handsome.

Which I wasn't.

Good, I said. School's good. I like school.

That was quite a few words.

Is your teacher nice?

I nodded. Very nice, I said. Ms. Macbride.

And she gives you milk and crackers, and then you take a nap? Dad asked.

I nodded again.

Macbride, Dad said. That must be Scottish.

What's Scottish?

It's a place. Scotland. Like Ireland in many ways, only not so green, he said.

Henry, Mom called from the second floor, and Dad called down, Up here. Talking with Trey.

His voice was as big as thunder, calling down. You could hear it a long way away.

Tell me about Ms. Macbride, Dad said.

I wanted to tell him how she jumped from the floor to the top of the desk, how she had squatted down in the hallway in front of me. I would never forget that. I would remember it when I was an old man.

But I didn't say that.

I said, She's very pretty, and she's only out of school two years.

Ah, he said, and laughed.

And the other kids?

Many other kids, I said. Max and Major, Hannah and two Sarah's.

Two Sarahs, he said. Do they look alike?

No. One's fat and the other's skinny.

Dad laughed again. I had never heard him laugh much. Only once or twice, I thought.

I wondered if he was going to hit me. He had only hit me a few times, but you could never tell why he'd hit you or when or where. It was as fast and surprising as a crack of lightning. Then it disappeared. But there was a boom of thunder deep in your head.

He reached for me, and I flinched. But he only put his hand on top of my head, and ruffled my hair a little. He did that as though he liked me. He was being nice to me.

I wanted to ask him about his brother John, who died. I wanted to ask him if that made him sad or angry, even though it was a long time ago. I tried to imagine Dad when he was seven years old, younger than Nora. I tried to picture him walking on the side of a hill, picking between gray rocks, crying for his dead brother.

But I couldn't. Dad wore black and white, and the lower part of his face was always darker from where he shaved his beard. His teeth were a little crooked, and they were not white the way Nora's and my teeth were white.

Dad was powerful, and did not smile often, and maybe he never cried.

Mom said he never, ever wanted to go back to Ireland. Mom said she would go, but she was not in any hurry.

Dad said, I understand your mother was talking to you about Ireland. She was telling you about my brother John.

I didn't say anything, but my eyes must have been very wide.

That was a long time ago, he said, when I wasn't much older than you. I was only seven years old, and that's younger than your sister.

He said it wasn't unusual for kids to die then. For babies to be born dead, or to die within a few weeks or months of being born. And while kids were less likely to die after they were a year or two old, they still died, at three or five or seven or nine years old. It wasn't unusual at all.

Dad looked at the window, where the air was bright, and it was like he was seeing something that I couldn't see. Like he could see the small Connemara farm, and the small house, and the dark rooms.

He said even though they had electricity and running water by then, there were only a few lights inside, and water just in the kitchen. They used an outhouse to do their business, and it was outside in back, near the toolshed. Late at night, and in the cold weather, you had to put boots and a coat on, and you had to follow the path even when you were half asleep.

There were spiders in the outhouse, and to this day, he said, he had a terrible fear of spiders. He still had a dread of going to the bathroom in the middle of the night.

What's dread? I asked, and he said it was a powerful, slow-burning fear.

But we weren't so afraid of death, back in Ireland, he said. It was just part of life. It was like taxes and the rain and rocks and like getting a cold, only a really bad cold.

People died at home, not in hospitals or nursing homes. They died at home and they had a wake from home and then they went to the churchyard to be buried. The priest said a few prayers, he said dust to dust and ashes to ashes, and then they shoveled dirt over the coffin.

People of all ages died, Dad said. Newborns, and babies a few months or a few years old. Teenagers died, young mothers or fathers died, people in their middle years died.

We didn't have the good nutrition, the good food that we have nowadays. The good sanitation, in the outhouse, or the water, and we didn't have the medical care. The nearest hospital was twenty-five kilometers away. That's fifteen miles. Even more.

You only saw a doctor when you were very sick, and that meant travelling on two or three buses, and paying a great deal of money. And then the tests, the medicine. By God, the expense.

I had not said a word in a long time. Dad looked at me, and then he looked out the window.

He said, John was a lovely, sweet little boy. He had been sick for a while with a cold, and maybe the flu, and then the diarrhea.

And then, Dad began, but he stopped.

And then, he said again.

His eyes were wet, were brimming. He stared out the bright window, and I wanted to do something.

But I lay there, looking at his big hand on the covers of the bed. His long fingers were gathering into a fist, squeezing, then unclenching, over and over.

I tried not to look at his face.

Fifteen

WHENEVER NORA TALKED ABOUT it, she whispered. Even if it was just the two of us, in her bedroom or my bedroom, or walking to school, the two of us, she still whispered, as though this was the darkest, most silent secret in the world. As though even God wasn't supposed to hear.

Nora said that I was the only other person, aside from her, who knew, and that if anyone found out, especially Mom or Dad, we were toast. Toast meant we were a slice of bread that was pushed down between the red coils of the toaster, and turned from tan to brown.

I didn't know if it was bad to be toast, but Nora said it meant that you were finished as a regular piece of bread. It meant that you were finished and done. You were kind of dead, like the bodies in the basement and on the first floor.

And that's what *it* was. *It* was the basement and first floor of our house, the Burnes Funeral Home. It was not going down there, under any circumstances. Not ever. Not even by accident.

That's what Mom and Dad said, because that's where they did their work, that's where they did what they did, and that's where the dead people were. And that was as dark and as silent as the secret between Nora and me.

Nora had been to the first floor two times. Once when she went down, looking for Mom or Dad, she found Dad standing near a dead person in a casket. And the funny thing was, Dad was not upset that she was down there. Not at all.

She said he was relaxed and smiling, and actually picked her up. She said it was as if the dead body made Dad a little happy and calm.

The other time was when she went to the first floor with Mom to see Alice, the little girl. Alice was dead, for sure, Nora said, but she was very pretty, even dead. She wore overalls, and her hair was clean and curly, and she held a purple elephant in her hands.

She wore sneakers with red flashing lights in the heels. Which might be flashing now, underground, all this time later. If there was a slight tremor in the earth, or if a heavy truck drove past, and everything trembled.

Alice was pretty thin, from having been sick, but she otherwise looked good, Nora thought. Better than a lot of the kids we went to school with.

Some kids had dirty hair or fingernails, or they smelled a little funny, like in a barn with cows or sheep.

Nora said that back in Ireland, when Mom and Dad grew up in the country, that probably they went to school with dirty hair and fingernails, and they must have smelled like cows and sheep.

She said it wasn't their fault, because they didn't have much running water, and no showers, and they worked with the animals on their small farms.

Trey, Nora said, we have to do it. We just have to.

I said, What?

But I was pretty sure she was coming back to the *It* question.

You could never trick Nora and get her to think and talk about something else. When Nora got on to something, something she wanted to talk about or do, she never let go. She was a dog with a bone or a cat with a mouse.

You know what, she said. Go to the first floor, and go to the basement.

Nora, I began.

But she said, I know you're scared. I know you don't want to do this. I mean, Nora said, then she stopped.

You mean what? I asked.

You're young, she said. Five and a half. I'm almost nine. I'm way older.

I nodded.

If we got caught, Nora said, they'd be way madder at me than you.

No, Nora. They're always madder at me. Always, no matter what.

That's 'cause you never say anything, Nora said. They think you don't like them.

Do you like them?

Nora looked worried for a moment.

Of course, she said. They're Mom and Dad. Yes, I like them. I love them.

Maybe I do too, I said. But I don't know it.

We were in Nora's room, and Mom and Dad had gone out somewhere. Her room had two windows, about fifty stuffed animals and Christmas lights pinned to the ceiling above the windows. The lights were red, green, blue, orange and purple.

The stuffed animals were dogs, a lion, a green cat, snakes, a tiger, a salamander, a spider and two fish, a shark and a small gray whale, and a green frog. There were many others, too, but sometimes it was hard to tell what kind of animal they were.

The Christmas lights were on, the way they were on almost all the time, except when Nora was at school. The lights were grand, Dad said, and Mom thought they were very pretty. Even in the summer, when Christmas was far away. They brought sparkle into the world, Mom said.

A year or two earlier, Mom and Dad would never have left us alone in the house, unless one of them was home too. They thought we might burn down the house, or run away, or get kidnapped by bad guys.

Kidnapped was when they grabbed a person, a kid, and took them away. Then they'd send a note or make a phone call, and say, We have your kid. Pay us money, or you'll never see your kid alive again.

That happened, especially with the children of very rich people, because the rich people could pay a lot of money.

But Nora said that kidnapping didn't happen very much anymore, not like in the old days. And it wouldn't ever happen to us, she was pretty sure.

Now we would be in the huge house, on the second or third floor, and there would be no sounds anywhere. Even if both Nora and me were there, it felt as though nobody was there. There were just creaks and small groans, and somewhere outside, a few streets over, a dog might bark. A small yappy dog, with a high thin bark, or a bigger dog that would woof and woof, a few times, and then grow silent.

Cars and trucks went by, a boy on a skateboard passed, two or three boys walked by, or girls, or sometimes girls and boys together in a group.

We never went into Mom and Dad's bedroom, which was a big bedroom at the back, on the third floor. Nora said they would know if we had been in there. Their bedroom was not as forbidden as the first floor or the basement, but it was still pretty forbidden. Even if we were sure there were no dead people there.

For some reason, maybe because she was so smart, Nora knew things and noticed things that regular people didn't know or notice. When she was sitting in the den or the living room on the second floor, when she was in the kitchen or dining room, looking at her phone or reading a book or magazine, she looked like she was absorbed by the page or screen.

She was absorbed, but she also wasn't absorbed. She said she had trained herself to always notice pretty much everything, almost all the time.

She noticed what they said, she noticed the look on their faces, she noticed what they wore and how they paused.

Nora had been doing this as long as she could remember. Maybe since she was three or four, which was as far back as she could recall. She didn't know how or why she did this, but it seemed extremely important, and it was fun too.

She had listened to Mom and Dad for years. They sat, and they sometimes drank their whiskey. Nora would be reading a page or a screen.

She said that after a few minutes, with Nora never taking her eyes from her reading, it was like Mom and Dad forgot she was there. They didn't think she knew or noticed anything.

They talked about dead people, and they talked about the families of dead people. They talked about Nora and they talked about me. Once in a while they talked about Dilkey, who sometimes helped them with funerals.

Nora knew, from being down there twice, that the first floor had an office, a few long rooms with rows of chairs, and very high ceilings, and lamps on tables. At the front of the two long rooms were big heavy tables where they put the dead people in their caskets.

There were some smaller windows with colored glass that looked like flowers. Nora said that was called stained glass. She said it was pretty. One window looked like a red rose.

She knew all this from being down there twice.

The basement was something else.

She didn't know anything about the basement, except for what she'd heard. And even though she always tried to listen closely and carefully, she sometimes got information that didn't make sense. She heard one thing—that the basement was huge—and then a little bit later Mom or Dad would say that the ceiling was too low and that they might have to get someone to dig down to make the basement ceiling higher.

Nora thought there were at least two big, finished rooms. One where there were caskets on display. Five or ten or fifteen caskets. Wood caskets and metal caskets. Grey, brown, and black caskets, even one that was yellow.

Who, Nora asked, would want a yellow casket?

I didn't know. I had never even thought you could go to a funeral home and pick a casket for your loved one.

Maybe yellow seemed bright and cheerful, and would make you feel less sad to lose a loved one.

Did they make red caskets, bright as a fire engine? Did they make purple caskets? Or caskets with flags on them? Caskets with the picture of a movie or sports or television star on them?

Mom and Dad were still not home, and being in Nora's room was so much fun. The stuffed animals were pretty and soft, and her room smelled of cinnamon and vanilla, and some perfume that was like the smell of October, when the wind was blowing and leaves were flying from trees.

I didn't even know what to call that smell. Just October, maybe.

Being in Nora's room was the safest I ever felt, and it always made me think that there was fun in the world. That there were different clothes to wear, and pictures to look at, and little cards and notes from Nora's friends to read. Like the world was big and there was air and light for everything.

Nora said she'd heard Mom and Dad talk about how inside each casket was a puffy mattress to lay the dead on, and a small pillow to put under the dead guy's head. But before they put the body in the casket, when they were just showing the casket to people to buy for their loved one, the price of the casket would be printed on a card and put under the pillow.

You went from casket to casket, admired each one, and then looked under the pillow at the card, and pretended not to be shocked by the price.

Nora said caskets could be anywhere from three or four thousand dollars, to ten or fifteen thousand dollars. Even more. That's what Dad had said.

The other room, the really creepy room, was next to the casket room. This was the room with the sign on the door that said it was illegal to go into the room unless you were Mom or

Dad. That meant that you would go to jail for going into the room.

Nora said this was the preparation room, or the embalming room, and she said this was where they laid the body on a steel table. She was pretty sure they took the clothes off the body and washed it.

But she wasn't sure about embalming. She knew it involved formalin, and she knew it meant draining the dead person's blood. She didn't know how, though. How they got the blood out and the formalin in.

Maybe through the nose or mouth, the ears, but that didn't make sense, she said.

She hoped they didn't put it in though the openings where you peed or pooped. That would just be so terrible, she said.

I asked Nora if we could talk about her friends. About Asia and Asia's little sister, Pippa, who was in my class.

Maybe they cut a hole in the dead guy's chest, Nora said. Maybe they put a tube in that way.

She said that maybe they used a pump. They forced air in.

Does Pippa like me? I asked Nora.

If they force the blood out, using air, then they could pump the formalin in, Nora said.

Nora, I said. Does Pippa like me? Does she think I'm okay? Does she think I'm weird?

Nora looked at me and looked at me some more. Then she was back in the room. Here on the third floor. You could tell from her eyes.

I think she does, Nora said.

We were silent a minute or two.

We're gonna have to go down there, Nora said. Sooner or later, we're just gonna have to go down there.

Sixteen

I'M STILL UNDER A cloud, in banks of fog, and it's the drugs that cause this. It's not my brain.

I swallow my pills at the back window of the nurses' station, then I sit and say very little in the day room. Me, the chair, the rug, the windows, the walls and ceiling. I don't sneak any of the pills into my cheeks or under my tongue, to spit out later.

I've thought of it, but so far, I swallow the pills, and feel the chemicals spread through every part of my body, especially my brain. From my stomach, into the bloodstream, and then everywhere inside—to my heart and liver, to the muscles and fat, the tendons, every piece of tissue, the lungs, the pancreas, and then to so many parts of the brain. The cerebrum, the brainstem, and the cerebellum.

That's the world, right there.

Not the heart, which is a pump and a muscle.

The brain has everything, pretty much, which makes us human. Love and hate and fear and desire. It has all the memories, all the sensations, for everything we've ever experienced.

It's where the soul would be, if we had a soul.

And it produces chemicals too. The brain chemicals mix with the pill chemicals, and they try to make something new.

The new thing is sleepy and tired, most of the time. It's the mist and fog, and these memories, or images, of things from the past. From way past, when I was little, to the recent past, just before I was brought here. When I'm pretty sure I was already seventeen.

I see leafy shadows on the ceiling. I see angles of light from cars passing out front, on the walls and ceiling. I see faces looming above me, as I lie in bed, or as I sit on the rug in the den on the second floor. There's a brown leather couch, there's a ticking clock on a mantle.

Sometimes, someone plays an oboe, plays long sad notes that rise then slide. Maybe a slow cello will begin, and it's more beautiful and sad than anything I've ever heard. Sad and full of longing, because something you love, that the player loves, has gone away. Something will never ever come back again.

My eyes are closed, hearing the music in my brain, and someone sits down next to me.

Very slightly, I open my eyes, and it's Maggie. Of course. Not of course, really. It could have been Amanda or Clea or Bobby Collins. But the movement was light, and the smell of talcum powder, of hazelnut shampoo, is Maggie.

Maybe it's not hazelnut. Maybe it's vanilla. I don't know.

She does not look different because of the shock therapy. She still looks sad, and she's wearing red tights and a black skirt, and a yellow hoodie. I've never seen her in so much color.

I look at her for a little while, for thirty seconds or a minute, and she looks back at me. Her eyes are as big as they've always been, and her hood is up, but it's sitting loosely around her head. Her dark hair still frames her face.

She says, Trey, and I say, Maggie, and we speak so softly it's hard to tell if we've actually made a sound.

She begins to talk, and that's strange. Maggie speaking in a whispery voice.

They came early, she says. They came when it was still dark outside, and even though I knew they were coming, and I even knew the time they'd come, it was pretty weird.

She bites her lower lip lightly. Her teeth are like a dove or snow or summer clouds.

There were two nurses in surgical scrubs. Blue scrubs, and they wore little bonnets to cover their hair.

They were almost like angels, Maggie says, but more like angels of the night than anything else.

But she says she didn't mind, she didn't care.

Another nurse, a night nurse, had woken her up around three or four in the morning and gave her a pill to make her even more sleepy. So she was still groggy when the two nurses came for her.

They were nice, the two nurses. They were not from the Behavioral Sciences Unit, but from a medical floor of the hospital. They whispered because they did not want to wake people up.

They told her that she wasn't allowed to eat or drink anything, because of the anesthesia they'd be giving her before the ECT. And it would be twilight anesthesia, which meant that she wouldn't necessarily be completely unconscious. She might go all the way under, but she might be seventy or eighty percent under.

But she almost certainly wouldn't remember much, if anything, afterwards.

That's because one of the drugs they were giving her. Versed would make her relaxed, but it would also induce amnesia.

The nurse who said that was tall and thickly built, and she smiled most of the time. The other nurse was shorter and a little older than the first nurse, and not as thickly built.

She smiled too, but not as often as the first nurse.

Maggie couldn't tell if the second nurse was overweight, or if she just seemed skinnier next to the other nurse.

They got her to use the bathroom in her room, and then they sat her down in a wheelchair they'd brought.

She was floating and relaxed and things seemed a little funny. She knew it was from the pill they'd given her earlier, and she hoped they'd give her another one.

The skinnier one said, Okay, sweetie, we have to put a line in on the back of your hand. Is that good with you?

Maggie smiled and said, Why not?

She was feeling looser and happier than she'd felt in a while.

The second nurse put a surgical bonnet on Maggie's head and tucked the loose hair under it. Then the first nurse turned on a small light next to Maggie's bed, and she sat on the edge of the bed, with Maggie in the wheelchair in front of her.

The nurse took some small white packages out of her pocket, tore them open, and set them on the top of her leg.

It was still dark outside, and still very early. Maggie didn't know for sure, but it might have been five-thirty, maybe six.

There was no movement out in the hall, where the lights of the ward were dim. In her room, outside of the small circle of light from the lamp, the room was dark. Sometimes, a car's headlights, from a parking lot on the far side of the hospital, would sweep over the floor and ceiling.

She said she felt very warm, and she thought that might be from the two nurses, who were being so nice to her. Maggie said they both smelled like mint, maybe from soap to wash their hands.

They weren't just nice, Maggie said, but they seemed to really know what they were doing, and she had the feeling that they liked her, that they wanted her to get better.

The skinnier nurse swabbed the back of her hand with an alcohol pad, and then said, You'll feel a little prick.

Maggie looked away, and the big nurse smiled at her and said, Don't wanna look at the needle going in? Can't imagine why.

She laughed, and Maggie laughed.

The big nurse took Maggie's other hand, and massaged the top of the hand with her thumbs. Maggie felt even more warm, she felt as though she was surround by love, that either one of these women could be her mother.

Then she felt the needle, and it hardly hurt at all.

Great, the skinnier nurse said. You have good veins, young lady.

The nurse taped the needle in place.

The big nurse was standing behind Maggie in the wheelchair, and the nurse began to rub her shoulders and neck. It was deep down, like she'd hardly ever been touched before.

Maggie is talking and talking, which is stranger than anything. She talks quietly, and she hardly moves her head, but every word is clear and distinct.

I say, Yes, and, Right, and, Really.

Once in a while, as she talks, maybe without realizing it, Maggie puts her hand on my hand, and keeps it there for a few moments. Twice, her hand squeezes my hand.

Is this what love is? I wonder. Is this the thing everyone talks about?

Did Maggie love the nurses? Did the nurses love her?

I want to know, of course. I'm dying to know, but I can't ask her.

There are so many times I want to say things, about what I feel or see, and I think that next time Maggie pauses, I'll actually say something. I'll tell a story about a time I woke up very early in the morning, to study for a test, or the time I had my tonsils out, and had to be at the hospital, at this hospital, at five in the morning.

And how, at three-thirty or four in the morning, the world looks very strange. The rooms are the same, the walls, the doorways, the furniture, are unchanged. But they look entirely different, even if they're in the same place.

For one thing, the windows are deeply and wholly black, deep deep black, in a way you don't see at any other time. Like the black is a kind of creature or force, that it's everywhere, and that only the black itself knows how incredibly dark it can be. That it can take over the world. That it closes in, surrounds you, smothers you. That it leaves you swimming in ink.

Familiar rooms look strange in the dark, and stranger still when you've had little sleep. A bed, a couch, a mirror on a wall, look like they arrived from somewhere else. And this is all more weird because they all look vaguely familiar, but very different and changed too.

You're in a dream. You've made the whole thing up. But none of it is yours. You're in control of nothing.

After they taped the needle in place on the back of her hand, Maggie goes on, the smaller nurse took a capped syringe out of her pocket.

This is Versed, or midazolam, the nurse said. To help you relax, and also, to induce amnesia, so you'll have trouble remembering anything about the next few hours.

I'm pretty relaxed, Maggie said she said, and both nurses laughed.

This'll make you really really relaxed, the big nurse said. It may well put you to sleep, and that would be okay.

The small nurse took the cap off the syringe, and put the needle into the line on Maggie's hand, and pushed the plunger down.

Almost immediately, Maggie felt a warmth, a happiness that she hadn't felt in years. In ten or thirty or fifty seconds. It was so fast that she doubted it could be the drug she was feeling. More that there was love knitting together the universe. And she was at the center of it, moving the needles.

She wanted almost to laugh, to sing, to get up and dance, but she was too far away, too sleepy to do anything but smile. She sat back and told herself to stay awake as long as she could.

Maggie looks at me, and for twenty or thirty seconds she holds my hand.

I think of how, at that moment, I might have been holding her hand right before the ECT. I wondered if she was scared, or if she thought of the black black night as a form of her depression. As something you could never escape from.

Was she thinking anything?

So they turned off the small table lamp, and they pushed her out of the room, around the nurses' station, and through the big front doors of the Behavioral Sciences Unit. First a big single door, then through double doors that swung open like moving walls.

There were long tubes of light in the ceiling, Maggie says, and her head had fallen back on the wheelchair. Her head was lolling, if that was the word, she says. It felt as though it were barely attached.

She didn't know where they were or where they were going. Just down a hall, with a silver band in the wall that you saw in hospitals.

She heard a ding, ding, ding, which she thought was an elevator. But they didn't get on the elevator. They passed it, and then paused at a door.

The big nurse knocked, they went in, and Dr. Manchin was wearing scrubs, and there was a table, there was another nurse who wore scrubs too, and Maggie said she wanted to say, Where are my scrubs?

Everyone wore scrubs except for her. She wore sweats.

They got her onto the table. The three nurses and Dr. Manchin half lifted and half steered her. The nurse who'd been in the room covered her with a white blanket from her feet to her chest.

The room nurse took a syringe from a cabinet, said, This is Demerol, and injected it into the line.

Holy shit, Maggie says. I mean, Trey. Holy fucking shit.

She didn't think she could possibly get any more high, but Demerol pushed her very far and very high.

It was like the top of her head was cold, and the rest of her was warm.

Then someone was holding her hand. Someone was brushing her forehead with something cool.

Is she out? a nurse asked.

I think so, Dr. Manchin said quietly.

She felt something on each side of her forehead. She heard a sound, then felt her brain do things.

Then she was so far away. She was past the moon and planets. She was drifting, and doing slow summersaults. She was waving, and it was utterly black except for pinpricks of light.

And lightning bolts, she said. Like a storm of bolts, but no rain. Just bolts and bolts and more bolts. Plus wind.

Almost everywhere.

Seventeen

MISS LEVY WAS MISS Levy in first grade. Not Ms. Levy. The Ms. was for many teachers, but not for her. And she wore skirts or dresses every day. She never wore pants, like almost all the other teachers.

Miss Levy wore scarves at least half the days, and she wore them even when it wasn't cold out. They were sort of the same color as her skirt or shirt, or they were different—when she wore a red scarf with a black shirt, or an orange scarf with a brown skirt.

Nora said that Miss Levy really knew how to dress.

Miss Levy was quiet and beautiful, but not beautiful the way some of the other teachers were beautiful. She would never have jumped from the floor to the top of her desk the way Ms. Macbride did. She didn't have bright blond hair like Ms. Lukeman.

Ms. Macbride moved around almost all the time, from the door to the sink to the windows, and she could talk loud sometimes. She could talk like she was on the side of a mountain and she was calling to her friends in the valley.

Most of the time Miss Levy almost whispered, and everyone grew quiet just to hear her. Her voice was soft, her voice was steady, and somehow it always got through the noise in the classroom.

Miss Levy had short black hair, cut around her head like a helmet. She had bright green eyes, which stood out even more against her black hair. And her cheekbones, Nora said. Her cheekbones were to die for.

Cheekbones were very important, Nora said. They were under your eyes and to the outside of the eyes, and the higher they were, and the more they stuck out, the better.

I felt my own cheekbones, but they weren't especially high. They stuck out a little, but that was because I was skinny.

Don't worry, Nora said. It doesn't matter as much for a boy.

Miss Levy also had a bow for a mouth, according to Asia, and perfect small white teeth.

We were walking home, Pippa, Asia, Nora and me, and Pippa and me were not saying anything. We didn't know a thing about beauty and style. Until a month or two ago, we had not even known they existed.

Nora and Asia were in the fourth grade, the second to highest grade in our school. After fifth grade, they'd go to middle school, and when Pippa and me were in third grade, they would no longer go to our school. That would be strange, like the color of the sky changing, but it was a long way off.

Pippa and me had been in the same class for all of kindergarten with Ms. Macbride, and we were in the same class with Miss Levy. We could never talk directly to each other, I think because she was a girl and I was a boy.

I liked her and I think she liked me, but that didn't matter, I guess.

I didn't speak much, and Pippa didn't speak much either.

I knew what her voice sounded like, and she knew what mine

sounded like. We'd say Yes or No or Maybe or Okay, but that was about it.

Maybe that was what school was for. To get you to talk to people. To help see if there was a voice buried inside you.

Your voice was deep deep inside. In your throat or your brain or in your leg, or somewhere else. Maybe the toes or the fingers. It could be anywhere, pretty much, but when you told it to say something, there was no sound. You could tell it two or three times to say something, but it was no good.

Your voice was too far away. It was silent. There was no sound at all.

The kids in the classes changed around from kindergarten to first grade. There were two classes for each grade, from K to five. K was short for kindergarten because kindergarten was such a long word.

Half the kids in your K class went to one first grade class, and the other half went to a second first grade class. So the kids were mixed around a little bit, and that changed what Nora called the class dynamic.

We had Owen and Toby, we had Madeleine and Cora, we had Nelly and Lucas, a Christine, a Bob, a Colleen, a Luke. Plus kids from K too. One Sarah, Hannah, Major but not Max, Pippa, and Trey, who was me.

Our classroom was not at the end of the hall, the way that K classes had been. We were about halfway down the hall now.

By third grade, we would move to the second floor, where all the big kids were. Third, fourth and fifth grade were upstairs. K through second was downstairs, but in different rooms along the hall.

We would only go to the second floor to visit the library, where there were so many books. The cafeteria and gym were on the far side of the first floor, past the front desk and the principal's office.

The principal was Ms. Yancy, and she was nice, but very serious. You did not want to have to go see her in her office. A third grade boy named Larry had to go to her office the first week of school because of throwing pebbles on the playground. Larry's mother had to come to the school, and she and Larry met with Ms. Yancy in her office. Then Larry and his mom had to leave the school in the middle of the day, before lunch, even.

Larry would not have to come to school for a whole week.

Larry, Nora said, did not have a father. Larry's mother worked two jobs.

Nora had heard.

Nora heard things all the time. She seemed to know things, at least some things, about all the kids and all the teachers. She talked to everybody, or almost everybody, and they told her things.

She knew that Robert in fifth grade took medicine for depression, which meant you were very sad. Many many kids, almost half the kids, took a drug to pep them up and then slow them down. The drugs were called Adderall and Ritalin.

She said half the boys took peppy drugs, and that the pep drugs sped them up, made them go faster, and then slowed them down.

Nora said that Ms. Macbride was a mountain climber, and had a girlfriend.

I said, Everyone has a girlfriend, and Nora looked at me with her big eyes, and laughed.

Girlfriend girlfriend, Nora said, and I had no idea what she was talking about.

I kept looking at her.

She said, You'll understand when you're older, and I hated that.

There were things every day that were a mystery, and that I'd understand when I got older, but I didn't want to wait till then.

How much older? Second grade, fifth grade, eighth grade?

Then Nora said something really mysterious. She said that Miss Levy's family was from New York City, and that Miss Levy's family was very very rich. They were bankers and owned apartment buildings in the big city.

We're rich too, I said. The Burnes family. We're very rich.

I told Nora we lived in the biggest house on North Tioga Street, and that no other houses were even close to as big. There were four rooms on the third floor, not counting the bathroom, and we didn't even need the fourth room.

Nora laughed and laughed. We were walking along North Tioga Street. Asia and Pippa had turned off onto Tompkins Street toward their house, and now it was just me and Nora.

There were red and yellow leaves on the trees, and soon there would be no leaves. There would only be bare branches reaching toward the sky, looking spooky when the sun was starting to set. They looked like the legs of a spider.

In the winter the branches would have snow and ice on them. They looked like they were in pain and would soon die, but in the spring most of the branches were growing leaves. I didn't know how they survived.

Maybe life was stronger than death. For a while anyway, because Nora had said that everything that lives has to die.

Nora said that Miss Levy was rich rich. Like New York City rich. Trips around the world. A big apartment in the city, another in London. Houses in Connecticut, in the Adirondacks, in Virginia. Boats and cars and planes, Nora said. Anything you could want.

But she's so nice, and she's shy, I said. She's the nicest person there is.

She can afford to be, Nora said.

Why? I asked, and Nora said to never mind, that I would understand when I grew up.

We're not rich? I asked Nora, and she said, No, not the way Miss Levy's family was rich. Miss Levy's family had money from a long time ago, and they were growing their money like an orchard of fruit trees. More and more branches growing apples and peaches and pears and plums.

I saw our house up ahead, and I thought that it still looked big. The sign still said, Burnes Funeral Home, and you could see it from blocks away. If you died, this is where they brought you, though I had recently learned that there were other funeral homes in our city. It cost a lot of money to die. That's why I thought we were rich.

I had heard Mom and Dad talking about hundreds and thousands of dollars. Pretty soon, in the years in front of us, that could be millions of dollars, and that was a huge deal of money.

We went up the front steps at the Burnes Funeral Home. I was Trey Burnes. Nora was Nora Burnes. Mom and Dad were funeral directors or morticians. Nora said mortician was a fancy word for someone who looked after the dead.

Nora took a key out of her pocket, and unlocked the front door. As soon as we were in the hall we could smell the formalin. We went through another door, then up the steps on the right to the second floor.

The ceiling and walls were white, the leather couch was brown, there was a deep red chair with big arms where you could put your elbows. There was a deep red stool for your feet. Everything was bright and very clean.

Mom loved to clean, and almost nothing was out of place for very long. Mom would never let me and Nora clean because we didn't know how to do a proper, thorough job. That's what she said. Proper and thorough.

I kept thinking of Miss Levy, and I thought about Ms. Macbride too.

Nora had said that it was more than likely that I loved Ms. Macbride, and I guessed that was probably true. She was the nicest, most interesting person I think I had known. Nobody could ever replace her, I thought.

But if I had probably loved Ms. Macbride, then I was sure that I loved Miss Levy. Because she was just as beautiful as Ms. Macbride, and maybe more so. Her voice was soft like water in a brook, and she sometimes put her hand on my shoulder or my head.

Trey, she said. Trey, Trey.

Now that she was rich, my world grew bigger. It was mysterious, it held things I couldn't imagine.

Eighteen

THE CLOSET IN MY room on the third floor was not big, but there were lots of clothes hanging on the bar that went from one end of the closet to the other. My shirts and a jacket and sweaters, but Mom and Dad's clothes too. They couldn't fit everything in their closet, so they hung them in my closet. Black suits and dresses, white shirts, black pants, and some things in long thin black plastic bags that were like a body, only with no arms and legs and no head. Just a metal hook at the top that went over the old wood bar.

Sometimes, late at night, the closet door would be closed and I imagined things in the closet. I imagined small people with red or yellow eyes and weird grins hiding under the clothes, and poking each other, wondering if they should open the door and explore what was outside the closet.

I pictured the plastic bags, hanging there, growing like mushrooms in the dark. Dad had told me that mushrooms grew in the dark, in moisture, and they were good to eat. But some were poison, and could kill you. So you had to know the difference.

But the plastic bags—they waited patiently night after night after night. They didn't move and they didn't make a sound. They stayed quiet in the dark, and when it rained and when it was humid, there was moisture in the air.

They grew long arms and long legs, and then slowly, so slowly that nobody noticed, they grew new heads. They grew the arms and legs and heads of dead people who were coming back to the world above the ground. Their hair was combed, and their eyes opened, and their arms and legs moved, very slowly in the dark and quiet of the closet, in the dark and quiet of the night.

I was never sure what they wanted. If they were lonely, the dead people. If they were forgotten. If they wanted company, or if they wanted to capture a living person to take to the place of the dead. Because everyone had to die anyway, and they were lonely now. Not months and years in the future. But now.

Maybe they were angry to be dead. Maybe they hated to be dead, and they hated that living people were alive, and in sunshine and air. They had died too soon, and they had died with terrible pain, and that was not fair.

Little Alice, who was so young. She was younger than me, and she was dead from the cancer. She had red lights that blinked on her sneakers. Did they still blink in her coffin? If a giant truck drove on the small roads of the cemetery, near her grave, and made the earth shake, and made her sneakers blink red and red and red.

Just for a moment or two.

During the night, I always kept the door of the closet closed tight, and I put my school backpack against the door to the hall so that I would hear if someone tried to open the door. Then I could run to Nora's room, and she would know what to do.

Would they be able to talk, I wondered, the people just back from the dead? Would they be able to move their arms and legs?

They would be stiff, after not being moved for a long time. Their arms and legs would creak, their voices would be full of rust.

Then I went into the closet, though never at night, at least in the beginning. I kept the door open at first, and just sat in the doorway, with my bum on the closet side. The dresses and jackets and black plastic bags brushed my shoulders and head, and they almost tickled.

They smelled funny too. But funny nice, like wool and the sheep wool came from. And like people who had worn the clothes. Sweat and perfume, and even formalin, the smell of my childhood.

When I put my nose in the fabric of Mom's dress, it was like she was there with me. Her flowery perfume, which was like the smell of lilac bushes, in spring, on the side of our house. And like some old, deep smell from a long time ago, some room nobody had lived in for many years. The smell was a little scary, but it was also a little sweet.

When I could, when nobody was around, and always in the day, I went into the closet. I would go all the way in and to the right or left. There was plenty of room for me to fit.

I sat down, and my head found a place in the hanging clothes. Plastic and cloth, and bits of sweater and the legs of pants. They surrounded my head like a shroud, like the thing they used to put around dead people about to be buried, Nora had told me.

A shroud, she said, was like a cloud. It surrounded a body.

I was all the way in a corner, in the far right, back corner, and when I pulled my legs up to my chest, it was almost like I was buried.

There were footsteps on the stairs, and Mom called, Trey. Trey, where are you?

She stood in the doorway of my room, and said, Where is that kid?

Nora, she called, but Nora wasn't home. Nora went to Emma's house after school.

Damn that boy, Mom said, and I could hear her going back down the stairs.

I think that I might have smiled, because I was finally more invisible than I had ever been. I was here, where almost nobody would ever look for me.

There was a moment almost of panic, because I thought that I might be taken for a dead person. That I wouldn't be able to say anything, and they would take me down to the basement. They would put me on the steel table, and they would do things to me with shiny sharp tools.

But the panic went away quickly. I was just there in the closet, and no one knew. Nobody could see or hear me.

The walls were white plaster, and had never been painted, I was pretty sure. There was a wood baseboard all around the bottom of the wall, between the wall and floor, and I don't think that had been painted either.

Nobody bothered with a closet, except to hang clothes, and then everyone forgot about it. This was like discovering a new room no one knew. No one but me.

I lay down on the floor of the closet, and stretched my legs out. I put my legs together, my toes pointing at the ceiling, and laid my head down, and folded my hands on my belly. I closed my eyes, and thought, This is how they'll find me. Exactly like this.

Then I started to think of the massive house, here on North Tioga Street. I started to think it was a giant ship on the ocean, floating away from the land. The basement was underwater, but it was sealed tight against the water.

I was at the top of the ship. And I could see for miles and miles.

There was a bang out on the street, like a gunshot on TV, but then I heard a heavy truck rumble by.

I reached over, and pulled the door of the closet closed.

Everything was dark. It was darker than the middle of night. There were no streetlights shining in, just a very thin line of light at the bottom of the door. So thin that it was like a single hair. It was like the last piece of light in the world.

I had died of the cancer, like Alice. And soon, I'd meet her.

I had died from a bad heart, because I was a nasty, smelly kid.

I had died of old age, because even though I was only six years old, and would be seven before too long, I didn't have friends and I spent the days by myself like a lonely old person. Eating cans of soup. Talking to people, in my empty apartment, who had been dead a long time.

There were so many ways to die, and I had heard of many of them from Nora, or from the television or radio.

You could die of drowning or from guns. You could die from knives or starvation, from bombs, or from car crashes.

There was a whiff of formalin in the clothes, and then there was wool and perfume like flowers and the earth in springtime.

The hard floor was digging into the bones of my back and butt.

I shifted slightly, and things didn't hurt anymore.

Then I lay very still, my eyes closed and clenched, my legs together, my hands still on my stomach. I thought to say a prayer for myself, for having died, and gone somewhere else, but I didn't.

That was selfish, and I didn't ever want to be selfish. That was one of the worst things to be.

I would just lie there, on the floor of the closet at the top of the house. Somebody might find me. They would have to begin looking first.

This was an hour or two after school, and school had gotten out a little before three. Dinner would be soon, I thought. There would be green beans with butter. There might be hot rolls. There could be potatoes. Maybe meatloaf, with onions and mushrooms in it.

There would be a glass of milk, so cold to drink that it almost hurt your teeth.

I'd been in the closet a while. An hour, maybe two hours. I could stay a long time. But if I had to pee I'd be in trouble. And I was getting hungrier and hungrier.

Dead people in their graves stayed a very long time. They stayed pretty much forever. They stayed until the heavens opened and angels playing harps and trumpets came down to the ground through the sky, and everybody on earth rose up to heaven. There was a kingdom up there.

The angels wore white sheets and they had wings. They were very nice. But God was not so nice. He had a big gold stick, and he could shoot thunderbolts with his stick, which was called a staff.

God had a long white beard.

I heard about God and angels and heaven in little pieces. I wasn't sure of much of it.

There was a devil down below, and that was hell. There was fire in hell, almost everywhere down there, and I didn't know if there was one devil or many devils.

The devil, if there was only one devil, was red and had a short beard. He had horns and a tail, and he carried a pitchfork like a farmer, and he had cold cold eyes, even if he lived around fire pretty much all the time.

Nora said that all of it, heaven and hell, angels and devils, were just stories people made up. She'd heard that somewhere, and she thought it was probably true.

But I didn't know. Sometimes Nora heard things, and she repeated them in her own voice, and she sounded very grownup.

Sometimes I did that too. I wasn't sure of what I was saying, but when Nora said things to me, I always thought it was true. It sounded so good. So grown-up.

Nora said, Really. It's official.

Official meant that God and every grownup in the world agreed that something was true.

Way down below, on the first floor, I heard footsteps on the front porch.

I didn't hear them so much, but I could feel vibrations on the floor of the closet. Someone was there. Someone had walked up the steps, and then the door opened and closed, and there were more vibrations from someone moving up the front stairs.

It had to be Nora, coming home from Emma's house.

There were voices, but they were low and far away, and I couldn't tell who was talking or what they were saying.

The voices went on for a minute or two, and then there were footsteps.

Sometimes it was hard to tell where the voices began and the footsteps stopped.

Then it was only footsteps, and then footsteps coming up the stairs to the third floor. They were lighter than Mom or Dad's and I knew they were Nora's.

I breathed out a little, and breathed back in, slowly and quietly.

Was this what it was like in a coffin, in a grave?

Only you didn't have to bother to breathe.

Did an angel or a devil come to your coffin and ask if you wanted to join them in heaven or hell?

Would they give you wings or horns and a tail? Would you get a pitchfork or a gold stick to shoot thunderbolts?

Could a devil beat up an angel? Or was an angel stronger and tougher?

Were devils really angels that had fallen from heaven?

Nora and I had talked about these things. I asked questions, and Nora talked.

But I was never sure how to remember. There was someone named Lucifer and another named Michael.

There were two Michaels in the grade above me in school.

I had never known a Lucifer.

For a long time, I stayed very still, lying in the corner of the closet. I kept my hands folded, and I thought that an angel flying by, or a devil creeping around behind bushes and trees, might see me and think that I must be dead.

They would want to take me away to heaven or hell.

The footsteps on the third-floor stairs were still for a few minutes. They might have gone to Nora's room.

Then there were no footsteps, just a light sliding sound like slippers on wood.

There was a tap, then another tap, on the closet door.

C'mon, Trey, Nora said. Let's go. Time for dinner.

I waited for five, for ten seconds. Then I said, Okay. Be right there.

Nineteen

S UE, THE NURSE, GIVES me one white oblong pill, three white tablets, a yellow and red capsule, and a light green triangular pill.
I'm not certain, but I think that the capsule is different, and that the
triangular pill used to be pink. The capsule was blue and green, or
tan and orange. It definitely wasn't yellow and red.

I don't know, but I'm pretty sure.

It's hard to tell, sometimes, if something happened in my
head, or in a dream, or if it happened in the world, on the ward.
Sometimes, what I picture in my mind, or what I dream, is so imme-
diate and vivid that I'm sure it had to have happened. For real.

Then I have to trace back, to what I was thinking, or to a dream,
then I begin to think that it was in the infinite space of my brain,
which contains everything from this and every world. My brain contains trillions of miles.

And every one of those miles is real. A real thought, a real
memory, a dream, a fantasy. They jumble together and they mix in
and around the things that go on, here on the ward, and last week,
and ten or fifteen years ago.

Every minute, every second, every hour and day, every week and month and year. I carry them all, in the little space between my ears. But it's more like a portal, a way into something so huge that you can't even begin to measure it.

There are rooms and closets in that space, there are people, there are trees and flowers, cats and dogs, boats and trains, a blue sky, a cloudy sky, a night sky full of stars that are stacked, layer after layer, like massive cliffs of tiny lights, that wink and wink and wink.

I swallow the pills, all six of them, and I try to feel them melt in my stomach, then seep through the wall of my stomach into my blood. I wait to see if they'll take me up or down or maybe sideways, but it takes between a half hour and an hour to see what the pills will do.

I sit in the dayroom, and I try to remember if I've seen Dr. Manchin lately, or if I've seen Cara, my social worker. I try to remember the last time Nora came to visit me.

I haven't seen Dr. Manchin more than three or four times since I've been here, but then I haven't been here all that long. I don't know if it's a month, or three months, or even a year, though I'm pretty sure I haven't been here a year.

Dr. Manchin told me to write everything down quite a while ago. At least a month ago.

I've been doing that every evening after dinner and meds, and I don't even know where that takes me. It takes me some place, it takes me to a lot of places, but I have no idea what it means.

It's like my dreams and fantasies, it's like memory, and I do it, crouched over a notebook on my bed. The bed is in the room, the room is on the Behavioral Sciences Unit, the unit is on the fourth floor of the hospital, and the hospital is in the city in upstate New York where I've always lived.

This is on the planet earth, and earth is in the Milky Way.

I'm trying to figure all this out, and to see if there's a place for me here. I need to know if I have to stay inside the world of my brain, or if I can push out into a larger world.

In the day room, I sit in my usual place, and the usual people sit or move around. Amanda, Dennis, Juliet, Clea, Bobby Collins.

Maggie has been sleeping for a few days, it seems. She had E.C.T., she talked more in an hour than I'd heard her talk in months, like she was a new person because of the lightning in her brain, and then she went to her room to sleep and sleep.

Amanda says that that's typical, to sleep like that. Because of the drugs, and because of the bolts.

Amanda doesn't know long she'll sleep, just that it won't be forever.

At least not forever for now, I think. Forever as in death. Then I say to myself, Don't even think that. Maggie's only sixteen or seventeen.

Gawd, I want to say.

There's a clock on the wall inside the glassed-in nurse's station. A big clock like the ones in school. White face, thin black hands, except for the second hand, which is red.

Sometimes I watch the clock here the way I do in school. The red hand moving all the time, and the minute and hour hands moving much more slowly, so it's hard to tell if they're moving at all.

I concentrate on the red hand for a while, and I try to figure if it always goes at the same speed. If it's faster coming down on the right, and slower moving up on the left. Sometimes I think it is faster on the right and slower on the left, but other times I think it always moves at the same speed.

It's never faster on the left, moving up. That's for sure.

The minute hand's more interesting, of course, and much slower. When I concentrate on the minute hand for a while, I have to block out the second hand. The red hand would just confuse things. So now and then I have to squint, and if the meds have settled me, have mellowed me out at least a little, I can see the minute hand move so so slowly.

Like ice melting, like the light outside very late in the afternoon in winter, with the black outline of geese moving steadily across the sky.

When I'm good, when I'm easy and relaxed and the fog has left my brain, I can follow the movement of the minute hand. I watch and watch and try not to blink, and it's gone from two-fifty-four to three-oh-three, and I'm proud of myself.

I think, You did it. You saw. You paid attention.

A few times, when I've been very sharp and very patient, which don't often happen at the same time, I've even been able to follow the hour hand. It's short and a little thicker than the second and minute hands. And it moves incredibly slowly, like a glacier, and slower than a cloud in the sky, slower than the tide at the beach.

You wouldn't even think it moves at all unless you knew that it did.

So I've tried. I've watched it, for a long time sometimes. The short black finger, halfway down on the right, just sitting there. The thin red finger moving, the long thin black finger moving, but much more slowly, and the short black one not seeming to move at all.

But it does. They all move, just at different speeds.

I've watched it from a little past the three mark on the right, halfway down on the right, and then it's past the mark. It's three-seventeen, and the hands move, they orbit the center of the clock, they sweep and sweep, and the short black finger, it's farther past the three mark, it's falling toward the bottom of the face, but slow as a planet in the sky.

Then it's three-twenty-four, and the hour hand is almost halfway to the four, and it's like I'm watching the planets, and they all move in their slow way around and around the sun, and I'm very excited. As though I'm watching the workings of giant worlds.

People walk past, and I hear voices, and doors opening and closing, but I don't look up. I keep my eyes on the hour hand.

Maybe people look at me, and they say to themselves, There's crazy Trey, on different meds, staring into space.

But it's more than that. I'm staring into space and time. It seems as though I'm learning things, but I can't say what. Something about how time moves both slow and fast, and light seems to bend or something, and maybe time bends, and space is very near and very far at the same time.

But the best thing, the important thing, is to look and notice and pay attention. All the time if you can. In every space.

Clea was a little chunky but is getting skinnier every day, it seems. She comes and stands nearby, three or four feet in front of me, between me and the clock.

I can't ask her to move. Maybe this is a sign that I need to stop watching time.

Hi, Trey, she says, and I say, Clea.

She says, You sitting here with all your friends?

For a moment, for less than a moment, I'm confused.

My friends? I wonder. What friends?

Then I realize she's joking.

I smile. I say, Every one of them.

Mind if I sit? she asks.

I pat the seat next to me, and she sits.

Were you staring at the clock? she asks, and I say, Sort of.

How come?

Just watching time, I say.

Clea smiles, and it's a lovely smile, one of those smiles that change everything.

Her smile is big, her teeth are shiny underneath her braces, and the smile is in her shiny eyes, in her flared nostrils, even in the strands of frizzy, dark blond hair.

Bobby Collins told me a while ago that Clea was thirteen. But that might have been three or four months ago. I can't tell, can't remember. Maybe it was a month ago.

She may have turned fourteen, but that would mean we had a little birthday celebration here on the ward, and I can't remember a celebration for Clea. We had one for Bobby, with cake and ice cream, and we had one for Juliet with more cake and more ice cream, but Juliet fell asleep in her chair at her birthday party, and Dennis dropped a plate of cake and ice cream.

Everything froze, and we all looked at the cake and the ice cream melting on the floor, and Bobby laughed, Amanda laughed, and John, one of the evening aides said, Okay, we'll get it.

Lisa, another aide, ran out to get some paper towels and a damp sponge, and Dennis said he wanted more cake and ice cream.

I'm sitting and thinking, here in the dayroom, that I like Clea. When she first came in she was sadder than a grieving widow. She stayed in bed for a long time, and then she started to rise. She started to move.

Another week or two went by, and her meds or something kicked in. When Maggie and I, or Amanda and Maggie and I, would be sitting in our chairs in the dayroom, Clea would stand ten or fifteen feet away. She wouldn't say anything, she wouldn't move, but she'd stand, swaying like a sapling in the wind.

First Maggie would ask her to come over and sit, and she did. Then Amanda said, C'mon over. Sit down, and Clea sat with us again.

She said almost nothing. But she looked relieved just to be with other people.

Often, we wouldn't say much either, except maybe Amanda.

Then one afternoon, Amanda said she felt sorry for her father, and Clea said, How come?

We all looked at Clea as though the cat had just spoken.

Just wondering, Clea said.

How come, Amanda? Maggie said.

I dunno, Amanda said. Maybe just that I've always been pretty mean to him.

None of us said anything for a little while, but ever since then, despite the age difference, Clea has been one of our crew.

She's four years younger than me and Amanda, and three years younger than Maggie, but the age difference doesn't matter as much in here. In grade school or middle school or high school, two or three or four years is huge. It's the difference between junior year in high school and seventh or eighth grade in middle school.

Clea says, When you gonna leave this place, Trey? You been here a while.

Her eyes are deep brown, and because her hair is dark blond, her eyes seem even darker and larger.

I move my head side to side.

Dunno, I say.

Cara and Dr. Manchin say I'm almost ready to go home, she says.

I look at her.

The meds have helped, Clea says.

They say when? I ask.

The idea of Clea leaving the ward kind of worries me. Clea, with her braces, with her frizzy blond hair, with her sadness, moving in the world, is terribly disturbing. The world could do anything it wants to her.

Where are your mom and dad? Clea asks, and I can't say a thing.

Where are Mom and Dad?

I don't know many things, but I definitely know they've never been to the ward to see me. In the two months or five months that I've been here, only Nora has visited me. She's been here two or four or six times, and I'm almost certain she's never mentioned them.

Nora goes to the university on the hill here, and she lives in an apartment in Collegetown, near the school's southern entrance. She happened to be staying at the house on North Tioga Street in July and August. Just by chance, Nora was there. Very, very late at night, Nora was awake. Nora was paying attention.

Could they have asked Mom and Dad questions?

Could Mom and Dad have run away to Canada or Mexico?

Did they go back to Connemara or Galway, to live on a small farm, among all the gray rock walls, the hills, the ocean in the distance?

Clea is still sitting here, but I don't say anything because I don't know.

Way far over on the other side of the big room, Maggie's door is still closed. She's in there, I think.

She wouldn't have left unless she said goodbye.

Twenty

IN THIRD GRADE, I was eight. I had Ms. Revisi, and our classroom was on the second floor. Ms. Revisi was not as beautiful as Mrs. Harcourt in the second grade.

Mrs. Harcourt had skin like coffee with milk in it, and she had a voice like a song. Mrs. Harcourt had a smile that went from her toes all the way up to her big dark eyes. Sometimes when she was sitting on her chair, she'd pull me up onto her lap and put her arms around me and put her face against my face.

Trey, she said with that sweet accent. Lovely, lovely boy, she said.

Why are you so lovely? Mrs. Harcourt asked, and I could never answer because I wasn't lovely at all. But to Mrs. Harcourt, all children were lovely.

We were precious, she always said.

Mrs. Harcourt smelled like oranges and lemons and limes. She was as fresh as a Sunday in May, and she made your tongue pucker. That felt funny at first, but then it made you smile and smile, almost from your toes to your eyes.

Ms. Revisi was pretty old. She was forty or fifty, and that was about as old as Mom and Dad. She was very thin and strong, and we learned that Ms. Revisi ran on trails in the woods every other day, and every year in August, before school began, she swam across the huge lake here. The lake was forty miles long, and a mile or two wide in some places, and our city was at the south end of the lake, down in the valley.

Ms. Revisi had short hair like a cap. It was a little black and a little gray.

Ms. Revisi didn't smile the way Mrs. Harcourt smiled. Her smile was quick and small, and didn't make you want to smile. Mrs. Harcourt's smile was as big as the day.

Going up the stairs felt funny at first. The only time we had gone to the second floor before was when we went to the library, once or twice a week. Then, Ms. Macbride or Miss Levy or Mrs. Harcourt was always with us. We would have to be very quiet, and if we talked at all, we would have to talk in whispers.

By the third grade, by the time I was on the second floor, Nora was no longer there. She had graduated from elementary school, and she was now in middle school, at Boynton, which was sixth, seventh and eighth grades.

Nora liked Boynton. She said it was nice. There were way more kids. Kids from all over the city, not just from Fall Creek.

Nora had had Ms. Revisi as a teacher, and she liked Ms. Revisi. Nora said she was firm but fair, and she was much nicer than she seemed.

Even though she didn't smile too much, and she never pulled you onto her lap, and she would never jump from the floor to the top of a desk. She was nice in different ways.

She was quiet and calm, and she liked kids in a silent way. She smelled like vanilla, and her hair was short as a boy's.

Her earrings were silver and long and dangled down the sides of Ms. Revisi's neck.

It took three years to get from one end of the hall to the other. Then it took six years to get from Fall Creek to Boynton, and three years to go from Boynton to the high school. After that you could go to college or join the Army or get a job somewhere.

Everyone went somewhere else.

Nora liked moving from Fall Creek to Boynton. It was a longer walk from home on North Tioga Street. It was twice as far. But there were always rivers of kids moving toward the schools on North Cayuga Street.

She walked with Asia or Emma, or sometimes both of them. She walked with newer kids too. She walked with Eliza and Greta, and she walked with a boy named Mitchell.

Mitchell, Nora said, was gay, so it was uncomplicated.

What's gay? I asked, and Nora said, Mitchell likes boys.

I didn't know what that meant, because I liked boys too. I liked girls, but I liked boys.

I didn't say that out loud. Just in my head.

Nora was getting taller and taller. Mom said she was shooting up like a weed.

Her legs were long, her arms were long, and she had a long neck. She was one of the tallest kids in her class, and she was a head taller than me.

That's what happened when you were ten and eleven and twelve and thirteen, she said. It was called puberty. You started to get a grownup's body. The voices of boys deepened, you got hair under your arms and in other places. Girls grew breasts.

It happened at night when you were sleeping. It was like your body was invaded, and there was nothing you could do about it, whether or not you liked it.

You were going from a kid to a grownup, and it happened, at first, all of a sudden.

I mean, she said, it took years. But things happened overnight too.

Nora at eleven was almost as tall as Mom. Nora said she was already five-foot, two-inches tall. Mom was five-four, so Nora had only two inches to go. Mom seemed to have slight breasts and a butt, and Nora didn't, but Nora said that would happen.

Probably at night, when she was sleeping. Right now, her chest and butt were the same as mine.

I was pretty tall for my grade. Sarah was the tallest kid in our class, and not just because of the frizzy blond hair piled on top of her head.

But after Sarah, I was the next tallest.

I had a big nose, and my ears stuck out, and my mouth in the mirror was like the line a pencil made on a piece of paper.

Sometimes my eyes were blue, and sometimes they were gray. They didn't seem to know what color they were.

The kids in my class liked me okay, and I liked them. They didn't make fun of me to my face.

But I walked home from school by myself, and kids didn't come to my house to play.

I didn't go to other kids' houses either.

Nora always reached home ten or fifteen minutes later than me, and in the morning, she left fifteen minutes before me.

Many people in our city were dying, and a lot of them came to our house.

In late October, almost near Halloween, there were three funerals in one week, and the next week, during Halloween, there were two more. Usually, Mom and Dad bought candy to give out, and they kept the light on the front porch lit. But almost no kids came to our house.

Trick or Treating began before six, and went till eight-thirty or nine, and waves of kids went by. The little kids came first, and we could see through the curtains on the second floor, or we could see when me and Nora went out with our empty pillowcases to get candy, that there were always parents with the little kids. Parents would usually stand on the sidewalk, waiting, and the small kids were always a witch, a princess, a devil, an angel, a ghost, a bee or a dog with floppy ears. One little girl was a cat one year, and whiskers were painted on her cheek, she had pointed ears, and she even had a tail. Nora said she was adorable.

After seven-thirty the bigger kids were out. The second or third graders, up through sixth or seventh grade.

The older kids came last. They only had a mask on, or some didn't have any costume. Just a big bag to fill with free candy.

Nora said these last kids, who were taller than Dad, were high school or even college kids.

Mom or Dad would tell them to not forget to vote in the election that was only a week away. Nora said that that was pretty funny for Mom and Dad.

But when there were funerals going on, all the lights on the first floor were on, the porch lights and the side and back lights were all on too. From outside, the house looked like a giant wedding cake, Nora said.

When we stood outside, which we sometimes did, the lights on the second and third floor were always out. So it looked like the top of the house was floating on the downstairs light. It looked like a big boat or a spaceship, and if you closed your eyes for a few seconds and then opened them, the whole house would be gone. Into the dark sky, or sailing on the dark watery streets of Fall Creek.

The dead person for the Halloween funeral was tragic, Mom said. She was a woman who was only thirty-seven, and she had been a professor at the university, and she had three young children. She had a husband who was crushed, Mom said.

Nora said that Mom meant that the husband was very upset by the death. He would have to raise the kids by himself, Mom said. Hard enough to raise kids with two parents, she said. But one man with three kids?

Mom scrunched her face. She looked quickly at Nora, then she looked at me for a long time. Her eyes pinned me, like a bug on a piece of white paper.

I wanted to squirm, but I couldn't.

The professor woman died of the cancer. It ate her up even while she was alive.

Cells, Mom said. Just going crazy. Cells eating cells.

She looked at each of us again.

The poor woman was seventy-nine pounds in the end. And she was a tall woman, Mom said.

Nothing left of her.

Nora just watched Mom. Nora's eyes looked like they had hoods on them. Like a hoodie sweatshirt. Like a winter coat.

Mom looked at us as though we caused the cancer in the dead professor. She looked at me some more. Like I made cells eat other cells in her body. Like the three small kids of the professor, the crushed husband, were my fault.

Here I was, alive and useless, eating food, breathing the air, taking up space, and the poor woman, the mother and the professor was dead. Each of her kids needed her, her crushed husband needed her.

Mom didn't say it, but I knew. Nobody needed me.

Dad said I was a smelly, snot-nose kid. Mom always asked if I had wiped myself. She said I smelled like poop.

Nora always said afterward that she didn't know why they were like that with me. She said I was okay. Perfectly okay.

She didn't understand why they hated me and not her.

Do they hate me? I asked.

They act that way, Nora said. But deep down, I think they probably love you. In their way.

She said there had to be some secret, some something. There had to be answers. Ten answers. Or maybe none. Some people just did what they did. Who knew, she said.

Whatever it was, though, it had something to do with the basement. Down there. Beyond the locked doors and the sign that said to keep out, Nora said.

She said that we had to go down there. We had to find out. Sooner or later.

We had to.

Twenty-One

MOM ALWAYS HAD MOODS. Every day or week. She went up, then she went down. She went sideways. She went in straight lines, she went in circles. Sometimes big circles, sometimes small or medium circles.

Now and then she zigged and then she zagged.

When she drank whiskey with Dad, or sometimes without Dad, her moods went all over the place. Once in a while she would hug me for a second or two, or she would sit Nora on her lap. She would tell Nora that she was beautiful, that she was beautiful and good.

You're the apple, Mom said to Nora. You're the peach, the flower, the diamond in my life.

Nora said, Mom, and she stretched out the word as though it was a very long word that went on forever.

Mmmmoooommmm.

Really, Mom said. Really, she said again.

Nora got away from Mom's lap, and Mom lit a cigarette with a dark blue lighter. The flame made Mom's face look like the rock wall on the side of a gorge.

We had deep gorges in our city, not even far from our house.

Dad was out somewhere, in his black suit and white shirt. Maybe he was at church or out drinking whiskey in a barroom. Maybe he was helping another funeral director with a funeral.

Sometimes he did that. He helped at the Magni Funeral Home. He helped at the Eames Funeral Home, at the Cutting Funeral Home. Mom and Dad helped them, and once in a while they helped here, at the Burnes Funeral Home.

Mr. Cutting was big as a tree, he had a giant belly, and his face was red, as though he was out of breath. As though he had just run five miles in his black suit. In his shiny black shoes.

Mr. Cutting was funny. He talked all the time when the family of the dead person was not around.

Mr. Cutting called Nora Gorgeous, he called me Sport. He called Mom Flossie, and Dad was Ace. Everybody had a different name with Mr. Cutting. Mom and Dad called him Rick.

When Mom was flying up, she hardly ever slept. Just an hour or two or three. She baked cookies at three in the morning. She hummed. She talked most of the time.

She talked about her mum, she talked about Da. They were both dead, but she still talked about them.

Will and Maureen were her favorite brother and sister. They were both still in Galway. They each had a family of their own now, and children who were cousins of Nora, and even of me.

Will had a beautiful red-headed boy named Seamus, and Maureen had a girl with curly black hair. Her name was Monica or Maeve.

Monica or Maeve wanted to be a doctor some day.

A day or two later, after talking so much and hardly ever sleeping, after moving around and not stopping, baking chocolate chip cookies in the middle of the night, Mom would seem to hit the big wall of a forest. There were so many trees and vines, so many bushes and plants, that she couldn't move any more.

No light came into the forest, it was so dense. Monkeys screamed in the trees, birds tweeped and cawed, and Mom was just really really tired. She felt very hopeless and sad. Her legs weighed a hundred pounds each, and it was like there was a deep thick fog in her brain, Nora said.

There was no hope for her, and there was no hope for the world.

Dad said, Ellen, then he said her name again.

Mom was on the couch, under a white and brown wool blanket that had come all the way from Ireland. She wore red socks, and her feet stuck out at the bottom of the blanket.

Dad asked if she was taking her medicine, and Mom said, Henry. Oh, Henry.

Mom said, Jaysus, and sounded Irish.

When Mom was tired or when she drank whiskey, she sounded more and more Irish. She sounded like she had been born and raised in the wild west of Ireland. In Galway, on the River Corrib, in the province of Connacht.

It was so beautiful at dusk there. At Christmas. It was like God smiled down on the waters of Galway Bay.

On the counter in the kitchen there were two little brown bottles with white caps like a flat mushroom. On one bottle it said, lithium, and on the other it said, Seroquel. One bottle said, Take two in the morning and one at night, and the other said, Take one in the morning and one at night.

Nora said that was Mom's medicine. She said it was for moods, and for feeling very sad. Mom had told Nora that the medicine helped, but not all the time.

Nora said that every once in a great while, once a year, or even once every two or three years, Mom would hear voices that were not even real. They were just voices in her head, but it was hard to tell sometimes.

Once, a long time ago, when I was just a baby, Mom had to go to the hospital for a week or two. It was so long ago that Nora could barely remember. I couldn't remember at all.

In this house, in all these rooms, even down in the basement with the dead people, there was no Mom for a week or even two weeks. There was just Dad in his rubber apron, Dad boiling hot dogs for us on the stove. He put the wet boiled hot dogs on the kitchen table, Nora said, and we passed around a small bottle of mustard, dipped a hot dog into the bottle, and ate it that way.

I was in a highchair that Dad dragged to the table.

Dad laughed and said we were like lashings of Tinkers.

He said that Mom was getting a nice rest.

You kids, he said. You kids wear her out.

I don't remember any of it. Not the hot dogs or the mustard, and not any of what Dad said.

Later, when I was in third grade and eight years old, Mom was pretty steady most of the time. Nora was eleven and she went to Boynton Middle School. Nora got an A in everything.

Once in a while, though, Mom would stop taking her medicine. She would forget, or maybe, Nora said, she got bored. She missed having all that energy. She missed not having to sleep, and she missed being able to work or talk or move around for sixteen, eighteen hours a day.

It didn't take long for her to fly up there. Just stop the medicine for three or four days, then zoom. Mom was up near the ceiling, Nora said.

Dad's face got very tight and white.

He said, Ellen.

Mom said, Henry.

She called Dad her wild colonial boy. She sang, The Night That Paddy Murphy Died. She sang, The Rocky Road to Dublin.

Dad said he did not, he absolutely did not want her down on the first floor during a wake.

For the love of God, he said, and she said, For the love of Henry.

I went up to the third floor, and lay on my bed for a while. This was evening time, and I could hear laughter and singing. I could even hear Nora laughing.

She liked them and they liked her.

The night grew later and darker, and when there was silence for a half minute, I thought that maybe they were talking about me. Maybe they were saying things.

I went to the closet, and crawled in, under and behind the wall of clothes. They were soft as feathers sometimes. They brushed my face and arms.

The floor was hard, and I could feel the bones in my backside grind against the floor. There was no meat, no cushion, on my butt.

I was skinny as shoelaces. Dad said I was all bone. Mom said that if I turned sideways, she couldn't see me.

Nora always said not to listen to them.

She said they were only kidding.

For a little while I didn't close the closet door, and I could still hear the singing and laughter. Even Nora sang a little bit about a wild rover.

Then Mom and Dad were singing together about the pipes calling from glen to glen. It was sad and beautiful, and I thought they must be drinking a little whiskey. Maybe they even gave Nora a few drops of whiskey in a glass of water.

I pulled the door closed, and then their voices were just a low vibration coming up from the floor.

If there was a little door in the back of the closet, if there was a door in the floor or the ceiling, then I could go away. If the door was so small that I could barely fit through, then nobody, not even Nora, could follow me.

I could crawl between the walls, around the space between floors, past electric wires, and heating and water pipes, and eventually I'd come to a space where there was fresh clean air seeping from another small door. That would be the outside, and in October, because this would happen in the fall, when the leaves everywhere were dying on the trees.

I'd go through this final door, into the darkness, into the night.

There would only be a few streetlights, and square yellow windows in houses. A little bit of light shining on dark parked cars.

If a car went by on the street, I would move quickly behind bushes or around the side of the house.

Dogs would bark, but if I waited a while, the square yellow lights in houses would wink off. And then later, there would be no moving cars on the streets.

I could go anywhere. I could go everywhere.

I thought about walking through dark back yards, climbing fences, checking to see if the doors of houses were locked. If there were windows that were not locked.

People forgot to use locks, people didn't worry. Some did worry, and some did use the locks. But some did not.

In the closet, where nobody could see me, where I was invisible and was no longer in the house at all, I could go anywhere and do anything. I could be outside in the dark when almost everyone was sleeping. Where some doors were unlocked.

Dogs were the worst thing, I thought. Dogs in backyards, or dogs in the window, looking out.

Dogs didn't sleep much at night. Dogs slept during the day. They curled into a circle, and even their tails stopped moving.

But they could see in the dark. They could smell you all the time. They could smell you three blocks away, Nora said. Even if you had just taken a bath or a shower. They knew where you were and who you were.

Many people had cats instead of dogs. Cats would not bite you, and they would not bark and growl. They just looked at you and they might mew. If they were inside the house they would sit in windows, and they watched the dark. But they were so still you almost thought they were a picture or a statue.

A cat could sit and not move pretty much forever. You could go away for an hour, could come back, and the cat was exactly the same. Maybe they could sit and watch all night long.

The door of the closet was still closed, but I heard footsteps on the stairs to the third floor, and they were light and quick. Not like Mom or Dad, who were tired all the time. They were kind of slow.

It had to be Nora.

She went into her room, and I think she was changing for bed. She changed quickly. Then she was in the bathroom.

I went again to the backyards in my invisible mind, and in one backyard of a big house, almost as big as our house, there was a deck. I went quietly up the stairs to the deck, and there were no dogs, no cats, no lights.

Just dark windows, all the way up to the third floor. There was a table with an umbrella and chairs on the deck, and I sat down for four or five seconds. The chair made small squeaking sounds like a mouse, but I didn't think anyone could hear me. They couldn't see me.

This was scary and exciting at the same time. I wanted to run away in the dark and hide behind bushes. I wanted to climb over fences because I was a quick and good climber.

I stood up from the chair and went to a back window. There was a couch and coffee table and some big chairs that looked like they were crouching. They had fat arms. But no heads.

If they had heads, I wondered, what would they see? A kid with big ears, with a nose like half a banana, with a mouth so thin it almost wasn't a mouth?

Would they scream to see this pale face just outside the window?

I could hear Nora tinkle in the bathroom, then I think she was washing her hands and brushing her teeth. Nora never forgot to wash her hands or brush her teeth.

Nora did one thing, then another thing, then another thing. She didn't waste time between each thing.

Nora was so quick and smart.

There was a dead television set in the room with the couch and chairs, and beyond that was a big dining room washed in moonlight. There was a shiny table with candles in the middle, and wood chairs all around it.

Beyond that was a hallway with a polished floor, and I couldn't believe I could see so well. The moon helped, just sitting up there like a glowing ball. Almost full, except for an edge that was a little flat.

But my eyes had been in the dark so long that I was used to the thin light. I was silent and invisible as a cat. A Ninja.

I turned the knob on the back door. It turned all the way, and the door made a creaking sound, and my heart was so loud I was sure someone could hear it.

The door opened an inch or two, and I could hear the refrigerator just past the small hall. There were coats hanging on hooks, there were shoes and boots in a line along the wall.

Then I heard Nora in the doorway of my room.

Trey, she said. Then a second time. Trey.

She stepped in, and she came right to the closet door. She opened the door, and she saved me from going farther into the house. She got down on her hands and knees, crawled into the closet.

Her feet were near my face and her head was near my feet.

Hi, Trey, she said, and she didn't ask what I was doing in the closet.

She pulled the closet door closed.

I thought you hid in here, she said. Now I know.

I didn't say anything, but this warmth went all through me, filling every part of me, like sunlight, like a warm bath, like blankets on a cold night.

This was perfect, I thought. I could stay like this forever.

They're going to New York City in three weeks, Nora said. The two of them.

We could do it then, she said.

Do what? I whispered.

But I knew, even though I didn't want to know.

Nora's eyes were glittery in the dark.

Twenty-Two

BOBBY COLLINS IS TALKING again. Bobby Collins is saying that as far as he's concerned, he could stay here forever. Not that he'd want to, and not that they'd let him. But this place is okay by him.

Bobby is still short and skinny, but not as skinny as he was a month or two ago. He eats a lot at breakfast and lunch and dinner. He eats one plate, then another plate, and sometimes he'll eat a third plate. Bobby eats as though he has hollow legs, and the chewed-up food just goes down and fills the empty space.

Bobby eats like he hasn't seen warm food in a long time.

He still taps with his fingers and feet, and his head twitches like he's a deer sniffing the wind.

You and me, Bobby says. We've been here the longest.

Amanda too, I say.

Sometimes I say a few words now. Sometimes I even say a full sentence. In the middle of the day usually, depending on the meds.

But never in the morning, after meds, and never in the evening either, again after meds. The meds seem to change every few days. The colors of the pills change, their shape, their size.

I still get them at the window of the nurses' station. The little white cup of pills, the little white cup of water. Once in a while, I don't even look at the cup of pills. Mostly I do look, I notice. But then I'll take the cup, now and then, throw it back into my mouth, and chase the pills with water. No-look, like a pass in basketball on television.

Then I try to tell, by the way I feel, how the pills have changed or not changed. Whether I glide up or down or sideways. Whether I'm sleepy, or buzzed like coffee, or if everything's the same.

If a pill goes from pink or orange to green or blue, the day can go from sunny to cloudy. Just like that.

Bobby says, What's not to like?

I'm not sure what he's talking about.

What's not to like about Bobby?

What's not to like about the chairs we're sitting on? About the people on the ward? The staff? The patients?

There's everything to like about Bobby. Bobby's funny and it's pretty much always okay to be around him. Even when he talks so much that he makes you tired.

But he knows he's making you tired, and so he'll get up, say, Catch you later, and he'll pace or find someone else to talk to.

Bobby has no mother. Or if he has one, she's nowhere around. She's never been around.

He thinks she might be in prison. For crack or meth or opioids. For Fentanyl or Oxycontin. But he doesn't think she's dead.

She's not even old, he says. She was fifteen when he was born, and he's fifteen now, so she'd only be thirty, if she was alive, wherever she is.

Fucking A, Bobby says.

I don't know what A stands for.

Alone? All right? Answer? Autumn? Anything?

Bobby lives in a trailer with his dad. On Buffalo Road, out in the country.

The old man's all right, he says. Used to be a druggie like his mom, but he cleaned up after Bobby was born and the mom had his little brother, and then went off to wherever she was going.

Derek's his brother. Pretty good kid most of the time.

Except when he's not, Bobby says and smiles. His top two teeth in front overlap by a lot.

His old man's name is Scrubs. He used to work in a carwash for a few years, and the name comes from there. The name stuck.

Now he works construction, and his real name is Neal. But nobody calls him Neal.

In the winter, there's not much work in construction because of the weather. So money's tight, especially after Christmas. The trailer gets very cold, and they walk around inside wrapped in blankets.

They eat government cheese and government peanut butter. Cheese comes in a big block and peanut butter in a big tub.

Bobby's fingers are tapping the arm of the chair. His legs are bouncing.

Scrubs gave up drugs, Bobby says, but boy does he like to drink. He can drink beer all weekend, pretty much from Friday night to Sunday afternoon. Sometimes he'll fall asleep on the couch, and soak the cushions with pee. Just pisses himself and the couch, all over.

Too drunk and too asleep to wake up and use the sink or the toilet.

Still wearing his dusty and muddy work clothes.

In here, Bobby Collins says, in here. Are you kidding?

Clean sheets. Changed once a week. Three squares a day, with orange juice, lemonade, coffee even.

Waffles on Sunday with maple syrup.

Heat in winter, a/c on warm days.

Are you shitting me? Bobby says. This is cake. This is vacation on a sunny island. Palm trees. White sand.

And pretty much everyone is okay. Is pretty nice, at least, and mostly more than nice.

I mean, Trey, he says and looks at me. His eyes are big and they glow, like something's burning inside him.

Let's get real, he says. Right. Can you fucking believe it?

Even the rich kids. The kids who have mothers who are doctors and professors and lawyers, Bobby Collins says.

They do good in here. Ya know. They do just fine.

At home, he says. Jesus. We have holes in the floor. You see ice on the ground through the holes. All winter.

The windows leak like a mother. The cold whistles in. All night, and then all day.

You can smell the old man's Camels all the time. You can hear him coughing constantly. Just hacking and hacking like his lungs are gonna come up.

And Derek is weird. He doesn't mean to be. He's mostly okay, but he's still pretty weird.

Mom drank and did crack when she was pregnant with him. He's not normal. His head is kind of small. Not very bright, and when he gets pissed off, oh shit. Watch out.

He throws things, he breaks things. Breaks windows, punches the TV screen, fires plates like they're Frisbees. He screams, Fuck and shit and cunt. He's got foam around his mouth, snot running out his nose.

He's jerking and twitching like a lunatic.

He's never picked up a knife, or gone for one of the guns. But Scrubs and me, we usually have to tackle him on the rug and then just stay on top of him. Hold him down before he really hurts himself or totally wrecks the place.

My God, Bobby says.

Derek's not very big, and he's not too strong. He's way skinnier even than me, Bobby says. But he's full of the rage, and that makes him big. That makes him twice his regular size.

When it's all over, when he's finally calmed down a little, at least enough so that you don't have to hold him down anymore, you get up and look at all the damage. You pick up pieces of glasses and plates, you duct-tape cardboard over the broken windows. Right before Bobby came here to the ward, there were five broken windows in the trailer.

In January, you leave a cup of water out overnight on a table, and it'll freeze by morning, Bobby says.

He sleeps in a sweatshirt and coat, in two pair of socks, in a ripped sleeping bag.

The whole thing. God, he says.

A real shit-show, a cluster-fuck. A full-blown debacle.

Bobby's tapping like crazy now. Fingers, feet, elbows, knees, the heel of his hand. He's blinking his eyes constantly, his jaws are clenching and unclenching.

So, yeah, he says. This place is cherry.

No Scrubs pissing the couch. No Derek fits.

And when they're not drunk or having a fit, they stare at the TV all the time. Hours and hours. Mouths partway open. They're mouth-breathers.

Fuck, Bobby says.

His eyes look a little wet, and so I look away. I can't tell if they're wet because he's almost crying, or because he's been talking so much.

We don't say anything for a minute, for two then three more minutes. We're quiet except for the tapping, which isn't loud.

Where's Amanda? I finally ask.

Bobby thinks she had a meeting with her parents and the social worker.

Is she leaving? I ask. The idea makes me breathe fast and shallow.

I dunno, he says. Could be anything.

Another minute or two go by. I resist the urge to look at the clock. It's up there on the wall in the nurses' station, but I refuse to look.

Maggie, Bobby says. She still sleeping?

He looks at me, but I avoid his eyes. I don't want to see if there are tears in his eyes.

I think so, I say. She's getting E.C.T. three days a week. Monday, Wednesday, Friday. I think. It might have been twice a week, but they maybe increased it.

She okay? Bobby asks.

I dunno. I hope so.

I look over and Maggie's door is closed. Somebody has taped a sign on the door that says, DO NOT DISTURB.

What's today? Bobby Collins asks.

Hmmm, I say. Trick question?

No.

Monday, I say. Thursday?

He smiles.

It's not the weekend. Cara's at a desk in the nurses' station, and she never works weekends.

Bobby says, Okay, then he stands up and says, Catch you later. He turns, and begins the big circuit around the ward. Around the dayroom, the nurses station, around the long hallway, past bedroom doors. Bobby can do a hundred laps a day. Sometimes he'll do two or three hundred. He'll pace till he drops, or until somebody stops him.

When I look over I notice that someone has opened Maggie's door. Not all the way, but a foot or two open.

It's dark in the room, but I think I can make out a lump under the covers of her bed. That must be Maggie, right?

I mean, who else could it be?

My eyes are closed because I don't want to start watching the clock again. Once I start I don't ever seem to want to stop. I'm also tired, and I feel my eyelids settle, heavy and still, as though I'm in for a long, deep sleep.

After a while I feel, more than hear, someone sit down where Bobby had been sitting. I feel light footsteps, the swish of air, the movement of someone fairly small, settling into Bobby's chair.

Trey, a voice says softly, and it's Clea, I'm pretty sure.

I open my eyes, and it is Clea. I swear, in only weeks or a month, she's lost weight, she's grown taller. She looks like the full teenager.

Hey, I say.

Trey, she says again. Is Maggie okay?

Sure, I say. But I really don't think about it. I kind of assume she's all right.

Why? I ask Clea.

All she does is sleep. Then they wake her up to zap her again. Then she goes back to sleep.

She talked a lot one day, I say.

That was it, Clea says.

How long's she been getting E.C.T.? I ask.

Three weeks? A month?

Is that long?

I don't know, Clea says.

We sit for a few minutes without saying anything. Clea's face is alert, strands of hair rim her head with light. She looks worried, a kind of pure worry that only a kid seems to feel.

A month ago, two months ago, Clea was so far inside herself that she didn't seem capable of worrying much about anyone but herself. Does getting better mean that you feel more pain?

I hate to think of her in pain. You want her to feel, but not too much.

Is it always about balance?

I don't know. I wish Clea knew.

But she seems so much better than she was a few months ago.

You could ask Dr. Manchin. Dr. Altemio, I say.

Hmmm, Clea says.

Then my eyelids come down again, and every part of my body wants to stretch out on a bed. It's like fog and mist, veils, are surrounding my head.

I'm moving. My brain is moving underneath something. Under grass, under water, and then so far under the water that my brain pushes through to air. To clear and cloudless blue sky, then across the sky to a part where it's deeper blue, sunless, where a white moon gilds the sky with light that is a lesser kind of dark.

Trey, a voice says. Trey, wake up.

Trey, the voice says again.

I blink and blink, but it's very bright when I try to open my eyes.

It's Cara, she says.

Cara, I say, fumbling to get my mouth around the name.

Trey, she says, there's a social worker from Malvern here. Mainly to see some patients in the adult unit. But she said she'd be happy to talk to you about Malvern. About their programs, and about transferring to the state hospital.

It's like a jolt. Like E.C.T. Then ice water poured down my back, then poured down the front of my pants.

I think of heavy wire mesh on all the windows. I think of locks on all the doors.

No, I say. No, thank you.

She's very nice, Trey, Cara says.

I open my eyes and she's staring at me hard. Warm brown eyes. Warm but firm.

What's she thinking? Why me?

Send someone else to Malvern.

Beyond Cara, I see a tall woman with short hair standing in the nurses' station. She's smiling in my direction, and she holds a black notebook in one hand.

You're gonna be eighteen, Trey, she says. You can't stay forever.

I know, I say, but I don't really know.

So why don't you meet with her? Cara asks.

No, thank you, I say. But thanks for thinking of me.

You're sure? she says.

I nod. Close my eyes again.

Feel Cara stand up, feel footsteps moving away. Hear the big door open and close a few minutes later.

Feel ice water all over. Shaking.

Twenty-Three

SIXTH GRADE. MIDDLE SCHOOL. I was eleven, and it was much easier to hide in Boynton Middle School. There were just so many kids. Twice as many as at Fall Creek. Three or four times more kids.

The building was huge.

When we changed classes every forty-five minutes, it was mobs of kids, parades of kids, moving with wild energy in the halls. Yelling, singing, pushing, talking, laughing, shrieking like monkeys in trees in the jungle.

Nora was gone by then. Nora had been there for three years, while I was still in Fall Creek, on the second floor, moving from third to fifth grade, closer each year to the door. Closer each year to leaving for good.

And all the kids from my class were at Boynton too. Major and Max, the two Sarah's, Hannah, Dylan, Luke. Pippa also. Pippa had come to Boynton, and she was still nice to me, in a quiet, shy way.

In six years at Fall Creek, from kindergarten to fifth grade, we had never really spoken more than a few words at a time to each other. But I always thought that she was the closest thing I had to a friend.

Pippa's real friends were Skinny Sarah and Dylan, who was a girl. Pippa ate lunch with Skinny Sarah and Dylan, and she usually walked to school with them also.

But once every two or three weeks, Pippa would walk to school alone, and she and I would walk together, hardly saying anything. We might say, Hey or Hi. We might ask, How's school? You like Boynton?

We'd say Hey or Hi back. We'd say, School's good, and, Yeah, I like Boynton. Then we just walked, our shoes or sneakers crunching the leaves on the sidewalk.

It was October, maybe, and the leaves on the trees were gold and red and orange. Halloween hadn't happened yet, but we were at an age where we wondered if we should go trick or treating, or if we were too old now that we were in middle school. In middle school we weren't little kids anymore.

Or maybe it was November, and Halloween was already past, and the leaves on the sidewalks and lawns were brown, mostly. The early morning walk to school grew colder and colder, at seven-thirty.

Nora was in ninth grade in the high school, and she was three inches taller than Mom. I was growing tall too, but not as tall as Nora. In fifth grade, at the top of Fall Creek School, I was the tallest kid in the school. But not at Boynton. There were almost a million kids there. Many of them were taller.

The high school was right across the creek, and we passed it on the way to Boynton. One time, a bunch of high school kids were on the green bridge over the creek, and one kid saw me and yelled, Noodle.

I didn't know at first if he meant me. And I didn't know what Noodle meant.

Then two or three said, Noodle, as I walked by.

Then I knew.

A noodle was very long and very skinny. It was pale.

I was a noodle. Of course I was.

We changed classes all the time at Boynton. There were blocks of time for each class, and there were A, B, and C lunch blocks, because all the kids couldn't sit in the cafeteria at the same time.

Nora said it was the same in high school. The same blocks of classes, only there were five lunch blocks, A to E. That's how many kids there were at Boynton and the high school.

At home, everything was pretty much the same as it had always been. I still didn't talk much, at school, on the sidewalks, but especially at home with Mom and Dad. The safest thing was to say nothing, and to go into the closet.

One night, almost in early winter, Mom and Dad had a viewing for a dead person and the family and friends. After everyone had left, Mom and Dad drank whiskey at the kitchen table. I stayed in the den because I thought they were tired and would leave me alone.

They still wore their funeral clothes. Black everything, except for a white shirt and white blouse. Dad's black tie was loose.

I was reading a book about a boy and girl who went off to find their missing father, and how when you wrinkled the surface of time you could travel across time. I think that's what it was about. I wasn't sure.

Then I could feel someone standing in the door. I was on the couch.

It was Mom, with this tightness in her face. Holding a glass.

What're you reading? she said. Her voice was thin, and I thought her voice was dangerous.

A book, I said.

Of course it's a book, she said. I can see that.

About a boy and girl. About a scientist.

You don't have anything better to do? she asked, but it wasn't a question, really.

I didn't say anything, and I could feel her getting more and more angry.

Her eyes were black diamonds.

I sat on the couch, and hoped she'd go away.

Nora was at Emma's house, at a sleepover. If Nora had been there, this wouldn't have happened.

You know? Mom said. You know?

I didn't want to know. I didn't want to have anything to do with what she was going to tell me.

You were a mistake. A terrible mistake that we have regretted ever since, she said.

What did she mean? What did it mean to be a mistake?

Like you got the wrong answer on a quiz. Like you had written down white, and the correct answer was black. Up or down, inside or outside, love or hate. Whatever you had written down, the opposite was the correct answer.

The person who made up the test, who was grading the test, knew the answers. And you were supposed to guess the correct answer. The answer that the giver of the test had decided on.

Your job was to read their mind. Because love or hate, hot or cold, winter or summer, fat or skinny—any of them could be the right answer. Or the wrong answer.

Maybe my face was blank. Maybe there was no expression on my face, and it was blank as a white wall. A wall with a big banana nose, with a thin line of a mouth, with ears that stuck out like clown ears.

Ugly as sin. That's what Dad said about some things.

Noodle Burnes. A pencil neck, a scarecrow, a skeleton.

I'd heard those things, but sometimes it was hard to tell if they were talking about me. If they were talking about somebody else.

Noodle was definitely about me. The high school kid looked right at me and said, Noodle. Then other kids laughed. Other kids said, Noodle, too.

They laughed. Big ho ho's. Bigger than Santa Claus.

The first kid, the kid who made it up, had dirty blond hair that was long and falling down the front of his face. He had pimples on his face, and he wore big boots. Tim boots, for Timberland.

Shit-kicker boots, some kids called them.

The first kid was big. He was twice as big as me. Taller by a little, and way wider. Wide as a truck.

The other kids wore baggy jeans, and they wore sneakers or Tims. Their hair was long too, and one of them, a short kid, had a little bit of a mustache. Just a thin line of hair on his upper lip.

Ha ha, ho ho. Fucking A, they said.

Fucking A was all over the place, whatever it meant.

Did it mean you got an A on a test? Or did it mean, Okay? All right? Sure? Maybe?

Words could have so many meanings, and you could never really tell what they meant.

When they said, Sticks, and looked at me. Did they say that because I was so tall and skinny? When they said, Skeleton, and looked at me, was that because I was so skinny, like a skeleton? Or was it because I lived in the Burnes Funeral Home? With the dead bodies? Because maybe skeleton meant death, like a skull and crossbones.

Maybe both, or maybe neither one. Like the exams, I could never tell. I couldn't read minds.

I wished I could. Life would be easier if I could.

I couldn't even read faces, most of the time.

But with Mom, I could almost always.

She stood there in the doorway to the den, and those eyes, dark as midnight, pinned me to the couch. I held the book on my lap, and put my long skinny hands over it, because I was ashamed to be reading a book about time, and about a girl named Meg who was searching for her scientist father.

Mom said, We wanted your sister. We planned for her. But we weren't going to have five or eight or ten snot-nose brats like all the people in Ireland. Pulling their families down, with their howls, their hunger, into poverty.

One beautiful girl like Nora, she said. Just one, and she would be everything.

Then you, you sneak, coming along three years later.

We were just starting out, and Nora was everything we wanted. Then this red, howling creature shows up. The nose and ears as big as turnips.

Mom sipped her whiskey. She sipped once, then she sipped a second time.

Her eyes got wet for a moment.

God help me for saying it, she said. God help me for even thinking it. It's not your own fault, for heaven's sake. But you've done fucking little to win us over.

The word fucking, coming from my mother's mouth, was a shock. You only ever heard it on the playground, or on the sidewalks near school.

It's like she was different. It's like she was lower.

She said, It's not that we don't love you, Trey, because we do, God knows.

We love you because you're our son, and every last day that you've been here, we've fed you, cleaned you up, tried to teach you right and wrong, put clothes on your back, and covered you with blankets at night. We've done everything a mother and father can do.

We've waited for you to grow, to flower, but you're a weed, Mom said. You can't turn a weed into a rose. You just can't do that.

You stare at the floor when you're not staring at us. And when you do look at us, which isn't very often, you never look us in the eye.

Your father and I, we can tell. We know how you feel about us, and we don't know why you hate us. We stopped asking why a long time ago.

We knew we were never going to get anything we wanted from a son like you.

No warmth or affection, no appreciation, no gratitude, she said.

We'd get more from the stones in Ireland, and believe me, there are plenty of stones in Ireland. There are millions and millions, everywhere you look, Mister.

I hated when she called me Mister. Like I was an old person who was a stranger. Like I was a person who walked in off the street, like I was someone she didn't know.

She sipped again on her drink, and she kept sipping more and more. I watched her throat moving up and down, and then there was nothing left in the glass. She even took the ice cubes into her mouth and crushed them between her back teeth.

She said, What we wouldn't have given for a normal boy. A

boy with a normal nose and mouth and ears. A handsome boy who spoke normally, and acted normal.

Instead, we have you sneaking around the house like a ghost or wraith.

She was in the doorway, and I couldn't leave. I wanted to crawl behind the couch, or under one of the chairs.

We were silent for a little while.

Then my mother looked different. She seemed to be looking up at a corner of the room, and her eyes were wet, they were glistening.

Was this possible? To go from cold to hot, from sky to earth, from ocean to mountain so quickly?

But there were. There were tears falling down the front of her face.

I think she said, God forgive me.

But I wasn't sure. Her breath was jagged.

Then she turned and left.

I took my book, and went out in the hall, and then up the stairs to the third floor. I didn't want to go into the closet, because I was going in almost every day. But I had to.

I left the book on the bed, and then crawled in, behind the coats and dresses, and I pulled the door closed. It was dark, of course, and the hems of the clothes were soft, and some of them smelled like moth balls.

For a moment I had the creepy feeling that the smell of moth-balls was a little like the smell of formalin. I thought, Oh God. Me lying down in the complete darkness, and someone pumping forma-lin into my veins.

Then I started taking slow, deep breaths. Slower and slower, deeper and deeper. I could control my breath, especially if I concentrated.

Then I was breathing very low and slow, almost like I wasn't breathing at all.

I could hear a car pass out front every once in a while.

I could hear the engine, and I could hear the sound of the tires on the surface of North Tioga Street.

The sound of one car would fade, then another car approached.

I don't know how long I listened. For three minutes or nine minutes or for a half hour.

It had to be late. It had to be after eleven or twelve o'clock, and Nora sometimes said that midnight was the witching hour. Midnight was when goblins, ghosts, witches, all came out. She said that midnight was when graveyards yawned.

She read that in a book for English class.

I heard them coming up the stairs. First Mom, who was lighter and slower, and then Dad.

My door was closed, but I could feel Dad approach the door.

Please, I thought. Please don't.

He tapped on the door, but the doorknob didn't turn.

I didn't breathe.

Goodnight, Trey, he said. Sleep tight.

Then his footsteps went away.

I didn't know what he meant. I didn't know if he was joking or serious.

I stayed in the closet for hours. I stayed there in the dark, wishing I knew what people meant. Until there were no more cars passing on the street.

Twenty-Four

NORA AND I BOTH sat on the edge of the bed in her room, and everything she said was a whisper. Outside was rain, and outside was getting dark, and there was a viewing down on the first floor.

The rain got heavier for a few minutes, and the wind picked up, blowing water in sheets against the window, and pressing the side and roof of the house. As if the rain and wind meant to get inside.

We could hear the voices of people down on the first floor, and we could feel the front door open and close, the vibrations of footsteps, the coming, the kneeling, the standing, the going.

The dead person was a woman named Regina, and she seemed to have had a lot of friends, for an old person. Most old people had very few friends. Most old people had friends who were already dead.

Nora's room had pictures on the wall. Old black and white photograph posters of the Brooklyn Bridge, of the inside of Grand Central Station, of the top of the Chrysler Building. There was also an old photo of a street and steps in Paris, a long time ago.

Nora loved cities. She had been to New York City twice. Once with Emma and Emma's mom and dad, and once on a school trip, but she had never been to Paris. Someday, she said, she'd go to Paris.

Its nickname was the City of Light. It had more beautiful women than anywhere in the world, Nora said.

Paris had wide streets and lovely parks and buildings that looked like wedding cakes.

While the rain fell and the wind blew, Nora whispered that she had something to tell me, and that it was top secret. So secret that if anybody found out, she and I might have to go to jail. Maybe for a long time.

I whispered that I hadn't done anything, as far as I knew.

She said it didn't matter. That I was part of a conspiracy.

A conspiracy, she said, was when two or more people whispered together about breaking the law.

Her voice was a soft hiss. Her voice didn't sound at all like her regular voice. It was like a new Nora. An older Nora, a bigger Nora. A secret Nora.

She was fourteen already, and Nora had breasts that were small but definite. She had really long legs. Her hair was short, and cut in angles around her face. Parts of her hair fell on her forehead, and there was a purple streak in the piece that fell between her eyes.

Nora, if you didn't know her, might seem scary.

You promise not to say anything to anybody? Ever? No matter if your life depended on it? she asked.

I moved my head up and down. I nodded and kept nodding.

You have to say it, Trey, she said.

You promise? You swear? she asked.

Yes. I promise. I swear, I whispered.

But I felt nervous. I felt suddenly cold all over. I was pretty sure I was trembling.

184

What would jail be like? I wondered. What would happen when the police put handcuffs on your wrists and stuck you in a police car? Where was jail and how long did they make you stay there? For conspiracy? For knowing things you were not supposed to know?

Regina's family, her son and daughter, called Mom early in the week and said their mom was dying at the Lakeview old peoples' home. She would be dead in a day or two at most. That's what the doctor told the son and daughter.

Nora heard Mom tell Dad, and Dad said they would pick up the body when they got a call from Lakeview.

So I knew they'd be gone, Nora whispered. I knew I'd have an hour or two to explore.

I started to tremble more. I started to shake.

Jail, and now the basement.

Even though Nora had been talking about the basement for years, I didn't ever think that she would really go down there.

I don't know why I thought that. Nora pretty much always did what she said she'd do. She didn't have any fear, not that I could see.

I mean, she must have been afraid. But I could never tell. She was just tall and smart and brave.

So Nora waited through the weekend for Lakeside, and they called late Sunday morning, when it was clear and cool outside, when the sky was blue. When most people were home drinking coffee.

Nora, I said, you shouldn't have done it. You should have just stayed up here.

Don't be a baby, Trey, she said.

Then she pushed my hair off my forehead, to let me know she loved me. To let me know I was still her brother.

I went down the back stairs, she whispered, and her voice was suddenly very soft. So soft that it was little puffs of air pushed out from between her lips.

She got to the landing, where there were three doors. One, straight ahead, went outside to the back, where the van, the hearse and the limo were parked. The hearse and limo were black, the van was white. The door on the left went into the first floor, and the one on the right was around the turn, and went downstairs.

The one on the right went to where all the secrets lived. That door was locked almost all the time, but Nora said that more and more, Mom and Dad forgot to lock it, or didn't bother to lock it.

Nora tried the door, and the handle turned, and when she whispered that, whispered that the door was unlocked, I was afraid that I would pee my pants. I could feel my heart thumping, as though it would shatter in my chest.

I almost couldn't sit still where I was sitting. I had to get up and run, and turn in circles, to get Nora's words away from me. But I didn't. Didn't get up and didn't get her words away from me.

I watched Nora, and her eyes were like my eyes, only they were shiny and they blinked, and I could see them moving around in her room, seeing something, moving along, seeing something else, pausing, moving some more.

Those same eyes had been in the basement.

The stairs and hallways were carpeted, and there were no sounds from her steps. Sounds were muffled.

She opened the door and went through and down some steps, and there was another hallway, and another door, this one with the Keep Out sign in red. State laws said that you could not enter, that unauthorized personnel would be in violation of the law and would be prosecuted.

Nora said that the sign meant that unless you were a funeral director like Mom and Dad, you shouldn't and couldn't be in the room.

She tried the door, and I thought I would have a heart attack.

Don't, Nora, I wanted to say, but I didn't make a sound.

It was like Nora wasn't in the room with me. She was in the basement again, and she was seeing and feeling all of it.

And if Nora was in the basement, then I was too. But I would do almost anything not to be there.

Except I didn't do anything. I stayed on the edge of the bed, next to Nora, and I hated that more whispers were coming from her. At the same time, I couldn't wait to find out what she saw and did down there. Like Nora, I needed to know.

I looked at the poster of Grand Central Station, a long time ago. In the nineteen-forties, I thought. The huge space. The huge high windows. People, shafts of sunlight. All the people moving, although they were frozen in the photograph.

All those moving, frozen people would be dead now, I thought.

Then I paused, and thought, Are they all dead?

Of course, I thought. That was just life. You lived, then you died.

But the door to the Keep Out room was locked. The door-knob wouldn't move.

So Nora moved down the wide hallway to the left, and there was a big room, the size of two living rooms, and it was full of caskets.

She was afraid at first. There were eight or ten or twelve caskets in the room, and she thought for a moment that there were bodies in every one of them.

The caskets were on stands, and about half or two-thirds of them were open, had the lid lifted, and the white puffy lining was showing. The small pillow, and Nora said they looked like jewelry cases.

They were made of metal, light grey, or dark brown, and two or three were made of wood. The wood ones were custom-made, Nora said, by a local carpenter. The wood was pale, and had a simple latch to close the top with the bottom.

Nora had heard Mom and Dad talk about the wood coffins. Mom had said that they should carry them for six months or a year, and Dad said, Or even longer.

There were at least two or three of them down there, Nora said. Maybe even four.

The metal coffins were very shiny, and the light from the high windows fell on the floors and walls, though the light seemed weaker in the basement.

And even though it was a basement, it didn't feel or smell like one. There was carpet on the floor, and the air was very dry.

But the other big room, Trey, the Keep Out room, she said. That's where you and I have to go.

I began to shake my head side to side.

I was never going down there.

We have to, she said. We just really and truly have to.

Not me, I said.

The rain spattered the windows on the third floor, and the wind moved branches in the trees. It felt like the wind was trying to blow the roof off the house. It felt almost like the end of time.

Where did birds and dogs and cats and insects go in the rain? I wondered. Did some of them drown? Did any of them keep dry?

Did they stand or perch or sit or crawl, and just let the rain fall and fall and fall on them? What did heavy rain feel like to an ant, crawling in the grass? Like a hurricane?

Did ants and bees and crickets die in rainstorms? And if they did, what happened to their bodies?

We heard footsteps on the second floor, and we didn't move. The footsteps were quick, and pretty light, but we knew somehow that they were Mom's.

The steps seemed to go into the den, then the kitchen. We heard a drawer sliding open, and I thought, A knife. My God she's getting a knife.

Nora said, Breath mints. She keeps them in the drawer.

Nora said, Mom's talking to the family and friends.

Farther down below, the big front door kept opening and closing. When you opened the front door you stood in a hallway. Straight ahead was a door, and a big flight of steps that went to the second floor.

During a viewing, that door was closed and locked so that the families and friends of the dead wouldn't go upstairs.

To the left was another big door that went into another, larger hallway. There was a wood stand with a pen and notebook on top, and that's where the viewers would sign their names, Nora said.

When there wasn't a viewing, the door on the left was closed and locked, and the door to the stairs was unlocked and open. It all depended on the dead. If the dead guy was in the basement, we'd smell formalin.

During viewings, we'd smell flowers. One smell covered up the other smell.

Nora said the coffin room was really big, and had a soft carpet, and had little cones for lights in the ceiling. The walls were painted white, but a nice creamy white that was soft like the carpet.

She kept whispering, even though the rain kept pounding the roof and walls and windows, and the wind whispered and whistled. The wind sounded a little like Nora.

All these big, shiny boxes, with silver handles on them, to carry them upstairs, then to carry them out to the hearse, then to the church, if there was a church service. Then to the hearse again, and then to the grave, Nora whispered.

And that was the end of it, she said. That's where everybody went when it was all over.

The priest or rabbi or a son or daughter or friend would say a few words, and then everybody would leave except for a few guys in work clothes.

Those guys, Nora said, usually stayed out of site behind trees or bushes. They had a thing called a backhoe, Nora said she'd heard, and when everyone else was gone, they came out from hiding and filled in the hole. Then, maybe, they'd plant grass seed.

Maybe there would be a big polished stone to put at the head of the grave, with a name and the dates of birth and death. The dates of the two biggest things in a person's life.

Nora didn't think of those things when she was down in the basement. She kept noticing the clean white walls, and the dark carpet, and the long shiny boxes.

That was the room where the families came and picked out the coffins. There were cards with prices under the small pillows of each casket, Nora said. That was where you chose the box your loved one would be buried in—forever and ever.

That's what priests and ministers said. Forever and ever.

As though they understood time, Nora said. As though they commanded time.

I wasn't sure I understood what Nora was saying. Sometimes I didn't understand what anybody was saying. They were talking fast or slow, and often above me. I was too young or too stupid.

The rain slowed to a pitter here, a patter there, and down below people weren't going in and out the front door so much. That must have been after eight in the evening, or even after nine.

People were driving home through the rain. They were undressing, using the bathroom to pee and brush their teeth. On the first floor, at the front of the long room, Regina was in her casket, surrounded by flowers, surrounded by the puffy white material they put in caskets. Her eyes would be closed, her hands folded on her stomach.

Nora said she tried the door on the Keep Out room a second time, but it was still locked.

Me and you, Trey, she whispered. We have to go down there, she said. Sometime.

I wanted to say, No. Never. But I couldn't.

Nora was the best person I knew. There was nobody even close to her.

Think about it, she said.

She looked at me. But not all the time, she said.

I almost smiled, because I already thought about it almost all the time.

Next to always.

Tomorrow, they would close Regina's casket and put her in her grave. The ground would be soft because of the rain.

The ground would welcome her in its arms. Regina would be back with her mother.

Twenty-Five

IT'S TEN-FORTY-SEVEN AT NIGHT, according to the clock in the nurses' station, and for us in here, for the ward, that's pretty late. I tell myself not to watch the clock, not to perseverate, and so I don't.

I'm in my usual spot in the dayroom, sitting and watching. Everyone is tired, even the staff, but for some reason I always get pretty awake around now. Nearly everyone has gone back to their rooms, they're reading or writing letters or writing in their journals, and I bet half of them are already asleep.

Lenny, the overnight guy, will be in at five till eleven. He always gets here at exactly five till eleven. He's an older black guy, and he's worked here over thirty years. He walks soft, and talks even softer, and he's always even and calm.

So even and so calm that people joke with him, they ask what drugs he's on. Prozac, Effexor, Zoloft, and a big dollop of Valium?

But Lenny just smiles. He's not on any drugs. He's just calm. Nothing anywhere to get upset about.

Amanda heard Dr. Manchin say, I want what Lenny's got.

The weekend overnight woman is Gloria, and she knits all night.

She's pretty calm too, but not as calm as Lenny. Gloria has three kids, and a husband who works for the city.

Three staff people are in the nurses' station, behind the glass, and they're all writing, either on loose pages, or in a notebook, and Christina, the evening nurse, is typing into a laptop.

Another nurse is named Carolyn, and the aide is Mike. Neither of them is full-time. They work something called *per diem*, which means they get paid for the hours they work, as needed. If someone on the regular staff is sick or on vacation, they call Carolyn or Mike, or both of them.

Earlier in the day, Wendy and Lisa on the day shift, said that it was late August, and I said, You mean this is late August now?

Now? Late August? I asked again, because I was sure that we were in the late winter or spring even.

This couldn't be the end of summer. We couldn't be getting ready for the start of fall.

They both looked at me.

Trey? Really? Lisa said. Her eyes were blue, and very clear, like cold January water. Even though Lisa was nice. Those eyes.

What month do you think it is? Wendy asked.

I'm not sure, I said. I've never asked.

I've hardly asked anyone anything, I think, and I almost never look out the window. When I do look out, it's usually dark and I look at lights in the distance. The hospital's on a hill, and it overlooks a giant lake.

There are lights along the edge of the lake, and at the city on the southern end of the lake.

Trey, Lisa said. Really. What month did you think it was?

March. Maybe May, I said.

Really? Wendy said.

How long have you been here? Lisa asked.

I shrugged and made an I-don't-know face.

Take a guess, Lisa said.

I shook my head.

I used to think a few months, but now I think it's got to be longer, I said. Five, six months?

Longer, Wendy said.

Quite a bit longer, Lisa said.

Hmmm, I think I said, then I thought that I'd been talking quite a bit. For me.

How long? I asked, because it felt like I wanted to know. I really wanted to know.

Almost a year, Lisa said.

Almost a year, and almost September, and pretty soon I'll be eighteen, and there's no way that I'm going to Malvern, not unless they force me.

The ward is empty, except for me. Christina, Carolyn and Mike are gone from the nurses' station. Lenny's in there, wearing his tan cardigan against the air conditioning, sitting and reading notes. His glasses have slipped partway down his nose.

Maybe I could ask Lenny what the date is. I mean, what month and year, and how old I am, and if I'll turn eighteen in the fall some-time, the way I turned fifteen and sixteen and seventeen in the fall in the past.

I'm sure he'd tell me in his soft voice. He'd tell me the truth, and maybe he could tell me how to avoid going to Malvern. Lenny would know.

Lenny makes the world safer.

But I don't want to disturb his reading, even if he probably wouldn't mind.

Most of the overhead lights have been turned off, and there are plenty of shadows on the carpet and chairs, and on the doors to the bedrooms. This is night lighting, and everything is quieter now.

I can feel Lenny moving through the ward now, stopping at each door, looking in, making sure everyone's okay and in bed.

He passes through the dayroom, and he puts his hand on my shoulder and squeezes lightly.

Hey, Trey, he says.

Hey, Lenny.

You doing okay? he asks.

Pretty good, I say.

Good, he says. Stay that way.

He goes back into the nurses' station, sits down and begins reading notes again.

Lenny knows when you want him to sit with you, and he knows when you want to sit by yourself. I don't get how he knows, but he does.

When everyone's gone, when there's only me out here and Lenny in there, it feels really different. Like there's been a party, or there's been a fair or a church service, and everybody's left. I don't know what a party or fair would be like because I've never been to either one, but I'm pretty sure it would be something like this.

I've been to church a few times, at St. Agnes, near downtown, but there aren't many people at St. Agnes.

A big place where there had been a bunch of people, talking and laughing and sitting, being with each other in a big group, and then the same place is empty.

There's only chairs here, and a few end tables, and the big nurses' station, and the hallway, the carpet, the partially closed doors. And the dim light. The light is nice. The dim light makes you feel calm. It almost makes you want to go to sleep.

For a while, for maybe an hour even, I sit, and I partly close my eyes. I don't want to look at the clock, or not much anyway, because I've promised to not get stuck in the face of the clock, with those hands circling and circling, carving up time.

I imagine the big lake, at the bottom of the long hill, behind the hospital, and how it's forty miles long, and a mile or two wide at some points. The lake is called Cayuga, after a long-gone Indian tribe, and it's one of a half-dozen or a dozen long thin lakes that look on a map like fingers.

That's why they're called the Finger Lakes. Because a long time ago, the Indians believed, God pressed his or her fingers into the earth and made the Finger Lakes. And most of them, the biggest ones named Cayuga and Seneca, are shaped like long fingers.

Seneca Lake, in some places, is six or seven hundred feet deep, deep enough to bury nearly anything.

Mostly Cayuga Lake is deep green or gray or even a little blue. Some days the surface is very smooth like a mirror, and reflects the sky and clouds. Other days it's wrinkled like paper or cloth, and there are whitecaps from the wind.

Always, every day except in fog, you can see the other side of the lake, the hills, the trees, the squares and rectangles of farms. There are thin gray roads, and houses, a few here, a few there. There are some barns and silos, and a car or pickup truck will move along the thin roads.

Lenny's looking at something on the computer screen, but I

can't tell what it is from here. My eyes pass over the clock, and it's twelve-fourteen.

I'm not supposed to look. I've promised myself not to look, but I can't help but see that the red second hand is still moving. Sweeping around and around.

But no. Stop, I almost say out loud.

And the minute hand is at twelve-fifteen, the hour hand is creeping away from the twelve.

Don't, I tell myself. Stop.

Not to the clock or to time, but to myself.

I close my eyes all the way, and the light is gentle on my eyelids, not like during the day.

I can feel the air conditioning in the vent, blowing lightly and almost not too cold. In another hour or two, it will make the hair on my arms stand up. I'll have to get a sweater or blanket.

Lenny's smart to wear his cardigan.

Old people feel the cold more than young people, I've heard.

I try to remember where I might have heard something like that.

Nora?

Maybe. Nora knows all kinds of random things.

Nora's in college now, up on East Hill. She has an apartment in Collegetown.

Maybe I could go to live with her. I could get a job or go to school.

I'll be eighteen this fall. In weeks.

I won't go to Malvern.

I keep my eyes closed, and I work hard to not think of Malvern.

That's funny. Nora told me a kind of joke. You say to someone, Don't think of polar bears.

And all they can think of is polar bears, of course.

When did I last see Nora? A month ago? Three, four months ago?

A door squeaks, and I look up, and it's Maggie, standing in the doorway, a blanket on her shoulders and draped down to the floor. The hood of her sweatshirt is up.

She blinks in the dim light, and looks around, and then she sees me. She smiles a slow, sleepy smile, but keeps looking around.

Then she starts moving slowly. A few steps, a pause. Almost like she's sleepwalking.

She goes down the long hallway, toward the locked door to the main entrance, and then she goes right, along a second hallway, then she takes another right, along the far side of the nurses' station.

Lenny looks up, smiles and waves to her. She smiles back, that slow, sleepy smile. As though she's still partway asleep. She's buried under the hood and the big blanket that wraps her like a mummy you see in pictures.

I don't know how long it's been since I've seen her, since any of us have seen her. More than a few days, more than a week. I don't think more than a month.

It's been at least two weeks, maybe even three weeks.

But I'm terrible with time. Time is a mystery.

The only thing I know is that time moves and flows like a river. It never ever stops. Not for anyone or anything.

I doubt that Maggie knows how long. We're pretty sure, Amanda, Clea, Bobby and me, that she's been getting the E.C.T. every day. Real early in the morning, before it's even light outside.

As though it's a secret. As though E.C.T. has to be done before it's light out, and before most people are awake. It's like her brain has been in darkness. Her brain has been asleep. So before dawn, they hit it with lightning bolts to try to wake it up.

She comes around the far edge of the nurses' station, near the window where we get our meds. She's moving slowly, and the blanket or her clothes or slippers, make a swishing sound that I wouldn't be able to hear if it was daytime. There would be too many other noises.

She goes to the far back corner of the ward, near bedroom doors, and then turns right again, into the dayroom, and behind chairs. Behind me.

I hope that she'll stop and sit down next to me. But she doesn't. She keeps walking slowly, and I think that maybe I could get up and walk with her.

I don't. If she wanted company she's sit down with me. We used to sit together all the time. Weeks ago.

I'm sure we did. We sat so close sometimes that strands of her hair brushed my face. Her hair smelled like honey or lemon.

I'm almost certain that happened. I didn't just dream it.

Maggie continues to walk. She approaches the door to her room, and she pauses.

Don't go in, Maggie, I almost say. We might never see each other again. You may leave, or I may leave.

I could be somewhere, months or years from now, and I would begin to wonder if you really existed. You might wonder.

If this was something we thought had happened, if we had sat together for hours, neither of us saying a word.

Maggie starts moving again, past her door, and again, down the big hall, toward the locked door.

She stops at the door, turns, and walks toward me. Slowly, the same smile on her face. Not a big smile. But a real smile.

My heart is a drum. My breathing is fast and shallow.

I could faint, I think. I could die right now.

With fear, with joy.

She glides to a stop, three or four feet in front of me. She stands there like a beautiful ghost almost. Her hood up and surrounding her face. The blanket like a big robe.

The blanket is deep blue, and has orange and red and yellow stripes at the top and bottom. Deep colors. Bold.

She still has the smile, and I'm thinking that maybe the smile is from the E.C.T. Maybe it's from some drugs she's on.

Could she be happy? Is that why she's smiling?

She stands a while, and looks at me, and some seconds and then some minutes pass.

Maggie, I finally say, my voice so low that I could be whispering.

She doesn't say anything for more seconds.

Does she remember me at all?

Trey, she finally says, and her voice is even softer than mine.

She seems to stand a long, long time. She's watching me. Her eyes don't leave my face.

She sits down in the chair next to me. She pulls her legs, her feet, up underneath her.

This is like before, I think. But different too.

I don't know how it's different, but it's not the same. I can tell.

Maggie says, I have to tell you a secret. Please don't tell anyone.

Okay, I say.

She leans over, cups a hand around my ear, and whispers. So soft that I have to concentrate to hear.

Her breath is warm on my ear.

My mom and dad, she whispers. They're sending me to a psych place in western Massachusetts.

She puts a tiny piece of paper in my hand.

This is my number, for when you get out and for when I get out.

When? I ask.

When am I going? she asks.

I nod.

Her hand is still on the side of my head, it's still cupping my ear.

In the next week or two, she whispers.

I nod, as if I understand. But I don't understand.

I like you, Trey, she whispers. I like you a lot.

I want to tell her I like her. Like her a lot.

Maybe I just said that. Maybe I did tell her.

Maybe I didn't.

Twenty-Six

THIRTEEN YEARS OLD AND everything was changing. Changing big and changing fast.

Eighth grade, and we were at the top of the school, just like fifth grade at Fall Creek. We were the biggest and the oldest.

I'd been growing tall, and I'd been growing pretty much all the time. The long bones in my arms and legs ached sometimes, especially at night, when I was trying to go to sleep.

Nora said that those were growing pains, and that the muscles and bones, the ligaments, were stretching out, were getting longer. She'd had growing pains, too, when she was twelve and thirteen, and even when she was fourteen. She said it was painful, but painful in a different way. In a sweet way. Painful in a way you didn't mind. Because you knew you were growing into your grownup body.

Nora was fifteen, she was almost sixteen, in a few months, and she was in eleventh grade. Next year she would be a senior, and she would apply to colleges.

Next year, I would be a freshman in high school. But already I was tall as a small tree. A maple sapling. Skinny, with long arms that were thin as twine.

I was taller than Mom, and I was about the same height as Nora and Dad. Mom was now the shortest, and if this kept up, if I kept growing, I'd be the tallest. But I'd be the skinniest too.

Nora said that I wouldn't always be skinny, but I thought she just said that to make me feel better.

I was still Noodle on the way to school. I was scarecrow, I was toothpick, I was bones.

The newest one was pencil. Pencil Burnes.

A short fat kid was bowling ball. His real name was Keith, and you could see him flinch when they yelled, Hey, bowling ball. He didn't know how to ignore them yet.

Nora now had hips and breasts like a grownup, but it didn't seem to change her any. She was still smart and sharp as a January morning. She was fast and accurate.

Her blond hair was cut short, and some of it fell down her forehead and over her eyes, and she'd push it up and back behind her ears with one hand. She did that hundreds of times a day, and I don't know if she meant it, but the move—hair in eyes, pushed back behind her ears—was adorable.

Nora had to be the most beautiful girl in the high school, or at least one of them, and she seemed to know almost everyone. Most people at Boynton and the high school didn't seem aware that Noodle Burnes was related to Nora Burnes.

It didn't seem possible. Noodle and Nora? Related?

A troll and a princess?

Even when we walked to school together, which wasn't that often, kids didn't seem to get it.

Maybe kids thought that Nora took pity on this toothpick, and let him escort her to school. But when we did walk together, nobody called me pencil or bones or noodle.

It's like Nora's beauty was a shield, a power, and nobody challenged it.

In almost every class, Nora got A's. Every quarter, every class, every year. A after A after A.

One time, sophomore year, in a chemistry class, Nora got an A-, then a B+. She didn't like the teacher, who talked about her mental health issues. The teacher, Ms. Kerrigan, had O.C.D. That meant obsessive-compulsive disorder. She washed her hands in the chemistry lab sink three or four times each class. Ms. Kerrigan thought that some of her students had O.C.D. too, even if they didn't know it.

Parents of Ms. Kerrigan's students called the principal to complain. They thought she was crazy, and that she was making her students crazy.

Ms. Kerrigan said the parents were discriminating against a disabled person. She didn't get fired. And Nora got an A- for the year in chemistry, the only time she got less than an A.

At home, at the Burnes Funeral Home and on the second and third floor, things were a little different, but mostly the same too.

The Cerelli Funeral Home had closed because old man Cerelli had died. And Mr. Mangino, whose funeral home was downtown near the Catholic Church, had a heart attack, and his son William, who was supposed to take over the business, didn't want to work with dead people.

So Mom and Dad were busier than ever. They sometimes had three or four funerals a week. The smell of formalin was all over the second and third floor, almost all the time. The smell of flowers was there too, and it tried to overcome the smell of formalin.

Formalin was a suffocating and sweet and powerful smell. You could recognize it anywhere, although the only place I found that smell was at home. I couldn't imagine how it smelled down in the basement.

Maybe because they were busy, or because I was tall, Mom and Dad sort of left me alone, most of the time. They hadn't hit me in a long while.

They didn't even say mean things. Hardly at all, and never the kinds of things that they'd say before. I did okay in school, and I tried to avoid Mom and Dad at home. I stayed in my room, and only came out when they were working in the basement, or when they were out, picking up a body or taking one to be buried or cremated.

Now that they were even more busy, with extra viewings and funerals, we could go days without seeing each other.

Even for dinner, Mom would make macaroni and cheese, with broccoli, and leave it on top of the stove, or Nora would make chili with ground beef, onions and garlic and tomatoes, and she and I would eat from bowls, sitting in the den.

Mom or Dad might come up, wearing a rubber apron and smelling like the inside of a bottle of formalin, and they usually ate, sitting on a stool at the kitchen counter, reading a piece of newspaper or a magazine. They smiled at Nora, they nodded at me.

Once in a while, in the cool or cold weather, Nora and I would make oatmeal chocolate-chip cookies. Well, Nora would make them, I'd stir everything together in a big bowl. She'd pour in flour, oatmeal, an egg or two, white sugar and brown sugar, vanilla extract, cinnamon, butter, and I don't know what else.

The oven would be preheating, to three-fifty, three-seventy-five.

The cookie dough was thick and hard to stir, and when we put in walnuts and chocolate chips at the end, I always thought that I'd never be able to stir and mix everything. But I always did.

Before, I had used a spoon, and it got stuck.

Now I used a butter knife to stir, because the blade cut through everything.

Then when Nora baked the dough, in neat rows of three, the smell was beyond delicious. It overwhelmed the formalin.

Nora and I smiled at each other. That was the best time. That was like sitting on the edge of one of our beds, talking. With the world outside our windows dark, with snow or rain or wind pressing the window glass. Cars and trucks passing down on the street.

When the first hot cookies came out of the oven, we waited a few minutes for them to cool on a rack. Then Nora handed me one, and when I took a bite, boy oh boy. It tasted even better than it smelled.

Nora didn't talk as much about going to the basement. Not as though she had lost interest, because she hadn't, but because she knew that it upset me. And she was pretty much always nice to me. She didn't want to make me more worried than I already was.

But every three or four months, when we were sitting on the edge of one of our beds, I'd ask.

She went down to the casket room more and more. She went down every month or two. Always when Mom and Dad were picking up a body or taking a body somewhere. Always when she knew they'd be away at least an hour.

The Keep Out room was always locked. In six or eight trips to the basement, it was never unlocked. Not once.

Nora would try the handle on the door, once, twice, three times, but it was only ever the same. Locked.

So she'd go left, down the hall, and the big shiny caskets, their lids mostly open, were always there. And three or four caskets that were made of wood, wood stained brown, and with black handles and a latch to keep the lid securely closed.

The wood caskets were from the local carpenter, Nora was pretty sure.

There was also a collection of urns on a few shelves. An urn was kind of like a big container, the size of a milk jug, only with rounded corners.

Nora had looked urn up. An urn was where you put the ashes of a dead man or woman, after you burned their body in a big oven. The oven was bigger and hotter that the oven we used to make cookies.

Nora said that this was called cremation. The ashes, she said, were called the cremains. The dead body was the remains, and when you burned the body you got cremains. One thing to another to another. Person, body, remains, cremains.

There was a small clock-radio on the table next to Nora's bed. It was playing low, playing a song that I thought was The Beatles. *Across the Universe.*

There was a new poster on Nora's wall, showing a beautiful city with stone towers and steeples, and down below, at the bottom of the poster, it said, Florence.

That was in Italy, I thought. It was famous for being beautiful. It was so famous, that sometimes girls were called Florence, although I had never met one.

The basement was a really nice place, Nora said. Clean and quiet and private. It was dry down there, and not damp and moldy the way you'd expect a basement to be, especially in a big old house. The lights in the ceiling were fancy, and you could make them bright or dim on the switch that turned the lights off and on.

And the big room with all the coffins, was almost like a show-room where they sold cars, Nora said. Not even almost like. It was a showroom for caskets. Big shiny boxes, long and sleek, a lot like cars. Fancy upholstery, to ride over to the far side of life.

Every one of them shined, even the wood ones, which had been stained, waxed and polished, until they gleamed like metal.

There were chairs, too, in the showroom. Between every second or third coffin, and on little tables spread around the room there were boxes of tissues.

That was because the bereaved were shopping for a coffin to hold the remains of their loved ones. That was hard, Nora said. The bereaved had just lost their husband or mother or sister or son, and no matter how unsurprising the death may have been, the bereaved were in shock. The bereaved were grieving, they were reeling in the face of death. They were crying.

Nora said that the bereaved all looked like they had been hit in the head with a rock. They looked like they belonged in the waiting room at an emergency room. They stared into space, and seemed to see things way off in the distance.

Sometimes Nora just sat in the room, and took a tissue from a box on a table, and she blew her nose. She said she could almost feel all the grieving people. Walking into the beautiful room. Standing and looking. Going from casket to casket, touching the upholstery, lifting the small pillow, pressing down on the thin mattress.

How much did these things cost? they may have wondered. This is where their daughter or mother would spend eternity. That meant all time. Until the end of the world.

And that must have been very hard to even imagine. Forever and ever, Nora thought, and she said it almost made her dizzy to think of eternity. Something without end.

How could something have no end? she wondered. That went against pretty much everything she knew and thought.

No end. Forever and ever.

She stayed in her chair, and took another tissue, and when she blew her nose again, the sound was loud and rude. It was out of place. Everything down there was so quiet, so close, so hushed.

She couldn't hear any noise overhead, and she couldn't hear any sounds from the street. Not even trucks.

She checked her watch, and realized that she'd been down there almost forty minutes. She had a rule to never stay down there more than a half hour.

She left, moving quickly and quietly, and went up the stairs, and a few minutes later, she heard the van pull in near the back door. She had barely missed Mom and Dad, by five minutes at the most.

The idea thrilled and scared her. What would they do if they caught her?

She just had to pay more careful attention to the time.

I said, Nora, you can't keep doing this, and she said it was fun.

She said, Don't you like hearing about it?

I said, Sort of, but I'd rather not hear about it. I'd rather she didn't go down there at all.

So all that fall, and into the winter, Nora didn't go to the basement, or if she did go, she didn't tell me.

Then in February, when Mom and Dad were really busy, when they had four funerals within ten days, they must have gotten a little sloppy.

They had gone to Pennsylvania, two and a half hours away, to pick up a body, and they would be gone most of a day. Nora had made some chili.

After lunch, I went upstairs to lie down, and I had fallen asleep.

Trey, Nora said. Trey, wake up.

My eyes blinked open, then closed again.

I went to the basement, Trey, she said.

I could hear the excitement in her voice.

She sat down on the edge of the bed.

I checked the door to the Keep Out room.

Huh? I said.

I turned the knob, Nora said. It turned all the way. It opened.

No, Nora, don't, I said. I don't want to know.

It turned all the way, Trey. I went in. I went into the Keep Out room.

Twenty-Seven

FOR OVER A YEAR, for even longer, Nora didn't tell me what she saw. I wouldn't let her. I kept saying, No. No. Don't. I don't want to hear it.

Stop. Please stop.

I even put my fingers in my ears.

I was finally in high school and fourteen years old. Nora was a senior and she was applying to go to college for next year.

She said, You really don't want to know?

And I said, I don't. But I do too.

She said, It's up to you. I won't say anything that you don't want to hear.

I had kept growing, and I was now the tallest person in the family. I was over six feet tall. Nora and Dad were about the same height, and Mom was the shortest. I was at least half a head taller than Mom, but she and Dad were still very powerful. They could be pretty scary, even then.

They both had eyes that were so dark they were almost black. And they were deep and empty, like an abandoned mine shaft.

At times their eyes almost seemed to smoke, or to flicker for a moment with red at the edges. Like there was fire inside. Like there was incredible heat and pressure in their brains.

And then when they looked at you. God. When they pinned you with their eyes you were an insect under the microscope. And they could pin you any time and for no special reason.

Just if you were sitting in the den, or at the table in the dining room.

Nora said she never felt pinned by their eyes, but she said too that she kind of knew what I was talking about. She'd see them looking at me, and she could feel the heat and power of their eyes. Like black lasers. Intensely concentrated light. Or maybe darkness.

I sometimes asked Nora why they were like this, and she said she didn't know. Mom and Dad were different people with her. They had never hit her, they had never said that they wished she hadn't been born. She had never disappointed them the way I had.

Maybe this had something to do with Dad's dead brother, John, and how he had died on a freezing night in the middle of winter, I said. Right next to Dad. And how Dad lay next to John's body, trying to keep it warm.

But he couldn't have kept it very warm. The only heat in the house came from a fireplace, a room and a half away.

I don't know, Trey, Nora said. I just don't know.

Nora said, What about Mom? Why's she so angry at you?

She said she didn't want a lot of kids, I said. She said that too many babies were the curse of Irish women. Too many babies were the reason people stayed poor. So many mouths to feed. Not enough food, no time or energy. Scraping the rocky ground to grow more turnips to eat.

Not a nice life, Nora said. A hard and flinty way to be.

But even Mom, when her medicines were right, could be almost normal, she could be almost warm.

Like I'd be sitting on the couch reading a book or a magazine, and she'd come in with a glass of whiskey. She'd stand by the doorway, she'd sip, then she'd sit on the couch, very close to me. She'd be looking at me, but it wasn't like the black lasers were there.

Her eyes would be regular.

You love to read, don't you? Mom said.

I nodded.

What's this one? she asked.

I told her it was a science fiction book about a planet where all the people were very intelligent and got along well, but where gases in the environment were building up, so the whole planet was going to explode. They had to decide to leave the planet and find a new place to live. If they stayed where they were, they would all die. It would mean the end of their civilization.

They only had a few more weeks to live on their planet.

That sounds a little frightening, Mom said.

It is, I said, but they'll escape. They usually do.

Mom laughed in this easy, warm way.

She was sitting very close to me. I could smell the whiskey, but I could also smell a little formalin, and maybe a little perfume or shampoo that smelled like honey or vanilla. Like the thing we put in cookies when we baked.

I looked over, and Mom had a small smile on her face. She was looking across the room, but I couldn't tell what she was looking at. Just that at that moment, there on the couch, she was relaxed and almost a little happy. Life had been pretty good for her, at least since she had left Ireland and come here to the United States.

Maybe that had been terribly hard.

The way we could hear Dad cry in his bedroom on the third floor, behind the door, every now and then. In a way it was almost impossible to imagine. Because he was so strong, and so severe about so many things.

Was Dad thinking about his dead brother John? Was that still as sad as it had been when he was a boy?

When all the kids in Ireland, especially the wild west of Ireland, in Connemara and Galway—when they were so painfully thin from not having much to eat. Their pale skin, their freckles, their patience in the face of poverty.

Were poor people really patient? Or were they just beaten down? Not much food, very little energy? Listless and defeated? No more hope that things might be different? No matter how hard you worked, no matter how constantly you tried?

Then it was late December, after Christmas, and there had been no deaths or funerals or viewings for almost a week. And that, after a fall of two or three funerals a week. Mom and Dad had begun to look tired, and when they were tired they became sort of mellow.

There were still four or five pill bottles on the counter in the kitchen, and they all said Ellen Burnes on the label on the side of the bottle. There was lithium, things called Zyprexa and Seroquel, and one or two others that I couldn't remember. Maybe the names of the drugs changed a lot.

Nora said they were for Mom's brain, for her psychiatric problems. Nora didn't know exactly what those problems were, but probably for her anger and mood swings. When Mom talked so much there seemed to be a loud radio in her head. And then when she wouldn't talk at all, when she seemed to be made of the stones of Ireland.

Nora had looked up the names of the pills on her computer, and lithium was to make her steady, to keep her in the middle of the emotional road. Zyprexa and Seroquel were both atypical anti-psychotic drugs.

Atypical meant not typical, and psychotic meant full-out crazy.

Mom was moody, but she didn't seem completely crazy.

She didn't think she was Napoleon or the Queen of England or Cleopatra.

The one who seemed to need help was Dad. He hadn't hit me in years, and he didn't say mean things anymore. But the times he went into his bedroom to cry seemed to increase. And the crying grew heavier and heavier. Like he was sobbing for all of his life, like the gasps for breath, the choking sound, were a sorrow beyond measure or words.

It was like he had just found out that John had died. Like his mother and father had just died. Like the sadness, the darkness, had overwhelmed all the light. And there was no way forward, there was no way through this.

But Dad, as far as we knew, had no pill bottles around. Nora had never seen any, and I had never seen any.

During the summer before her senior year, Nora had begun working as a waitress at a restaurant on the lake, and she often made more than a hundred dollars a night. After two months, she had enough money to buy a car, and she found a blue Civic that had just under a hundred thousand miles on it.

She loved her little car, and sometimes, in the evenings after dinner, she took me for long rides, out of the city and into the country. We went on small county roads, out of Tompkins County, into Chemung or Cortland or Cayuga Counties.

There were fields and farms everywhere. And even in late November, after a few small snowfalls, the fields were empty except for corn that had been cut, and the edges of the corn stalks poked at the dark sky.

There were usually lights on in the few houses, and I wondered if people were eating dinner, or watching television, or if kids were doing homework at dining room tables.

A car or a pickup truck was often sitting in the frozen driveway, at the side of the house, and a few times we saw a dog and a cat.

It was strange to think of all the life out there, only ten or twenty miles from where we lived. Mothers and fathers, grandparents, nieces and nephews, sons and daughters. All of them moving slowly through the days and nights.

We hadn't even known they existed, there on North Tioga Street, on the second and third floor.

Did a mother or father, at the far end of the day, lie down next to their young son or daughter, and read to them from a book, about an owl moon, about Frog and Toad, about how nice it was to plant a tree.

Did the six-year-old daughter, lying next to her mother or father, feel the deep comfort of their presence? The massed heat of their bodies? Smell the particular scent of her mother or father? The onion and garlic smell from her mother's cooking, tomatoes, oranges, olive oil, ginger?

Her father smelled like the barn, like engines, like cold November earth mixed with a spicy smell of deodorant or shampoo?

Did her father's voice rumble deep in his chest? Was her mother's voice lighter, quicker, and did it rise to the ceiling?

Was there a nightlight plugged into a socket near the baseboard on the far side of her room? Did it glow pale yellow all through the night?

Did they read to her every night?

When I was much younger, when I was four or five or six, Nora occasionally read to me as I was lying in bed, trying to get to sleep. She read a book about an oxcart man, she read the *Goodnight, Moon* book, she read a book about a girl named Madeline who was in school in Paris with nuns, and she lined up with the other girls in two straight lines.

I was always under the covers, Nora was on top of the covers, but both our heads were on one pillow. Nora read carefully and confidentially. Her voice was soft and clear, at the same time.

She held the book up over her head so that we could both see the pictures. Even though the lights were off, the streetlight on North Tioga Street was always on at night, and came in through the windows, through the curtains. It made patterns like snowflakes on the walls and floor and bed.

Sometimes our heads on the pillow knocked gently against each other, and her hair was soft like feathers. As she read, I could feel her breath go in and out, and I could hear the air deep in her thin chest.

I often liked to close my eyes and just listen, without looking at the pictures. It was always as though every part of me was held by her voice. That Nora, that Nora's voice, could hold up the entire world.

The world was warm then. The world was safe, there in the bed. With me lying down under the covers, and Nora reading. No matter where Mom and Dad were, Nora made a web, guided by her voice, and nothing could get through the strands of the web.

I would go deeper into the bed. My eyes would stay closed, and the oxcart man would drive his oxcart into the tiny village, to bring the things he and his family had made or grown on the farm, and trade for other things.

It seemed like fall in the book. It always seemed like fall. The heat of summer finished, trees flaming with color, the harvest done, the snow still at bay.

The oxcart man was probably making his last trip before winter, before the world closed in on his farm with ice and snow and freezing cold. The supplies he bought and traded for would help see him and his family through the coldest months.

Nora's voice would grow quiet, and then stopped, and I would only hear her breathe.

My own breath was so deep and slow and quiet that I seemed almost to have stopped breathing. Nora was warm against my side. Her head stayed on the pillow.

After a long time, after two minutes or ten minutes, she kissed me on the side of the head. She stood up, whispered, Good night, Trey, and tiptoed out of the room.

Then the room wasn't as warm, and it didn't feel as safe.

Much later, I was drifting along the line between sleeping and waking. My eyes were still closed, and I kept hearing Nora's voice as she read about the oxcart man, about Madeline, the girl in Paris, who stared without fear at a tiger in the zoo.

There were footsteps on the stairs. Heavy footsteps like Mom or Dad, and it must have been midnight, and I had never been awake that late. I didn't think so, anyway.

There had been formalin smells all day down on the second floor, and the smells came again, with the footsteps.

It had to be Dad, because there was no slight click in the shoes.

He stood in my doorway, and the smell was powerful, as though he had spilled formalin on his shirt or pants.

I could feel him looking, and I wondered what he might be thinking. That this kid in bed was his son. That this kid was an accident. That the kid was a stranger, and what was he doing here?

Then he turned and crossed the hall. He went into his own room.

My breathing was fast and shallow.

Back in the car with Nora, in very late December, with the fields nearly all empty, and surrounded by dark woods on the back and sides, we kept driving.

It was very cold outside, but the heater brought warm streams of air up from the floor.

Nora said, Trey, when I'm in college, I'll have my own apartment.

I didn't say anything. I watched the road in front of us, and black trees that covered the hills. There were so many hills and trees, there were so many miles of roads.

We were in Cayuga County, and the houses were spread even farther apart. We could drive pretty much forever.

So if you wanted to, Nora said. You could move in with me.

I might have said, Ummm, or, Hmmm.

I don't remember.

Think about it, she said.

Okay, I said.

We went up a long hill, and near the top there were dustings of snow—at the sides of the road, in thin lines in the fields.

The dashboard was lit up with red and white numbers that glowed in the dark of the car.

We had a lot of gas, and it was like a spaceship inside. We were warm, and we could go almost anywhere.

Twenty-Eight

TWO PEOPLE HAVE LEFT, and soon another will be leaving, and no new kids have come to replace them. So we're a very small group now.

The ward is the same size, the halls and rooms, but everything feels little, with so few kids. The halls echo a bit.

Bobby Collins left a week ago, and Maggie left this morning.

I don't remember too clearly, but I'm sort of sure that Bobby came in a few weeks after me, or maybe a few months after. So much from that time is muddy, is filmy and foggy and surrounded by veils. It's diaphanous.

Bobby was here for almost a year, or close to a year. He'd been sitting and pacing, tapping, talking. Bobby with his crooked teeth, with his gun, with the broken trailer he lives in.

Bobby went to an adolescent mental health home. A group home, they call it. The home is not in a trailer with smashed windows. His father, who tries, Bobby said, will not be there drinking.

Bobby said it was time to move on, and Dr. Manchin also said it was time to move on.

Me and Bobby, the night before he left, we talked for a while.

He said that the ward was a good place, that it was definitely good that they let you stay a long time, but you didn't want to stay forever.

What about you, Trey? he asked.

I said, What about me?

He said, Dude, you've been here a long time. Almost a year. Am I right?

I nodded.

That's the longest you can stay? he said. Right?

Yeah.

So you're not going to that state place, are you? Malvern? It's pretty raw, I hear, he said.

Bobby was tapping his feet and fingers on the carpet and on the arms of his chair.

I didn't say anything.

Plus you're gonna be eighteen, he said. That's the cutoff. You'll be a grownup.

I said, Ha. A real big grownup. Ready for the world.

In September, October? he asked.

Late September, I said. The big one eight.

Trey. Bro, he said. Those are coming at us, real fast. You don't take action, action will take you.

I know, I said.

Really, Trey. No shit. Don't ignore it, cause it's coming at you. Only a few weeks. You'll blink your eyes and it'll be right there, that hour of that day.

I think about it, I said. I've been thinking about Malvern for months.

And what do you think?

That I'm not going there.

Bobby looked at me, and I thought that his eyes were different than they'd been a few months ago. They were darker, calmer, maybe more clear. Even as he tapped, his eyes were different.

We sat for a while without saying anything. We sat for ten or twenty minutes, and I didn't look at the clock.

Cara was in the nurses' station writing things on a computer, and a new nurse named Jocelyn seemed to be counting meds. Jocelyn had dark hair and big shoulders like a swimmer. She had the tattoo of a star on the back of her hand.

Bobby put his hand on my shoulder.

Listen, Trey, he said. I worry about you, and I think you're a good dude. So I want you to get out of here. We can meet up on the outside, we can have a beer or two.

I watched him.

Okay? he said.

Thanks, Bobby. Yes.

Then there was more silence, and then we said goodbye, and that was the last time I saw Bobby. He left early the next morning, before most of us were up, when a case worker for the mental health house came to get him.

And Maggie, last night. God, that was hard.

She didn't have a hoodie on. Her dark hair was pulled back in a braid, but frizzy strands were dancing around her head.

We sat up late, after Lenny had come in. We talked a little, but mostly we sat and we held hands.

Our hands were kind of damp, and we couldn't let go of each other until one or maybe two in the morning.

She said that I was one of the most interesting people she'd ever met.

I think I smiled. I almost said that she was the best and most interesting person that I'd ever met.

Will we see each other? I said. After we're both out of these places?

She said definitely.

I had given her Nora's cell phone number because I didn't have a phone. And I had Maggie's number.

She said she didn't think she'd be in western Massachusetts for more than a month. Six weeks at the outside.

We can do things, she said. I have a car. My mom and dad are nice.

We were quiet awhile, then she leaned over and kissed the side of my face.

I think I was trembling. That was maybe the best thing anybody had ever done to me.

Her hair brushed my face, and her lips were soft and warm and cool all at the same time.

Without meaning to, I went, Oh.

She said, You okay?

I said, Yes. Very. I said, You don't know. You can't know.

And she said, Yes, I don't think I know. But I do know too.

Then we sat some more, and when Lenny came through to check doors, he smiled at us.

We sat until really late. Not until dawn, the hour when Maggie used to get her E.C.T. treatment, but still real late. No light in the sky in the east, across the big lake, but the light, the rising sun, was not far off. You could feel it, somehow. The morning was there, just over the lake and hills. A half hour, or maybe two hours away.

We stood up, in the end, and I still didn't look at the clock. Whatever time it told, I thought, it would still be the present.

We kept holding each other's sweaty hand, and we went to a far corner of the dayroom. Where there were tall and wide windows that looked out onto the lake, and the city, a few miles to the south.

We stood there, looking and looking, at the black night, and at the yellow and white and red lights dotted on the side of the lake, and in the south, the long lines of roads and lights in the small city. We looked as though there was some message for us, in all that dark.

But there wasn't. It was just night, and me and Maggie, not being able to say goodbye.

I was really tall by then, and she was shorter. The top of her head came to just above my shoulder. She leaned her head on my shoulder, and I didn't know what to do. I had never been near a girl who was not Nora. I had never been near any people, boy or girl, except Nora.

Nora was easy to be with, even if she was beautiful.

Was Maggie beautiful?

I think she was. Being gone, she's still beautiful in my memory.

We stood and stood, and both of us knew that this was it. This was goodbye.

If we stood almost forever, holding hands, we would still have to say goodbye in the end.

Maggie's mother was picking her up at six, to drive to western Massachusetts. She was discharged. She was going.

Sometimes we saw a car, moving down unlighted roads. Two white eyes in front, two red eyes in back.

The car would seem to move very slowly, a little piece of road in front of the car was lit up. But it was such a tiny piece in the great darkness of night.

Then it would go around a corner or over a hill, and it was gone. It was going somewhere. Maybe it had arrived.

One time we heard the whoop-whoop of an ambulance, arriving at the hospital, but we couldn't see it. The emergency room was on the far side of the building.

But we could picture the ambulance, with spinning red and blue lights on top, and even though it was out of sight, we knew it was there.

I said, You're gonna be exhausted tomorrow.

She said, I'll sleep in the car.

Then she put her arm around me, around the lower part of my back. Her hand and arm seemed strong.

I put my arm around her shoulders, and we fit somehow. Her arm, my arm, back, shoulders. Still staring at all the darkness, at all the small lights, which twinkled like Christmas, even though Christmas was a long way away.

Her head was still on my shoulder, her arm around my back.

I wanted to die, right there. With her. I wanted this moment to freeze and expand, and to never end. Just the two of us in the middle of the night, at the big windows.

I pressed my face to the glass, and it was cold. Then it was foggy where I breathed on the glass.

Pressing your face to the glass did not make you see better. You had to be at least a few inches away.

I kept thinking that I wanted to die. This was the best, the sweetest, the kindest, the warmest moment of my life. This was like nothing that had ever happened to me. I didn't know that a person, even a noodle, could feel like this. It was like floating and flying at the same time.

This was so beautiful it ached.

Everything I knew and thought about life could be over. It could end right there, at the windows, on the ward, and I would die happy.

But after a while, she dropped her arm from my back, put her hand on the side of my face, and she kissed me on the lips.

It was like the earlier kiss on my cheek, but then some. It happened before I knew it had happened. It made me flush, and ache some more.

I was afraid my legs were wobbly. I was afraid I would pass out with pleasure. I was afraid I would cry.

But we kept standing, and outside kept being dark. Then she said that she really had to go to bed.

I don't know what we said at the end. We hugged, she asked if I had her number, and I said I did.

I walked her to the door of her room, and we put our arms around each other, let go, then she went in, and I went to the day-room again.

Some time later, Lenny came through, and asked if I was okay.

I said I was fine, and he said, You're a good kid, Trey.

I didn't know if I would ever go to sleep again, because it was by far the best day and night of my life. It was sad too, but that helped it be the best day and night of my life.

And now. The ward is what? Different? Smaller? Emptier?

No Bobby. No Maggie.

Just me and Clea, Amanda, who is the only other old-timer, and some younger kids, or kids who don't talk, who don't get out of their beds or chairs. Who need weeks and months to let their meds lift them.

Amanda, too. She's leaving soon, but she doesn't know exactly when. In a week or two, maybe a month. But no more than that, she said.

Dr. Altemio has told her she's good to go, but that she just needs to figure out where she'll go, and what meds she'll be on, and if she'll be in school, or if she'll get a job.

Pretty soon everyone will be gone.

This is early September, and I'll be eighteen in a few weeks, on the twenty-third. Cara, the social worker, still talks to me about Malvern, but I've told her that I won't go there.

Cara always says, You've go to go somewhere.

They have heavy steel mesh on all the windows at Malvern, and very long halls that don't have carpet. They have linoleum, and the maintenance staff polish the linoleum once a week. It's always so shiny you can almost see yourself in the floor.

You look down, see your face, then you step on your face. I don't know if that would hurt.

At Malvern, there are lots of red brick buildings spread out on a hill, overlooking the big lake that's about thirty miles from our lake. They have their own graveyard at Malvern. Some patients go there, and they never leave.

Lenny told me these things. Twenty, thirty years ago, he worked there for a year or two.

He said, Trey, between me and you, don't go there. You don't want to go there.

Then he said I had to promise to say we had never talked about Malvern.

He didn't say anything especially awful, but I could feel it in his quiet voice. His voice was almost urgent when he said, Don't go there.

It was almost as though he was saying, Trust me on this. This is important.

So I've been in touch with Nora. We talked a while on the phone, and she'll come in to talk with Dr. Manchin and Cara and me. She'll tell them I can live at her apartment, that there's an extra room there, and I can go to school or get a job.

Nora will make sure I take my meds.

Nora was the one who took me to the hospital almost a year ago. Nora saved my life. So maybe it's right that Nora's the one who will pick me up.

I've hardly seen Dr. Manchin. Not for weeks or maybe months. I mean, I see him in the halls, or through the doorways of the doctors' offices, but he seems very busy. Always.

He covers many of the patients on the adolescent unit, and he covers the patients on the adult unit.

Dr. Manchin is always nice, always friendly.

He asks how I am.

I nod. I say, Good. I say, Fine. I nod again.

Good, Trey, he says. Keep it up.

Sometimes Dr. Manchin's shirt with the red or blue stripes is wrinkled. Maybe he should button his suit jacket, to hide the wrinkles.

Maybe I should thank him for the notebooks and the pens, because even though I can't focus much of the time, I've tried to write something almost every day. Two and a half notebooks are filled, on both sides of each page. And that's college-ruled. That's a lot of words. Many memories, especially of me and Nora.

I hope Nora wouldn't be offended by anything I've said. She's always been so good to me.

So Nora will come in in a few days, and I hope she doesn't forget. The alternative is Malvern.

Once again, for the thousandth time, I'm sitting in the dayroom, and it's late again.

The staff are all gone, except for Lenny, and outside the windows it's dark.

Then Amanda comes slowly down the hall, from the small dining room, and she's eating a small bag of popcorn.

228

Amanda's wearing gray sweats, but over the sweats she's wearing a yellow terrycloth robe that I haven't see her wear since last winter.

God, some of us have been here a long time.

It gets dark earlier each week at night, and it stays dark longer in the morning. And even though the temperature in here is controlled, you can still feel the heat or cold through the walls and windows.

Amanda and her robe are ready for the cold.

It feels as though I haven't seen Amanda in a while, although I have, sort of the way I see Dr. Manchin. In passing.

Amanda sits next to me, and says, Hey, Trey.

Amanda, I say.

She offers me some popcorn, and I take a handful. It's sprinkled with cheddar cheese.

I'm sorry Maggie left, she says. You must miss her.

I nod, and it surprises me that Amanda would even think of me and Maggie as a pair.

I'm not as homely as I was. Nora often said, around when I turned fifteen, that I had grown into my ears and nose. That I was becoming pretty good-looking.

I'm sure Nora was exaggerating. Nora would always lie to prop me up. But I was surprised that the face staring back at me in the mirror didn't repulse me.

Ten days, Amanda says.

Ten days what?

I'm leaving.

Oh boy, I say.

Amanda nods and smiles.

You, Trey? What about you?

Very soon, I say.

How soon? she asks.

Before the twenty-third. Before Malvern.

She's watching me. Amanda's smiling bigger and bigger.

You serious?

Yup.

She leans over and kisses me on the cheek.

Way to go, boyo, Amanda says.

Twenty-Nine

S o I WAS SEVENTEEN. I was almost grown up. I was very tall and still skinny, but not as skinny as I had been. I weighed a hundred and fifty-five pounds, and I was six-foot-two inches tall.

I didn't know what Mom or Dad saw when they looked at me. I had never known.

I had been sixteen for pretty much all of junior year of high school, and through the summer. Then when senior year began, I would turn seventeen a few weeks into the new school year.

Nora was twenty, and she was a junior at the university up on the hill. She was such a good student that they had made her a College Scholar. The school paid for everything, and they gave her money to live on. She could study whatever she wanted.

She had her own one-bedroom suite, in a big old dorm, on the north side of campus.

When she first left for college, I was afraid that I would never see her, that she would be gone from the world we shared. And for the first few months of the first year, we didn't see her very often. She was going to classes and making friends, and cooking her own meals in the apartment.

But then it was as though she missed me, missed Mom and Dad, missed the Burnes Funeral Home. She came home every weekend, or every other weekend, and she spent Friday and Saturday and Sunday nights on North Tioga Street.

Those were the only times all four of us ate dinner in the dining room together.

Then Monday morning, Nora walked or drove up Buffalo Street to her apartment, and then to her classes.

At first, I was afraid that it would be really bad, living on my own with Mom and Dad. That they would turn on me like in the old days.

But it was easier in most ways.

They were very busy almost all the time. There were funerals, viewings, a few cremations, and it seemed as though they never stopped working. Sundays, Tuesdays, Fridays. It didn't matter. People died when they needed to die. And Mom and Dad were always waiting, they were always ready.

When they weren't doing the funeral home, down in the basement or the first floor, they were eating sandwiches or soup in the den, or they were in their room with the door closed on the third floor. Strange to say, I didn't see them much.

I stayed in the kitchen or the big living room, or I stayed in my room on the third floor. Once in a while, if they were out for some reason, I sat in the den and looked around for evidence of their lives. Mom's smokes, a book or magazine left open to a certain page, an empty glass with nearly melted ice cubes, a pair of shoes or slippers under the coffee table.

There was no talk, the way there had been when Nora was around and chittering like a sparrow. Once in a while I'd hear them as though they were whispering, in the den or the dining room. Or on the third floor, I'd hear faint conversations in their bedroom, as quiet as mice in the walls.

I couldn't imagine what there was to talk about.

Mom or Dad made soup or chili, and left a big pot, warm on the stove. Each of us would eat when we wanted to. In the kitchen or den, the living room or dining room, even on the third floor.

One time I was in the living room, in front of the big bay windows that looked onto the street. I was watching rain, and how for a while, it made everything—houses, cars, leaves, street—shine.

I didn't notice anyone come into the room. The rain was heavier, and cars had their lights on, and cars were moving more slowly.

Then I felt a hand on my shoulder, and I almost jumped. Dad was at my side, and he had his arm around me.

He said, Watching the rain?

I said I was.

Kind of beautiful, he said.

Then we stood for I don't know how long.

I wondered if Dad watched the rain in Ireland, when he was a boy. Rain falling on rocks, falling on the green fields.

I wondered what he wondered. If he wondered.

Then after two or twenty minutes, he dropped his hand from my shoulder, and went somewhere else.

I kept watching the rain for a little while, but it was different.

Every now and then, I still went into the closet of my room. It wasn't quite the same as it had been when I was smaller, but I still liked the feeling. Behind all the hanging clothes, the plastic bags from the cleaners. The hems of clothes, and the plastic, kissed my face the way it always had. And the fit, especially since I had become tall, was tight.

But with the bedroom door closed, and then the closet door closed, it felt as though I had several levels of protection. I leaned my head against the far right corner, and Mom and Dad would never bother me.

I could feel more than hear the sound of doors opening and closing, of cars or trucks passing out front, of groups of kids going by. Kids with their laughter, with their bright loud voices.

Nora's classes had begun on Thursday, the last week of August, and after the first week of September, on a Friday around noon, she came in. Now that she was a junior in college, most of her classes were small seminars with four or five people in each one, or they were independent studies, one-on-one with a professor.

Nora had four classes in all, and they required very little class time, and far more time in the library, or at home, doing research and studying on her own. Her school week began Monday afternoon, and ended on Friday morning.

Her weekends, especially compared with most undergraduate students, were quite long.

As soon as she came in the front door, whether she had walked down the hill or driven, she dropped her coat and her purple backpack on the landing at the top of the second floor stairs. She stepped out of, or untied, her shoes, and left them on the landing.

I would still be at school, usually until two or two-thirty, but I'd see her stuff in a corner of the landing when I got home, and my heart would lift a little.

She still seemed confident and bright and happy, and she still talked like a bird in a tree, more or less declaring that she was alive and well.

You could even see a small change in Mom and Dad. They

smiled, and they talked with her, or mostly, they listened. She made everybody around her feel at least a little bit good.

The weather in early September felt mostly like summer, but that first weekend, when Nora came home, the temperatures dropped into the low fifties and high forties, and it was overcast and rainy, almost all the time.

Nora said, I brought the great weather with me, and Dad said that as far as he was concerned, this weather was much preferable to hot and humid.

Mom asked Nora about classes, and Nora said they were good. Just a lot of reading, and papers to write.

Mom said, I don't expect you'll have trouble with that.

We were in the big living room, and somehow, I found myself looking at Mom, while she listened to Nora. I thought, My god, she looks old. She was very small, and her hair was mostly gray, and there were deep lines at the sides of her mouth and eyes, and beneath the halo of hair surrounding her head, I thought I could see her skull.

Dad looked the same, but Mom was old.

She had never looked like this to me.

Nora still had light hair that had darkened just a little bit, but it was cut short, like a wedge at ear level around her head. She wore black tights, a red turtleneck, a green sweater with white snowflakes. She had a black scarf tied around her neck.

Nora almost always looked wonderful.

After a while, I was pretty tired and went up to my room for a nap. Lying down, I had the feeling that the house was lighter and less dangerous than it usually was, just from the presence of Nora.

I fell asleep listening to voices, and feeling the vibrations they made all through the house.

Then it was much later. It was full dark outside, and it might have been late. There were almost no cars on the street.

I turned over, pulled the covers higher, and tried to go back to sleep.

A single car was approaching, then passed, then I listened to it disappear north on North Tioga Street.

There was a tap on the door, and then I heard the doorknob turning.

Trey, Nora said.

Hmmm, I said.

Can I come it? she asked.

Sure.

Shove over, she said.

She was wearing sweatpants, and the same snowflake sweater.

You slept a long time, she said.

How long?

It's almost twelve-thirty.

Wow, I thought, but I didn't say anything.

She told me about school, and a friend named Micah, and a teacher, a woman named Professor Gerlach.

She asked about my school, but I didn't have too much to say.

We were silent a while. Me under the covers, Nora sitting on the bed, her back to the wall, her feet near my knees.

Then from nowhere, I said, Remember when you went into the Keep Out room?

Ages ago, Nora said.

What was that like?

You wanna know?

I nodded.

Is that a yes?

Yeah, I said.

It was strange and beautiful, Nora said.

How? I said, and I could feel my blood move, my heart bang.

Well, the door was closed, and I don't know how many times I'd turned the knob to find it locked. And suddenly it turned. It was unlocked. I thought I might pee my pants, Nora said.

I was afraid, lying there, that I might pee the bed.

So you opened the door? You went in?

I stood in the doorway a little, and I looked around.

The room was big. At least as big as the coffin room. There were white cabinets high up along two walls. There were shelves, and there were hooks on one wall where the rubber aprons hung. The smell of formalin was strong. It was almost hard to breathe.

There was a big sink, and there were machines on the counters under the shelves, the size of toasters. There were tubes, and there were trays of little knives and brushes, small containers of makeup, needles, thread. There were metal tools like nothing I'd ever seen. Long thin tools made of shiny silver, smaller than a toothbrush.

There were big plastic containers holding a clear liquid. The containers were bigger than a gallon of milk. The labels said, formalin.

That was the stuff. That was the smell of our childhood, Nora said.

She didn't want to turn any lights on, so the room was gray like dusk, like a gloomy blanket covering everything. It was half-light, but light enough to see.

And there on the left, she said, not far from one end of the counter, was the big steel table and a figure lying on the table. It was naked except for a small white towel that was covering its middle, covering its private parts, she thought.

At first, for at least a minute or more, she thought it was a life-size doll of an old man. She had never seen anything like this. It was very still, and the colors were strange. Pale white like a mushroom, but gray and yellow too. The skin almost glowed.

Except the nose, the ears, the lips, the fingers and toes, were dark blue.

This was a few years ago, Trey, she said. I was seventeen, I think, and I was still a kid, more or less.

I think I was a junior in high school, I'm pretty sure. I know I wasn't a senior yet. So for a long time, for years and years, really, I'd been thinking and even dreaming of getting into the Keep Out room.

So there I was, and it was so strange, so unlike anything I'd ever come across, that I didn't know at first what I was seeing.

Nora took a few steps closer to the table, and from maybe five feet away, she leaned over and looked.

She kept thinking that the doll would raise its arms, or turn its head, or sit up, but it was more still than the ceiling. Then she saw that the old man was unshaven, and that there was gray stubble on the lower part of his face and on his neck, like a harvested corn field. Cut stalks pointing at the sky.

She saw small brown birthmarks on the man's arms and chest, and she knew this wasn't a doll.

This was a person, an old man, who used to be alive. This was a dead person, and she almost laughed at herself.

A life-size doll in a funeral home?

Of course it was a body. This is what Mom and Dad did.

She said that she started to feel relaxed, as if she was just a person in a museum who was very curious. She was just looking around. The old man on the table didn't seem scary. This was just a dead body.

He was very thin, and he didn't seem tall. There were bruises on the back of his hand, and on the inner arm at the elbow. He might have been eighty years old, maybe eighty-five, and he must have been in the hospital, because they probably put needles in the back of his hand, and in his arm. The bruises were deep red and purple, with a little yellow.

He had small thin features, and almost no hair on his head, except for white wisps. His hands and feet and ears seemed large, maybe because he was so thin.

Nora took one more step toward the table, and she reached out. She put a few fingers on the man's arm, and she was surprised how cool it was. The skin was smooth, and a little rubbery.

She wondered if the old man had ever been in love or married. She wondered if he had children or even grandchildren. And if he had a soul, if there was such a thing as a soul.

Then Nora put her palms together, bowed her head, and stayed still for a few seconds. She stood next to the table, and finally turned.

There on a white cabinet was a black and white photograph, taped to the door of the cabinet. It was a little boy, maybe three or four years old, sitting on a low stone wall, with a small treeless field in the background.

He was very thin, and even though the photo was black and white, you could tell he had a lot of freckles. He wasn't smiling, just looking at the camera.

There were small holes in his sweater, and a giant hole in the elbow of the sweater on one arm, where his skinny pale elbow was poking though.

Who was it? I asked.

He kind of looked like Dad, and he kind of looked like you, Trey, Nora said.

I stared at her.

But I don't think it was either of you, she said.

My brain and voice were still. And Nora. She kept looking at me.

Thirty

We had been quiet, and almost entirely still, Mom and Dad and me. All that summer. The summer before senior year.

Nora was around too, at least some of the time. She would stop in, stay a day or two, and then would go back up the hill to her apartment on Buffalo Street. She worked her job as a waitress, and she read books that her faculty adviser had suggested. Books about American history. About the labor movement, about the lives of women on the Great Plains in the 1800s, about child labor in the factories of big American cities.

She said that all of it was extraordinary. She said it was endlessly fascinating.

Whenever Nora was around, she and I would usually end up talking for hours, late at night, on her bed or my bed, and sometimes in the big living room with the bay windows. We talked about nearly everything, and sometimes we went out for drives in the dark countryside. Passing sleeping houses, and moving through tiny towns, where there seemed to be no life, just a security light on a barn or above a rusting carport.

Sometimes a dog would appear from the shadows, and would stand

and bark at us, the sounds growing thinner and fainter as we passed and kept driving. Then there was no sound at all, as if the dog had never existed. There were only the wheels on the road, and fields where corn and hay grew quietly in the dark.

Mom and Dad were at home, of course, but in their way they were thin and faint and shadowy. They were in the basement, working with the dead people, or they were on the stairs, moving up or down, or they were standing in the kitchen, the den, or even the dining room, where we almost never ate anymore.

Nora had spoken to me about applying for college in the fall of senior year, and I guess I was planning to do that. College was one way of getting out of the house and on to a new life. She said she would help me with applications. She said I could apply to the university where she went to school. That way we could both go to the same school for a year.

Mom was close to fifty years old, and Dad was around the same age, though maybe a year or two older. Dad didn't seem any different than he had ever been, but Mom seemed somehow older and sadder and slower.

Mom's hair was half gray, and her shoulders were a little slumped. She moved a little less quickly, and she had fewer pill bottles on the counter in the kitchen. Nora said that fewer pills could mean that Mom was getting kind of better.

I wasn't so sure of that. Mom was tight like a spring, and her mouth was usually a straight line. Her hands were always at least a little clenched.

Dad was tight too, but he didn't seem so closed in on himself. He looked around a little, and once in a while he would smile. Mom pretty much never smiled, even when she was talking to Nora.

Mom's voice had grown lower.

In the house, it felt as though there was pressure everywhere. A tense, wound feeling in the air, no matter if it was the second or third floor, the den, Nora's room, the kitchen. Like something was pressing on you, and any minute, any hour, someone would begin to throw dishes or glasses at a wall, or would begin screaming, or would begin to swing their arms and fists at someone or something else. Punch windows, kick chairs, overturn the dining room table.

I didn't know where or who or what it was exactly. I couldn't name anything. But it was like light, or like the darkness. It was everywhere, and you could never escape it, except by leaving the house, or by driving around in Nora's car.

Then it was late August, it was the beginning of September. I know I hadn't begun senior year yet. Nora had started classes the week before, but she said there wasn't much work to do, that she wouldn't be busy until mid-September.

So Nora was home for the weekend. And it felt to me like we were getting ready for an explosion.

Nora was drinking a glass of wine, and it was getting late, and she poured me a glass of wine. I sipped and she sipped, and it got later still.

Then we were in my room. Pretty soon, I was light-headed and sleepy, and it wasn't quite midnight.

Then I was asleep and I don't remember falling asleep. I don't remember Nora leaving.

But I woke up, and the little red clock next to my bed said, Two-thirty-six.

I thought, This is the night to go downstairs. This is the night to go to the basement.

I was going to be a senior, and maybe now was the right time. I was years behind Nora. But it would be good for me. Maybe it would free me. It would make me less fearful. The wine helped my confidence.

Everything in the house was deeply, deeply quiet. There was a great hush, a thick blanket of silence.

There was air outside the windows, but I couldn't hear any cars, even in the distance.

There were little pale patches of light from the streetlight out front, but it was almost entirely black. Deep consuming black. A darkness at the end of the world.

I was wearing shorts and a tee shirt, and on the third floor. I could hear sleeping people through closed doors. The deep breaths, the murmur and sighs of dreaming. From Nora's room, from Mom and Dad's room.

Everyone, I thought, was deep asleep. They were all somewhere else in a dream. In Ireland, or at the university on the hill.

I got up and silently opened my door, and the sleep sounds were a little louder, but they were slow and deep and steady. They sounded as if a gunshot wouldn't wake them.

All I could hear was the dark air outside, the soft push and luff of wind. So often, late at night, the summer air seemed so gentle, so fresh, like a balm to anyone who breathed it. The air came to us from the woods and hills, from the farms and the giant lake.

I didn't put slippers or sneakers on. My feet would be more quiet if they were just bare. My feet were white in the powdery moonlight.

It was almost a little chilly, there at the very middle of the night. Nearly three o'clock, and I moved silently across the third-floor hall. I could feel the wood boards of the floor under my feet.

Then down the stairs, and there was only one tiny creak near the bottom of the stairs, but so small that nobody could have heard it. I was almost sure of it.

The kitchen had more moonlight because of the big windows behind the sink. The table and chairs, the counters, the refrigerator and stove, were all silent and still. What else could they be? I thought, but they were different than they were in the morning or afternoon.

I went down the stairs to the first floor, and in the hallway leading to the basement, I paused for a while. I watched and listened.

I could feel my heart, I could feel the blood moving in my veins, I could feel the faint sound of my pulse. A tap, a thrum.

The refrigerator had a faint sound, and the air outside was still making those tiny, soft sounds, like the wings of a bird. There was that, and the sound of my own breath, which was faster and more shallow than it usually was.

But there was nothing from the third floor, even though I couldn't hear anything overhead.

I went down the back stairs, and there was carpet, and that made me even more silent and stealthy. Like I was a soldier on a secret mission.

At the stairs to the basement, I opened the door, and it looked very dark down below. It looked like eternity, like death after life.

I went down, and at the bottom, the door to the Keep Out room was right in front of me. The door was locked.

Nora had told me so much about the basement that it was a little familiar, even though I'd never been down there.

I went down the hallway to the left, and then I was in a really big room, with a few square windows high up on the wall, and so many caskets I couldn't even count. There had to be ten of them. Fifteen, maybe even more. It was hard to tell.

Most of them were shiny metal, and they picked up light from the moon, coming through the curtains of the windows. Against the far wall, there were wooden caskets. Inside, all the ones with the tops open were lined with white fluffy material. Like ribbons and bows, padding and pillows.

I went toward the far wall, and I was standing and looking. My breath, the blood moving in my body, were quiet by then.

It was strangely peaceful down there.

Then I thought—

But no. That couldn't be.

A sound, way overhead. On the third floor maybe. Almost a vibration.

Maybe someone had woken up to use the bathroom.

No. There was someone. I had no idea who. Moving down the stairs. Then pausing on that landing.

A sound, a vibration. Something, someone, moving.

I looked to the side and there was an open wooden casket with a latch on the outside. I got into the casket, knees first, then stretched out on the crinkly white stuff. I carefully pulled the lid down.

There was a small pillow, and I lay down on my back.

Everything felt cushioned, but I could still feel the vibrations of someone coming down the stairs.

I didn't know if this coffin was watertight and airtight. How much air could there be?

Then the footsteps were in the coffin room. They were right there. They stepped this way, they stepped that way.

I had no idea who it was. Mom? Dad? Nora?

The steps got closer.

They paused.

They moved again. Then stopped, I was sure, right in front of my casket.

Then I felt some small noise on the outside. I heard the click of metal.

I knew, even without trying the lid, that the latch on my casket had been fastened.

I almost screamed or cried. I almost banged on the sides or top.

My heart was all in a commotion, my blood in a panic, and I had wild, fast, scary thoughts. That they would bury me in this coffin, whether I was alive or not. That I would suffocate, because I could feel that the coffin was strongly, tightly built.

I couldn't feel the movement of anyone anymore. It was the darkest black I had ever seen. There in the basement.

Ten minutes went by, a half-hour, maybe an hour.

Something detached, something split off, from something else inside me.

I must have passed out from fear or from not being able to breathe too well. In and out.

It was all drift and swirl. It was one part of me looking at the other part of me. Then it was smoke and darkness, and more drift, more swirl, and all the time, the air getting thinner and very warm from the air I breathed out. And my head light, and lighter still.

And kind of sleeping. Kind of thinking in sleep that this was where I would die, and that someone, sometime later, would find me.

Then five minutes or an hour later, after the vibration and the slight sound of footsteps going away, I thought in sleep, I seemed to have felt, the slight sound again, the vibration, of someone in the room.

Maybe this was a dream. The new footsteps. Or maybe the earlier footsteps had been a dream. These things were happening in some dream.

But I could feel the crinkly fabric all around me. The interior of the casket. The air was running out. It grew hotter and wetter, because this was nearly all my own breath, exhaled, by then.

Then. I knew. There were light, slight footsteps. But maybe that was a dream too.

There was a tap and small ping of metal on metal. The latch.

The top of the casket went up an inch. It went up all the way, and there was a flood of cool, fresh air, which was like something I had never felt. Like God had come to resurrect me.

Air and more air. Cool. Flooding over and in me. And the pale light in the room, that seemed almost bright after the inside of the casket.

Trey, Nora said. Jesus, Trey.

I didn't, I couldn't, say anything. I was trembling. I was shivering like a trapped bird.

Nora took me by the upper arm. She helped me out of the coffin, and I could feel the carpet under my bare feet.

What the fuck, Trey, she said, and she led me out of the casket room, and down the hall to the stairs opposite the Keep Out room. Then slowly and quietly, we went to the first floor, the second, and finally to the third floor. Nora's hand in the same spot on my arm.

Nora was shaking, and her voice trembled when she said, Who? What in the name of? she began, and had to stop.

Her voice fast, Nora said she had heard me get up earlier, cross the hall and go down the stairs. Then she thought she heard a second person get up, go down the stairs, then come back a few minutes later.

She lay in bed and wondered what was going on. Why were people moving around? she wondered. She might have gotten up to see if I was in bed.

Moonlight washed everything. It was powder and it was milk.

Everything about me was a long way away from the rest of me. There was me moving slowly with a shaky Nora, and another me on a different place on the stairs, the landings, and in the hall of the third floor. Part of me was to the side, then above, the things that were happening. Above all of this, watching Trey and Nora in the hallway.

Then in my bedroom. Nora pulled the covers back up on the bed. She got me to sit on the side of the bed. I lifted my legs under the covers. Then Nora settled the covers over me, up to my neck.

She sat on the edge of the bed. She said, What happened? Trey? What the fuck?

Her voice was high and sounded unnatural.

But I kept shivering as though I was very cold. As though it was January and not August or September.

Can you talk? she asked.

I turned to the windows. Streetlight and moonlight streaming in.

She pushed my hair off my forehead. She said, You need to sleep.

And for two or three days, I slept. I slept so deeply that I might have been dead. A few times, I got up to use the bathroom. I remember that, and I was nearly asleep as I moved between the bed and the toilet.

A few times Nora came to my room, to my bed, with crackers and juice, but I kept shivering, I kept drifting from sleep to something like dreams, to Nora saying, Trey, and back to a deep and utterly black sleep.

After a few days, Nora said that if I didn't talk, if I didn't get out of bed, that she would have to take me to the hospital.

I wanted to say no. Please, no. Not that.

There was no Mom or Dad. I didn't know where they had gone. There were almost no sounds in the house. There was wind very late at night, and the sound of a car or truck passing, and there were even the voices, usually of kids, down in the street.

I think I must have dreamed about driving with Nora in her car. There were enormous spaces, and there was the giant lake. Water, hills, sky.

Finally, Nora later told me, on the fourth day, she got me dressed, and she drove me to the hospital.

I don't remember that. Maybe just a patch or two.

Driving though downtown, then around the southern end of the lake, then up the long long hill. To the hospital. The only time I had been there was when I was born.

I couldn't stop shivering, and I couldn't speak.

Then in the Emergency Room, they put me in a cubicle with a curtain for a door. Nora went to talk to a doctor.

A nurse came in, said, This is to help relax you.

She put a needle in my upper arm.

In a few minutes, I stopped shivering.

In a few minutes, I was warm all over.

Thirty-One

OUTSIDE THE WINDOW, FROM up here on the ward, it's very dark, although it's morning. The sky's spitting a fine, thin rain that's making everything shiny. Leaves on trees, the face of roads. The lake, in the distance, has small wisps of fog or clouds on the surface. They hover over the water like specters or something.

I'm sitting in a deep corner of the dayroom, in a place I've never sat. It's like I'm already gone.

I can still watch, but it feels like nobody can see me. There are some new kids, but I don't even know their names. One is Benny, but I'm not sure which one.

I've heard the name.

There are two or three girls, one or two boys. They all seem quiet. They all seem inside themselves.

They're just kids, really. They just need a little help.

Clea comes over to sit with me for a few minutes. She says she's happy and sad to see me go.

You're the last of the old crew, Clea says. Everybody's gone. There's nobody here anymore.

Now you're the last one, I say. Now it's your turn to go.

She nods a little and bites her lip.

Clea says, I guess.

Then she says, I'll miss you, Trey.

She says, I already miss Maggie and Amanda and Bobby. I miss them a lot.

It's eight-twenty-two, and Nora's supposed to be here by quarter till nine.

Clea looks tired. She looks like it's three in the morning, and she needs to go back to sleep.

Maybe she's on new meds, and she hasn't gotten used to them yet. She might sleep for most of a few days, for a week even, and then she'll seem okay again.

Clea finally gets up. She leans over and kisses me on the top of my head, on the spot where my hair parts and there's a white line.

Bye, Trey, she says, and I take her hand, and squeeze it softly.

Clea, I say. I'll miss you.

She looks at me for a moment, for two or three moments, and it feels like she's about to say something. But she doesn't say anything.

She nods briefly, then walks slowly to her room.

On the side of the chair, on the floor, I have a green garbage bag with my stuff. Two pairs of pants, a few shirts, some socks and underwear. There are my notebooks and pens, a toothbrush and some prescriptions Dr. Altemio wrote for me.

Dr. Manchin has been out for a few weeks, either sick or on some kind of trip. I'd like to say goodbye to him, even though I haven't seen him in a while. Sometimes, I guess, you don't get to say goodbye.

There are also discharge papers in the bag. They say to keep taking meds, and to arrange to see a person in outpatient treatment. I'll live at Nora's apartment, and I'll find some kind of job.

I don't know how many people are still on the ward, but there seem to be very few. Wendy, the nurse, is at a desk in the nurses' station, and an aide named Michael is there too.

I take the bag of my things from the floor, and put it on my lap. It's not that big and it doesn't weigh very much either. I could stand up and walk out now, but the doors are locked. It's better to wait.

The clock in the nurses' station says eight-thirty-nine, and I wonder if Nora is driving here at the moment, or if she's here already. If she's walking through the parking lot, or walking down halls, or standing in an elevator.

There's a new kid standing in the dayroom, way over past the nurses' station. He's wearing gray sweatpants, a blue cardigan sweater, and I swear, he looks about twelve years old. He has very short hair, and full lips, and acne on his forehead and cheeks.

His eyes are scared, and I almost feel like saying something to him. Tell him to relax, tell him he's safe, tell him that he'll get better no matter what's wrong with him.

But I don't. Maybe he has to learn those things himself. I don't know. Maybe he's not safe, and maybe he can't or won't get better.

Now it's eight-forty-four, and I cinch the bag tight at the neck, and lift it to feel how light it is.

Then eight-forty-seven, and the buzzer from the outside door goes off.

It takes a minute or two or three, but finally there's Nora, with her wedge-cut hair, wearing almost all black, with a bright red scarf. She's with Wendy, the nurse, and Nora smiles.

I stand up, go to the door of the nurses' station, and Nora hugs me. I hug Nora.

Without Nora, what? Malvern?

Wendy says, You all set?

I nod, Nora says, Great, and Wendy says, I'll be walking you out.

We go to the front of the ward, and Wendy takes keys out, and we go through one door, then the second door.

It's big and bright. There are people and things moving. A voice on an intercom says, Dr. Law, line four-nine-two. Dr. Law, please.

This even smells different.

Nora has some tiny drops of rain in her hair. As though she's walked through mist. The rain outside must be so fine that it's almost fog. It's almost not rain at all.

We stand and wait for the elevator. Small red lights track the elevator's progress, and when the light reaches our floor, it bings, and the door opens. A small woman, wearing surgical scrubs, steps off. She's got one of those surgical caps and some kind of light device around the top of her head.

Nora puts her arm around my waist in the elevator, and Wendy hits the One button. I keep thinking, I'm out. I'm not going to Malvern.

Wendy looks at the two of us, and she's got this small smile on her face, as though she approves of us.

The first floor halls are busy with people. Someone in a wheelchair, someone being pushed on a gurney. Nurses, doctors, staff people, walking singly and in pairs. Some of them have stethoscopes hanging from around the backs of their necks.

Then we're on a big main hall that goes from the back to the front of the building. There are paintings on the walls, posters, and doors and hallways that lead off the main hallway. It's not even nine in the morning, and this feels like a bus or train station, like a mall before Christmas.

Nora's holding on to my arm now, right near the elbow. It feels good. It feels like Nora isn't ashamed to show that she's with me.

I think of Maggie, of Bobby, of Amanda, who each walked this walk in the last few weeks. I wonder where they are at this hour, this minute. I wonder where Dr. Manchin is, and if he's sick, and if he'll get better. He never read any of the words he asked me to write, but I don't think that matters. It mattered to write the words down. It mattered to Trey. It mattered to me.

We get to the big waiting area at the front of the hospital. It's two stories tall, and is all glass at the entrance. There are banks of chairs like the airport, and people sit, people stand, people walk quickly from one door or hall to the next.

Near the doors, Wendy stops. She says, Okay. Now.

Wendy says, You have everything?

I nod.

Your discharge papers? Wendy asks.

Yup, I say.

Good luck, Trey, she says. She pats me on the arm.

Nora has her car keys in her hand.

Thank you, I say, and Nora says, Thanks.

Wendy nods, then she turns and goes back the way we came.

We go through the door to the outside, into the air. My God, it's amazing. So rich and fresh. So cool. Like it's the beginning of fall. With the smell of leaves and grass and cars.

It's still very dark, and the rain isn't rain so much anymore. It's more like some mist or fog or low cloud.

Nora points the key at a distant parking lot of cars.

What do you want to do? she asks.

Not much, I say. Maybe walk around by myself.

Here? she asks.

Maybe downtown. Maybe you could drop me, then I could walk up later to your place.

It's our place.

I nod, and we get to the car. The same old Honda.

It's twenty-two fourteen Buffalo Street, she says.

Okay, I say.

Second floor.

I nod again.

Then we get in the car, and as we drive down the long hill on the west side of the lake, the air goes from veils and fog to a very fine mist. If rain wasn't hitting the windshield, I don't think I'd see it at all.

You feel okay? Nora asks.

I nod, see Nora squinting at the road, and say, Yeah. Pretty good.

Then we don't say anything. Nora drives, I watch, and the mist keeps coming down, smearing the windows.

All the cars have their lights on.

We go through a traffic light. We cross the inlet, go straight, then left on the Route Thirteen strip, then right on Buffalo Street.

We're about eight blocks from downtown. And then the big hill to Collegetown.

Nora drives slowly and carefully. All the cars seem to be going slowly. Lights on, windshield wipers on, the heat of cars on to get the fog off the car's glass.

Then we're near downtown. Nora says, Where should I drop you?

How about Buffalo and North Tioga?

She nods. She says, What's our house number?

Twenty-two fourteen Buffalo.

Good, she says.

We go another block, then she pulls in near the old post office.

Leave your bag, she says. I'll bring it in.

She leans to kiss me, misses my cheek, and kisses me on the ear.

Maybe I'm blushing. I don't know, and I probably don't care. It's hard to see.

I say thanks, she says, See you soon.

Then I'm on the sidewalk, and the mist surrounds me. I watch the red taillights of Nora's car stop at the traffic light at the bottom of the big hill. Then the light changes, and the car disappears in the fog on the hill.

So, I think.

There's almost nobody out walking.

So, I actually say out loud.

So, I say again.

I walk away from downtown. I go on North Tioga Street, and I'm moving north. I stop at Court Street, wait for traffic, then cross, and keep walking. There are still no people out now, and almost no cars either. The mist has picked up to a fine rain, and it's cold on my face and hands. Just like fall.

I'm in Fall Creek, my old neighborhood, and the streets are all the same. Utica, Marshall, Tompkins, Lewis, Tioga. These are the same streets where I walked to school, and came home after school. The houses with their windows and trees and bushes. Their driveways and front doors, their yards and flowerbeds and porches.

The rain is only mist now, and there are wisps and strands of fog along the ground. Everything smells clean and clear, fresh and cold as an October morning.

I'm remembering my first-grade self and my seventh-grade self. I picture Nora and Asia, Pippa and Emma, and Talia, who I barely knew. Ms. Macbride and Miss Levy, Ms. Ravesi and Mrs. Harcourt.

For some reason I think of Regina, the old woman who died, and Kyle, who was only eighteen. I think of the old man who seems to have died alone, and how almost nobody came to his funeral. Only a priest, all in black, came to pray.

And Alice. Most of all Alice. In her blue overalls, her shirt with clocks on it, holding a purple stuffed elephant in her dead hands. Her white sneakers. Tiny Alice.

Everything's alive in my brain.

Then I see the sign, the small rectangular sign. Burnes, I see. Burnes Funeral Home. The sign is lit.

I slow down at the sign, then I go quietly up the front walk, through small patches of fog. I'm silent, and I might be invisible in this dimness, in this rain and mist.

I stand on the porch, in front of the double doors. There are white gauzy curtains on the inside that you can almost see through. You can see shapes and colors. You can see the big staircase going up.

Then I push the doorbell, and wait. Nothing.

I push it again, and wait again.

I can feel and almost hear a door at the top of the stairs. Opening slowly.

Then someone's coming down the stairs. Slowly, like they're very very old.

Wearing black, I think.

Almost floating, like a ghost. Like something from before. Like something that's here now.

I think of Alice and her sneakers winking red.

Everything that used to breathe is somehow here.

Winking red. Saying, We're alive. We're alive. We're alive.

Right here. This instant. Right now.

Fomite

About Fomite

A fomite is a medium capable of transmitting infectious organisms from one individual to another.

"The activity of art is based on the capacity of people to be infected by the feelings of others." Tolstoy, *What Is Art?*

Writing a review on Amazon, Good Reads, Shelfari, Library Thing or other social media sites for readers will help the progress of independent publishing. To submit a review, go to the book page on any of the sites and follow the links for reviews. Books from independent presses rely on reader-to-reader communications.

For more information or to order any of our books, visit:
http://www.fomitepress.com/our-books.html

More Titles from Fomite...

Novels
Joshua Amses — *During This, Our Nadir*
Joshua Amses — *Ghatsr*
Joshua Amses — *Raven or Crow*
Joshua Amses — *The Moment Before an Injury*
Charles Bell — *The Married Land*
Charles Bell — *The Half Gods*
Jaysinh Birjepatel — *Nothing Beside Remains*
Jaysinh Birjepatel — *The Good Muslim of Jackson Heights*
David Brizer — *Victor Rand*
L. M Brown — *Hinterland*
Paula Closson Buck — *Summer on the Cold War Planet*
Dan Chodorkoff — *Loisaida*
Dan Chodorkoff — *Sugaring Down*
David Adams Cleveland — *Time's Betrayal*
Paul Cody— *Sphyxia*
Jaimee Wriston Colbert — *Vanishing Acts*
Roger Coleman — *Skywreck Afternoons*
Marc Estrin — *Hyde*
Marc Estrin — *Kafka's Roach*
Marc Estrin — *Speckled Vanities*
Marc Estrin — *The Annotated Nose*
Zdravka Evtimova — *In the Town of Joy and Peace*
Zdravka Evtimova — *Sinfonia Bulgarica*
Zdravka Evtimova — *You Can Smile on Wednesdays*
Daniel Forbes — *Derail This Train Wreck*
Peter Fortunato — *Carnevale*

Greg Guma — *Dons of Time*
Richard Hawley — *The Three Lives of Jonathan Force*
Lamar Herrin — *Father Figure*
Michael Horner — *Damage Control*
Ron Jacobs — *All the Sinners Saints*
Ron Jacobs — *Short Order Frame Up*
Ron Jacobs — *The Co-conspirator's Tale*
Scott Archer Jones — *And Throw Away the Skins*
Scott Archer Jones — *A Rising Tide of People Swept Away*
Julie Justicz — *Degrees of Difficulty*
Maggie Kast — *A Free Unsullied Land*
Darrell Kastin — *Shadowboxing with Bukowski*
Coleen Kearon — *#triggerwarning*
Coleen Kearon — *Feminist on Fire*
Jan English Leary — *Thicker Than Blood*
Diane Lefer — *Confessions of a Carnivore*
Diane Lefer — *Out of Place*
Rob Lenihan — *Born Speaking Lies*
Colin McGinnis — *Roadman*
Douglas W. Milliken — *Our Shadows' Voice*
Ilan Mochari — *Zinsky the Obscure*
Peter Nash — *Parsimony*
Peter Nash — *The Perfection of Things*
George Ovitt — Stillpoint
George Ovitt — Tribunal
Gregory Papadoyiannis — *The Baby Jazz*
Pelham — *The Walking Poor*
Andy Potok — *My Father's Keeper*
Frederick Ramey — *Comes A Time*
Joseph Rathgeber — *Mixedbloods*
Kathryn Roberts — *Companion Plants*
Robert Rosenberg — *Isles of the Blind*
Fred Russell — *Rafi's World*
Ron Savage — *Voyeur in Tangier*
David Schein — *The Adoption*
Lynn Sloan — *Principles of Navigation*
L.E. Smith — *The Consequence of Gesture*
L.E. Smith — *Travers' Inferno*
L.E. Smith — *Untimely RIPped*
Bob Sommer — *A Great Fullness*
Tom Walker — *A Day in the Life*
Susan V. Weiss —*My God, What Have We Done?*
Peter M. Wheelwright — *As It Is On Earth*
Suzie Wizowaty — *The Return of Jason Green*
Poetry
Anna Blackmer — *Hexagrams*
L. Brown — *Loopholes*

Sue D. Burton — *Little Steel*
David Cavanagh— *Cycling in Plato's Cave*
James Connolly — *Picking Up the Bodies*
Greg Delanty — *Loosestrife*
Mason Drukman — *Drawing on Life*
J. C. Ellefson — *Foreign Tales of Exemplum and Woe*
Tina Escaja/Mark Eisner — *Caida Libre/Free Fall*
Anna Faktorovich — *Improvisational Arguments*
Barry Goldensohn — *Snake in the Spine, Wolf in the Heart*
Barry Goldensohn — *The Hundred Yard Dash Man*
Barry Goldensohn — *The Listener Aspires to the Condition of Music*
R. L. Green — *When You Remember Deir Yassin*
Gail Holst-Warhaft — *Lucky Country*
Raymond Luczak — *A Babble of Objects*
Kate Magill — *Roadworthy Creature, Roadworthy Craft*
Tony Magistrale — *Entanglements*
Gary Mesick — *General Discharge*
Andreas Nolte — *Mascha: The Poems of Mascha Kaléko*
Sherry Olson — *Four-Way Stop*
Brett Ortler — *Lessons of the Dead*
David Polk — *Drinking the River*
Janice Miller Potter — *Meanwell*
Janice Miller Potter — *Thoreau's Umbrella*
Philip Ramp — *The Melancholy of a Life as the Joy of Living It Slowly Chills*
Joseph D. Reich — *A Case Study of Werewolves*
Joseph D. Reich — *Connecting the Dots to Shangrila*
Joseph D. Reich — *The Derivation of Cowboys and Indians*
Joseph D. Reich — *The Hole That Runs Through Utopia*
Joseph D. Reich — *The Housing Market*
Kenneth Rosen and Richard Wilson — *Gomorrah*
Fred Rosenblum — *Playing Chicken with an Iron Horse*
Fred Rosenblum — *Vietnumb* \
David Schein — *My Murder and Other Local News*
Lawrence Schimel — *Desert Memory: Poems of Jeannette L. Clariond*
Harold Schweizer — *Miriam's Book*
Scott T. Starbuck — *Carbonfish Blues*
Scott T. Starbuck — *Hawk on Wire*
Scott T. Starbuck — *Industrial Oz*
Seth Steinzor — *Among the Lost*
Seth Steinzor — *To Join the Lost*
Susan Thomas — *In the Sadness Museum*
Susan Thomas — *The Empty Notebook Interrogates Itself*
Sharon Webster — *Everyone Lives Here*
Tony Whedon — *The Tres Riches Heures*
Tony Whedon — *The Falkland Quartet*
Claire Zoghb — *Dispatches from Everest*

Poetry - Dual Language

Vito Bonito/Alison Grimaldi Donahue — *Soffiata Via/Blown Away*
Antonello Borra/Blossom Kirschenbaum — *Alfabestiario*
Antonello Borra/Blossom Kirschenbaum — *AlphaBetaBestiaro*
Antonello Borra/Anis Memon — *Fabbrica delle idee/The Factory of Ideas*
Aristea Papalexandrou/Philip Ramp — *Μας προσπερνά/It's Overtaking Us*
Mikis Theodoraksi/Gail Holst-Warhaft — *The House with the Scorpions*
Paolo Valesio/Todd Portnowitz — *La Mezzanotte di Spoleto/Midnight in Spoleto*

Stories

MaryEllen Beveridge — *After the Hunger*
MaryEllen Beveridge — *Permeable Boundaries*
Jay Boyer — *Flight*
L. M Brown — *Treading the Uneven Road*
L. M Brown — *Were We Awake*
Michael Cocchiarale — *Here Is Ware*
Michael Cocchiarale — *Still Time*
Neil Connelly — *In the Wake of Our Vows*
Catherine Zobal Dent — *Unfinished Stories of Girls*
Zdravka Evtimova —*Carts and Other Stories*
John Michael Flynn — *Off to the Next Wherever*
Derek Furr — *Semitones*
Derek Furr — *Suite for Three Voices*
Elizabeth Genovise — *Where There Are Two or More*
Andrei Guriuanu — *Body of Work*
Zeke Jarvis — *In A Family Way*
Arya Jenkins — *Blue Songs in an Open Key*
Jan English Leary — *Skating on the Vertical*
Marjorie Maddox — *What She Was Saying*
William Marquess — *Badtime Stories*
William Marquess — *Because Because Because Because Because*
William Marquess — *Boom-shacka-lacka*
William Marquess — *Things I Want You to Do*
Gary Miller — *Museum of the Americas*
Jennifer Anne Moses — *Visiting Hours*
Martin Ott — *Interrogations*
Christopher Peterson — *Amoebic Simulacra*
Christopher Peterson — *Scratch the Itchy Teeth*
Charles Phillips — *Dead South*
Jack Pulaski — *Love's Labours*
Charles Rafferty — *Saturday Night at Magellan's*
Ron Savage — *What We Do For Love*
Fred Skolnik— *Americans and Other Stories*
Lynn Sloan — *This Far Is Not Far Enough*
L.E. Smith — *Views Cost Extra*
Caitlin Hamilton Summie — *To Lay To Rest Our Ghosts*
Susan Thomas — *Among Angelic Orders*

Tom Walker — *Signed Confessions*
Silas Dent Zobal — *The Inconvenience of the Wings*

Odd Birds
Micheal Breiner — *the way none of this happened*
Bill Davis — *Cheap Gestures*
J. C. Ellefson — *Under the Influence: Shouting Out to Walt*
David Ross Gunn — *Cautionary Chronicles*
Andrei Guriuanu & Teknari — *The Darkest City*
Gail Holst-Warhaft — *The Fall of Athens*
Roger Lebovitz — *A Guide to the Western Slopes and the Outlying Area*
Roger Lebovitz — *Twenty-two Instructions for Near Survival*
dug Nap— *Artsy Fartsy*
Delia Bell Robinson — *A Shirtwaist Story*
Peter Schumann — *A Child's Deprimer*
Peter Schumann — *All*
Peter Schumann — *All, Nothing, Nothing At All*
Peter Schumann — *Belligerent & Not So Belligerent Slogans from the
                 Possibilitarian Arsenal*
Peter Schumann — *Bread & Sentences*
Peter Schumann — *Charlotte Salomon*
Peter Schumann — *Diagonal Man Theory + Praxis, Volumes One and Two*
Peter Schumann — *Faust 3*
Peter Schumann — *Planet Kasper, Volumes One and Two*
Peter Schumann — *We*

Plays
Stephen Goldberg — *Screwed and Other Plays*
Michele Markarian — *Unborn Children of America*

Essays
William Benton — *Eye Contact: Writing on Art*
Robert Sommer — *Losing Francis: Essays on the Wars at Home*
George Ovitt & Peter Nash — *Trotsky's Si*